T0244893

DOOMED
ROMANCES

DOOMED ROMANCES

Strange Tales of Uncanny Love

Edited by

JOANNE ELLA PARSONS

This collection first published in 2024 by
The British Library
96 Euston Road
London NW1 2DB

Selection, introduction and notes © 2024 Joanne Ella Parsons
Volume copyright © 2024 The British Library Board
'The Lady of the House of Love' © 1975 The Estate of Angela Carter,
reproduced with the permission of Rogers, Coleridge and White.
'The Glass Bottle Trick' © 2000 Nalo Hopkinson, reprinted
with permission of Donald Maass Literary Agency.
'Could You Wear My Eyes?' © 2000 Kalamu ya Salaam. Originally published as 'Can You
Wear My Eyes' in *Dark Matter: A Century of Speculative Fiction from the African Diaspora*.
'I'll Be Your Mirror' © 2021 Tracy Fahey, reprinted with permission of the author.
'Dancehall Devil' © 2022 V. Castro, reprinted with permission of Flame Tree Press.

Cataloguing in Publication Data
A catalogue record for this publication is available from the British Library

ISBN 978 0 7123 5555 1
e-ISBN 978 0 7123 6802 5

Frontispiece illustration by Sandra Gómez.
Illustration on page 304: A view of the heart, from F. Antommarchi, *Planches
anatomiques du corps humain executées d'après les dimensions naturelles* (Paris, 1826).
Cover design by Mauricio Villamayor with illustration by Sandra Gómez
Text design and typesetting by Tetragon, London
Printed in England by CPI Group (UK) Ltd, Croydon, CR0 4YY

CONTENTS

For my cousin, Laura

INTRODUCTION

Romance has a problem. It loves stereotypes. Fairy tale princesses who sleep peacefully until their princes wake them with non-consensual kisses. Elizabeths and Darcys who are enemies turned lovers (Jane Austen, *Pride and Prejudice*). Beatrices who need a Benedick to shut them up with a kiss (William Shakespeare, *Much Ado About Nothing*). Teenage Bellas who repeatedly require saving by the ancient vampire who stalks them (Stephanie Meyer, *Twilight*). We want the fantasy, and, as the Mills & Boon website boasts, "a hero who will command and seduce".* And yet, amidst the dreams of romance, threads of abuse weave their way through these narratives as obsession is framed as romantic, helplessness as feminine, and the death of a woman becomes a beautiful thing.

In the romance genre, there is nothing sexier than a dead woman. In fact, the dead, usually young, female body has been fetishized and romanticized throughout our cultural history. The unfortunate woman remains frozen in time, her loveliness never fades, and she is forever unobtainable. As Edgar Allan Poe writes, "the death, of a beautiful woman is, unquestionably, the most poetical topic in the world—and equally is it beyond doubt that the lips best suited for such topic are those of a bereaved lover".† The dead woman is silenced forever, and only lives on through the words of a man who reshapes and reconstructs her for public consumption. Consider the popular example of Pre-Raphaelite artist John Everett Millais's romantic and erotic

* Mills & Boon, "Write for Mills & Boon Modern" (Accessed 12th December 2023). <https://www.millsandboon.co.uk/pages/write-for-modern-series>.
† Poe, Edgar Allan, "Philosophy of Composition" (1846).

painting of the tragic death of Ophelia as she drifts down a stream strewn with flowers that symbolize her madness. Or Robert Browning's poem "Porphyria's Lover" (1836) in which the male speaker strangles Porphyria with her own hair before caressing her corpse. Love, it seems, is easier when the woman can no longer challenge or speak.

The stories I have chosen overthrow these patriarchal power dynamics and bite back. There are no Happily Ever Afters for my wayward lovers. Their Meet Cutes swiftly sour as these terrible tales of doomed dalliances reveal romantic horrors and unspeakable passions. Wrongs are righted in the most hauntingly horrifying ways. Romantic ideals are destroyed and the powerful become the powerless.

The tales in this collection are of course "weird". Supernatural, ghostly, and Gothic tales often challenge the status quo. They provide spaces through which to explore contemporary anxieties and play at transgressing moral, and sexual, boundaries. The darkness and the shadows of the macabre, the weird, and the world beyond the threshold of death reveal the abuses and inequities that exist in society, and this is particularly true for stories that deal with romance and love. Although to what extent they destabilize society's rules is very much up for debate. For example, while demons, witches, and vampires can have a lot of fun during their damnation, they are still exorcized, drowned, or staked in the end. Women must be punished for their sexual indiscretions. Think of the order of death in a horror film, for instance: the sexually experienced cheerleader will always die before the virgin.

This tension can be seen in the most famous of all the vampire stories. Bram Stoker's *Dracula* (1897) is a masterpiece of forbidden desire and rule breaking. We know that it does not end well for those who misbehave but what capers they have before the end! Dracula crosses the boundaries between male and female, hetero- and homosexuality. His sharp white teeth and "ruby-red" mouth engorged with fresh blood from a recent kill is reminiscent of a vagina dentata (toothed vagina) as it promises both sex and death. As we well know, Count Dracula loves to bite women under the covers of darkness and in the private spaces of their bedchambers. His female vampires exist in an orgy of sex and lustful power. In the novel, Mina, the "good Victorian wife", is bitten but survives and is saved, while her friend Lucy, who wishes she could marry all three of her suitors, is punished for her sexual greed with a stake through her blood-thirsty, lusty, and newly vampiric heart.

Women are not the only sex to be punished for "inappropriate" romances. Almost a hundred years later, the horror comedy film *The Lost Boys* (1987) and its homoerotic relationship between David, leader of the cool leather clad vampire gang and the object of his desire, Michael, revealed the contemporary societal anxieties and discrimination directed at the gay community during the AIDS epidemic. Michael is firmly in the closet and, no matter his night-time adventures, in real life there he must stay. However, *Twilight* aside, the figure of the vampire allows us to explore sexy forbidden passions, even if the romances must always be doomed.

While the vampires are denied their walk off into the sunset, usually the Happily Ever After (or HEA as it's known in the trade) is essential to romantic fictions. It reveals what forms of love are sanctioned by society. It tells us that, when we meet "the one", the stars will shine and fireworks will burst out in celebration. The sex will be equally explosive and will result in lifelong bonds. Sometimes it springs from an embarrassingly romantic public declaration: a flashmob (*Friends with Benefits*, 2011); a serenade accompanied by the school band (*10 Things I Hate About You*, 1999). There is no room for a "no" when a HEA is offered in front of others. And nothing can exist after one. The story stops. It is the end. "Reader, I married him" says Jane Eyre. And we are left to assume the lovers will spend the rest of their lives in some sort of blissful existence. However, in reality, as well as in some of the tales gathered in this volume, this is not always the case.

In the eighteenth and nineteenth centuries, a time when some of the stories in this volume were written, women were often trapped within the cruel confines of marriage laws that disadvantaged them in terms of divorce and economic rights. Vulnerable and unprotected, women lacked the freedom to choose love and instead had to make decisions, if they were lucky enough not to have a male relative chose for them, based on who would provide financial security and who they hoped would treat them kindly. Other women were treated like chattel and exchanged in return for land, power, and increased wealth and status. It is therefore unsurprising that many female writers used the Gothic and the ghostly as mechanisms to explore the terrors that haunted their real lives. In the eighteenth century, Ann Radcliffe's extremely popular Gothic romances sent their heroines into creepy castle ruins and terrifying mountainous landscapes, and into the clutches of a villain who they are expected to marry due to some misfortune or other, despite the fact that they are in love with a wildly dashing and honourable young man instead. While Radcliffe's supernatural often had a logical explanation in the end, the form allowed her to play with female rebellion and transgressive sexuality in exciting and new ways. Radcliffe's female protagonists, while victims, were often granted the power to defy men, thereby challenging the contemporary ideal of female submissiveness.

Female ghosts roam widely in nineteenth-century fiction as the afterlife granted them the freedom to enact the revenge denied to them in this world. Female authors, such as E. Nesbit (1858–1924), used the ghost story and supernatural fiction as vehicles to not only support themselves financially but to also, through their stories, avenge the lack of power and the hidden "rod of iron" wielded by husbands within the privacy and isolation of the home. While Nesbit was more famous for her children's books,* her ghastly ghost stories often reveal the brutalities of "love" and marriage through their depictions of controlling and obsessive suitors, who are haunted, and even killed, by the ghosts of their dead wives for the crimes they have committed against them. Patriarchal power can be subverted in the afterlife, and so the pages of Victorian periodicals are littered with avenging angels running amok in the ghostly shadows.

Later, in the twentieth century, Jilly Cooper, perhaps the sauciest of all the Bonkbuster writers, transports Ann Radcliffe's Gothic visions into the 1990s in *The Man Who Made Husbands Jealous* (1993). In this novel, the fourth in Cooper's Rutshire Chronicles series, the eighteenth-century Gothic castle becomes a peculiar sex tower owned by sex pest and famous maestro Rannaldini. However, while the women in Cooper's novels certainly have more sexual freedom than those in previous centuries, they still suffer the consequences when the predatory male conductor becomes bored of them. And let's not forget that the nineties were filled with women who were punished in real life for being seduced by more powerful men (Monica Lewinsky) or who had their most intimate romantic moments stolen and put on public display (Pamela Anderson). Divorce was easier and more acceptable but public slut-shaming and societal expectations still kept women in their place.

And this is all before we get to the lack of diversity and racism in romantic fictions, which results in bodies of colour/non-white bodies being either absent or objectified and fetishized. One only has to look at their covers to see that most romance stories are built around

---

* The most well-known are *The Story of the Treasure Seekers* (1899), *Five Children and It* (1902), and *The Railway Children* (1905).

white, heterosexual characters. It is an industry where publishers have, as Lois Beckett argues, "confined many black romance authors to all-black lines, marketed only to black readers."* These romances were often even shelved in separate sections in bookstores. Racist and stereotyped descriptions, such as of Black women as hyper-sexual or aggressive, expose our colonial past in uncomfortable ways. Some of my doomed romance stories reveal the traumas inflicted through slavery and colonialism as they use romantic entanglements as a mechanism for overthrowing both marital and colonial oppression. Other stories collected here use deviant desire, bodily horror, and folklore beyond the white Western world to unsettle their unfortunate lovers. Today, new and rediscovered voices are rising up in romance fiction, as well as its blood-curdling counterparts, to celebrate or curse their sweethearts no matter what form their appearance, culture, or passion takes.

The notions of romance and love are taken in their broadest sense in this volume, and so too is the otherworldly as some of the "hauntings" contained here take place in life. And, while ghosts, vampires, spirits, demons, and the dark arts abound, often the thing to be most feared is that which surrounds us in the here and now. So, if you are looking for tales of loving couples tragically separated by death, Romeos and Juliets, beautiful widows waiting for husbands lost at sea, then you should shut this book, return it to the shelf, and step away. The creeping Gothic horrors and "unquiet slumbers"† inside are not for you. There is no peace in the afterlife for my lovers. Instead, they

---

* Beckett, Lois, "Fifty shades of white: the long fight against racism in romance novels" (*The Guardian*, 4th April 2019): <https://www.theguardian.com/books/2019/apr/04/fifty-shades-of-white-romance-novels-racism-ritas-rwa>.
† Brontë, Emily, *Wuthering Heights* (1847).

are cursed to suffer eternal torment, aching loneliness, and unsettling discomfort. Others use their supernatural powers to enact the revenge and punishment denied to them in life. They upend their worlds and, in doing so, they challenge ours too.

A NOTE FROM THE PUBLISHER

The original short stories reprinted in the British Library Tales of the Weird series were written and published in a period ranging across the nineteenth and twentieth centuries. There are many elements of these stories which continue to entertain modern readers; however, in some cases there are also uses of language, instances of stereotyping and some attitudes expressed by narrators or characters which may not be endorsed by the publishing standards of today. We acknowledge therefore that some elements in the stories selected for reprinting may continue to make uncomfortable reading for some of our audience. With this series British Library Publishing aims to offer a new readership a chance to read some of the rare material of the British Library's collections in an affordable paperback format, to enjoy their merits and to look back into the worlds of the past two centuries as portrayed by their writers. It is not possible to separate these stories from the history of their writing and therefore the following stories are presented as they were originally published with minor edits only, made for consistency of style and sense. We welcome feedback from our readers, which can be sent to the following address:

British Library Publishing
The British Library
96 Euston Road
London, NW1 2DB
United Kingdom

THE INVISIBLE GIRL

Mary Shelley

One of the key figures of the Romantic movement, Mary Shelley (1797–1851) is, of course, most famous for *Frankenstein; or, The Modern Prometheus* (1818, revised 1831). This story was conceived during the weird summer of 1816, when volcanic ash clouded the sky and blotted out the sun following the eruption of Mount Tambora in 1815. This violent explosion created eerie changes in the climate, such as snow in June and unseasonable storms. *Frankenstein*'s Gothic monstrosity emerged in this darkness when Lord Byron urged his companions—his lover and Mary Shelley's stepsister, Claire Clairmont; John Polidori; and Mary and her husband Percy—to create ghastly ghost stories one gloomy evening in the Villa Diodati during their stay in Lake Geneva. The Gothic horrors of this stormy and frightening weather seep through *Frankenstein* infecting it with a disquieting significance. The weather is equally menacing in "The Invisible Girl", which was originally published in *The Keepsake* in 1833. At its core is the ghost of "a maiden who has lost her sweetheart" while in the "bloom of youth". "The Invisible Girl" is a very different sort of a story to *Frankenstein*; however, its monsters—the cruelties of the marriage laws—are no less terrifying.

This slender narrative has no pretensions to the regularity of a story, or the development of situations and feelings; it is but a slight sketch, delivered nearly as it was narrated to me by one of the humblest of the actors concerned: nor will I spin out a circumstance interesting principally from its singularity and truth, but narrate, as concisely as I can, how I was surprised on visiting what seemed a ruined tower, crowning a bleak promontory overhanging the sea, that flows between Wales and Ireland, to find that though the exterior preserved all the savage rudeness that betokened many a war with the elements, the interior was fitted up somewhat in the guise of a summer-house, for it was too small to deserve any other name. It consisted but of the ground-floor, which served as an entrance, and one room above, which was reached by a staircase made out of the thickness of the wall. This chamber was floored and carpeted, decorated with elegant furniture; and, above all, to attract the attention and excite curiosity, there hung over the chimneypiece—for to preserve the apartment from damp a fire-place had been built evidently since it had assumed a guise so dissimilar to the object of its construction—a picture simply painted in water-colours, which seemed more than any part of the adornments of the room to be at war with the rudeness of the building, the solitude in which it was placed, and the desolation of the surrounding scenery. This drawing represented a lovely girl in the very pride and bloom of youth; her dress was simple, in the fashion of the day—(remember, reader, I write at the beginning of the eighteenth century), her countenance was embellished by a look of mingled innocence and intelligence, to which was added the imprint of serenity of soul and natural cheerfulness. She was reading one of those folio romances which have so long been the delight of the enthusiastic and young; her mandoline was at her feet—her parroquet perched on a huge mirror near her; the arrangement of furniture and hangings gave token of a luxurious dwelling, and her attire also evidently that of home and privacy, yet bore with it an appearance of ease and girlish ornament, as if she wished to please. Beneath this picture was inscribed in golden letters, "The Invisible Girl."

Rambling about a country nearly uninhabited, having lost my way, and being overtaken by a shower, I had lighted on this dreary-looking tenement, which seemed to rock in the blast, and to be hung up there as the very symbol of desolation. I was gazing wistfully and cursing inwardly my stars which led me to a ruin that could afford no shelter, though the storm began to pelt more seriously than before, when I saw an old woman's head popped out from a kind of loophole, and as suddenly withdrawn:—a minute after a feminine voice called to me from within, and penetrating a little brambly maze that skreened a door, which I had not before observed, so skilfully had the planter succeeded in concealing art with nature I found the good dame standing on the threshold and inviting me to take refuge within. "I had just come up from our cot hard by," she said, "to look after the things, as I do every day, when the rain came on—will ye walk up till it is over?" I was about to observe that the cot hard by, at the venture of a few rain drops, was better than a ruined tower, and to ask my kind hostess whether "the things" were pigeons or crows that she was come to look after, when the matting of the floor and the carpeting of the staircase struck my eye. I was still more surprised when I saw the room above; and beyond all, the picture and its singular inscription, naming her invisible, whom the painter had coloured forth into very agreeable visibility, awakened my most lively curiosity: the result of this, of my exceeding politeness towards the old woman, and her own natural garrulity, was a kind of garbled narrative which my imagination eked out, and future inquiries rectified, till it assumed the following form.

Some years before in the afternoon of a September day, which, though tolerably fair, gave many tokens of a tempestuous evening, a gentleman arrived at a little coast town about ten miles from this place; he expressed his desire to hire a boat to carry him to the town of about fifteen miles further on the coast. The menaces which the sky held forth made the fishermen loathe to venture, till at length two, one the father of a numerous family, bribed by the bountiful reward the stranger promised—the other, the son of my hostess, induced by youthful daring, agreed to undertake the voyage. The wind was fair, and they hoped to make good way before nightfall, and to get into port ere the rising of the storm. They pushed off with good cheer, at least the fishermen did; as for the stranger, the deep mourning which he wore was not half so black as the melancholy that wrapt his mind. He looked as if he had never smiled—as if some unutterable thought, dark as night and bitter as death, had built its nest within his bosom, and brooded therein eternally; he did not mention his name; but one of the villagers recognized him as Henry Vernon, the son of a baronet who possessed a mansion about three miles distant from the town for which he was bound. This mansion was almost abandoned by the family; but Henry had, in a romantic fit, visited it about three years before, and Sir Peter had been down there during the previous spring for about a couple of months.

The boat did not make so much way as was expected; the breeze failed them as they got out to sea, and they were fain with oar as well as sail, to try to weather the promontory that jutted out between them and the spot they desired to reach. They were yet far distant when the shifting wind began to exert its strength, and to blow with violent though unequal puffs. Night came on pitchy dark, and the howling waves rose and broke with frightful violence, menacing to overwhelm the tiny bark that dared resist their fury. They were forced to lower every sail, and take to their oars; one man was obliged to bale out the water, and Vernon himself took an oar, and rowing with desperate energy, equalled the force of the more practised boatmen. There had been much talk between the sailors before the tempest came on; now, except a brief command, all were silent. One thought of his wife and children, and silently cursed the caprice of the stranger that endangered in its effects, not only his life, but their welfare; the other feared less, for he was a daring lad, but he worked hard, and had no time for speech; while Vernon bitterly regretting the thoughtlessness which had made him cause others to share a peril, unimportant as far as he himself was concerned, now tried to cheer them with a voice full of animation and courage, and now pulled yet more strongly at the oar he held. The only person who did not seem wholly intent on the work he was about, was the man who baled; every now and then he gazed intently round, as if the sea held afar off, on its tumultuous waste, some object that he strained his eyes to discern. But all was blank, except as the crests of the high waves showed themselves, or far out on the verge of the horizon, a kind of lifting of the clouds betokened greater violence for the blast. At length he exclaimed—"Yes, I see it!—the larboard oar!—now! if we can make yonder light, we are saved!" Both the rowers instinctively turned their heads,—but cheerless darkness answered their gaze.

"You cannot see it," cried their companion, "but we are nearing it; and, please God, we shall outlive this night." Soon he took the oar from Vernon's hand, who, quite exhausted, was failing in his strokes.

He rose and looked for the beacon which promised them safety;—it glimmered with so faint a ray, that now he said, "I see it;" and again, "it is nothing:" still, as they made way, it dawned upon his sight, growing more steady and distinct as it beamed across the lurid waters, which themselves became smoother, so that safety seemed to arise from the bosom of the ocean under the influence of that flickering gleam.

"What beacon is it that helps us at our need?" asked Vernon, as the men, now able to manage their oars with greater ease, found breath to answer his question.

"A fairy one, I believe," replied the elder sailor, "yet no less a true: it burns in an old tumble-down tower, built on the top of a rock which looks over the sea. We never saw it before this summer; and now each night it is to be seen,—at least when it is looked for, for we cannot see it from our village;—and it is such an out of the way place that no one has need to go near it, except through a chance like this. Some say it is burnt by witches, some say by smugglers; but this I know, two parties have been to search, and found nothing but the bare walls of the tower. All is deserted by day, and dark by night; for no light was to be seen while we were there, though it burned sprightly enough when we were out at sea.

"I have heard say," observed the younger sailor, "it is burnt by the ghost of a maiden who lost her sweetheart in these parts; he being wrecked, and his body found at the foot of the tower: she goes by the name among us of the 'Invisible Girl.'"

The voyagers had now reached the landing-place at the foot of the tower. Vernon cast a glance upward,—the light was still burning. With some difficulty, struggling with the breakers, and blinded by night, they contrived to get their little bark to shore, and to draw her up on the beach: they then scrambled up the precipitous pathway, overgrown by weeds and underwood, and, guided by the more experienced fishermen, they found the entrance to the tower, door or gate there was none, and all was dark as the tomb, and silent and almost as cold as death.

"This will never do," said Vernon; "surely our hostess will show her light, if not herself, and guide our darkling steps by some sign of life and comfort."

"We will get to the upper chamber," said the sailor, "if I can but hit upon the broken down steps: but you will find no trace of the Invisible Girl nor her light either, I warrant."

"Truly a romantic adventure of the most disagreeable kind," muttered Vernon, as he stumbled over the unequal ground: "she of the beacon-light must be both ugly and old, or she would not be so peevish and inhospitable."

With considerable difficulty, and, after divers knocks and bruises, the adventurers at length succeeded in reaching the upper storey; but all was blank and bare, and they were fain to stretch themselves on the hard floor, when weariness, both of mind and body, conduced to steep their senses in sleep.

Long and sound were the slumbers of the mariners. Vernon but forgot himself for an hour; then, throwing off drowsiness, and finding his rough couch uncongenial to repose, he got up and placed himself at the hole that served for a window, for glass there was none, and there being not even a rough bench, he leant his back against the embrasure, as the only rest he could find. He had forgotten his danger, the mysterious beacon, and its invisible guardian: his thoughts were occupied on the horrors of his own fate, and the unspeakable wretchedness that sat like a nightmare on his heart.

It would require a good-sized volume to relate the causes which had changed the once happy Vernon into the most woeful mourner that ever clung to the outer trappings of grief, as slight though cherished symbols of the wretchedness within. Henry was the only child of Sir Peter Vernon, and as much spoiled by his father's idolatry as the old baronet's violent and tyrannical temper would permit. A young orphan was educated in his father's house, who in the same way was treated with generosity and kindness, and yet who lived in deep awe of Sir Peter's authority, who was a widower; and these two children were all he had to exert his power over, or to whom to extend his affection. Rosina was a cheerful-tempered girl, a little timid, and careful to avoid displeasing her protector; but so docile, so kind-hearted, and so affectionate, that she felt even less than Henry the discordant spirit of his parent. It is a tale often told; they were playmates and companions in childhood, and lovers in after days. Rosina was frightened to imagine that this secret affection, and the vows they pledged, might be disapproved of by Sir Peter. But sometimes she consoled herself by thinking that perhaps she was in reality her Henry's destined bride, brought up with him under the design of their future union; and Henry, while he felt that this was not the case, resolved to wait only until he was of age to declare and accomplish his wishes in making the sweet Rosina his wife. Meanwhile he was careful to avoid premature discovery of his intentions, so to secure his beloved girl from persecution and insult. The old gentleman was very conveniently blind; he lived always in the country, and the lovers spent their lives together, unrebuked and uncontrolled. It was enough that Rosina played on her mandoline, and sang Sir Peter to sleep every day after dinner; she was the sole female in the house above the rank of a servant, and had her own way in the disposal of her time. Even when Sir Peter frowned, her innocent caresses and sweet voice were powerful to smooth the rough current of his temper. If ever human spirit lived in an earthly paradise, Rosina did at this time: her pure love was made happy by Henry's constant presence; and the confidence they felt in each other, and the security with which they looked forward to the future, rendered their path one of roses under a cloudless sky. Sir Peter was the slight drawback that only rendered their *tête-à-tête* more delightful, and gave value to the sympathy they each bestowed on the other. All at once an ominous personage made its appearance in Vernon-Place, in the shape of a widow sister of Sir Peter, who, having succeeded in killing her husband and children with the effects of her vile temper, came, like a harpy, greedy for new prey, under her brother's roof. She too soon detected the attachment of the unsuspicious pair. She made all speed to impart her discovery to her brother, and at once to restrain and inflame his rage. Through her contrivance Henry was suddenly despatched on his travels abroad, that the coast might be clear for the persecution of Rosina; and then the richest of the lovely girl's many admirers, whom, under Sir Peter's single reign, she was allowed, nay, almost commanded, to dismiss, so desirous was he of keeping her for his own comfort, was selected, and she was ordered to marry him. The scenes of violence to which she was now exposed, the bitter taunts of the odious Mrs. Bainbridge, and the reckless fury of Sir Peter, were the more frightful and overwhelming from their novelty. To all she could only oppose a silent, tearful, but immutable steadiness of purpose: no threats, no rage could extort from her more than a touching prayer that they would not hate her, because she could not obey.

"There must be something we don't see under all this," said Mrs. Bainbridge, "take my word for it, brother,—she corresponds secretly with Henry. Let us take her down to your seat in Wales, where she will have no pensioned beggars to assist her; and we shall see if her spirit be not bent to our purpose."

Sir Peter consented, and they all three posted down to ——shire, and took up their abode in the solitary and dreary-looking house before alluded to as belonging to the family. Here poor Rosina's sufferings grew intolerable:—before, surrounded by well-known scenes, and in perpetual intercourse with kind and familiar faces, she had not despaired in the end of conquering by her patience the cruelty of her persecutors;—nor had she written to Henry, for his name had not been mentioned by his relatives, nor their attachment alluded to, and she felt an instinctive wish to escape the dangers about her without his being annoyed, or the sacred secret of her love being laid bare, and wronged by the vulgar abuse of his aunt or the bitter curses of his father. But when she was taken to Wales, and made a prisoner in her apartment, when the flinty mountains about her seemed feebly to imitate the stony hearts she had to deal with, her courage began to fail. The only attendant permitted to approach her was Mrs. Bainbridge's maid; and under the tutelage of her fiend-like mistress, this woman was used as a decoy to entice the poor prisoner into confidence, and then to be betrayed. The simple, kind-hearted Rosina was a facile dupe, and at last, in the excess of her despair, wrote to Henry, and gave the letter to this woman to be forwarded. The letter in itself would have softened marble; it did not speak of their mutual vows, it but asked him to intercede with his father, that he would restore her to the kind place she had formerly held in his affections, and cease from a cruelty that would destroy her. "For I may die," wrote the hapless girl, "but marry another—never!" That single word, indeed, had sufficed to betray her secret, had it not been already discovered; as it was, it gave increased fury to Sir Peter, as his sister triumphantly pointed it out to him, for it need hardly be said that while the ink of the address was yet wet, and the seal still warm, Rosina's letter was carried to this lady. The culprit was summoned before them; what ensued none could tell; for their own sakes the cruel pair tried to palliate their part. Voices were high, and the soft murmur of Rosina's tone was lost in the howling of Sir Peter and the snarling of his sister. "Out of doors you shall go," roared the old man; "under my roof you shall not spend another night." And the words "infamous seductress," and worse, such as had never met the poor girl's ear before, were caught by listening servants; and to each angry speech of the baronet, Mrs. Bainbridge added an envenomed point worse than all.

More dead than alive, Rosina was at last dismissed. Whether guided by despair, whether she took Sir Peter's threats literally, or whether his sister's orders were more decisive, none knew, but Rosina left the house; a servant saw her cross the park, weeping, and wringing her hands as she went. What became of her none could tell; her disappearance was not disclosed to Sir Peter till the following day, and then he showed by his anxiety to trace her steps and to find her, that his words had been but idle threats. The truth was, that though Sir Peter went to frightful lengths to prevent the marriage of the heir of his house with the portionless orphan, the object of his charity, yet in his heart he loved Rosina, and half his violence to her rose from anger at himself for treating her so ill. Now remorse began to sting him, as messenger after messenger came back without tidings of his victim; he dared not confess his worst fears to himself; and when his inhuman sister, trying to harden her conscience by angry words, cried, "The vile hussy has too surely made away with herself out of revenge to us;" an oath, the most tremendous, and a look sufficient to make even her tremble, commanded her silence. Her conjecture, however, appeared too true: a dark and rushing stream that flowed at the extremity of the park had doubtless received the lovely form, and quenched the life of this unfortunate girl. Sir Peter, when his endeavours to find her proved fruitless, returned to town, haunted by the image of his victim, and forced to acknowledge in his own heart that he would willingly lay down his life, could he see her again, even though it were as the bride of his son—his son, before whose questioning he quailed like the veriest coward; for when Henry was told of the death of Rosina, he suddenly returned from abroad to ask the cause—to visit her grave, and mourn her loss in the groves and valleys which had been the scenes of their mutual happiness. He made a thousand inquiries, and an ominous silence alone replied. Growing more earnest and more anxious, at length he drew from servants and dependants, and his odious aunt herself, the whole dreadful truth. From that moment despair struck his heart, and misery named him her own. He fled from his father's presence; and the recollection that one whom he ought to revere was guilty of so dark a crime, haunted him, as of old the Eumenides tormented the souls of men given up to their torturings.

His first, his only wish, was to visit Wales, and to learn if any new discovery had been made, and whether it were possible to recover the mortal remains of the lost Rosina, so to satisfy the unquiet longings of his miserable heart. On this expedition was he bound, when he made his appearance at the village before named; and now in the deserted tower, his thoughts were busy with images of despair and death, and what his beloved one had suffered before her gentle nature had been goaded to such a deed of woe.

While immersed in gloomy reverie, to which the monotonous roaring of the sea made fit accompaniment, hours flew on, and Vernon was at last aware that the light of morning was creeping from out its eastern retreat, and dawning over the wild ocean, which still broke in furious tumult on the rocky beach. His companions now roused themselves, and prepared to depart. The food they had brought with them was damaged by sea water, and their hunger, after hard labour and many hours fasting, had become ravenous. It was impossible to put to sea in their shattered boat; but there stood a fisher's cot about two miles off, in a recess in the bay, of which the promontory on which the tower stood formed one side, and to this they hastened to repair; they did not spend a second thought on the light which had saved them, nor its cause, but left the ruin in search of a more hospitable asylum. Vernon cast his eyes round as he quitted it, but no vestige of an inhabitant met his eye, and he began to persuade himself that the beacon had been a creation of fancy merely. Arriving at the cottage in question, which was inhabited by a fisherman and his family, they made an homely breakfast, and then prepared to return to the tower, to refit their boat, and if possible bring her round. Vernon accompanied them, together with their host and his son. Several questions were asked concerning the Invisible Girl and her light, each agreeing that the apparition was novel, and not one being able to give even an explanation of how the name had become affixed to the unknown cause of this singular appearance; though both of the men of the cottage affirmed that once or twice they had seen a female figure in the adjacent wood, and that now and then a stranger girl made her appearance at another cot a mile off, on the other side of the promontory, and bought bread; they suspected both these to be the same, but could not tell. The inhabitants of the cot, indeed, appeared too stupid even to feel curiosity, and had never made any attempt at discovery. The whole day was spent by the sailors in repairing the boat; and the sound of hammers, and the voices of the men at work, resounded along the coast, mingled with the dashing of the waves. This was no time to explore the ruin for one who whether human or supernatural so evidently withdrew herself from intercourse with every living being. Vernon, however, went over the tower, and searched every nook in vain; the dingy bare walls bore no token of serving as a shelter; and even a little recess in the wall of the staircase, which he had not before observed, was equally empty and desolate.

Quitting the tower, he wandered in the pine wood that surrounded it, and giving up all thought of solving the mystery, was soon engrossed by thoughts that touched his heart more nearly, when suddenly there appeared on the ground at his feet the vision of a slipper. Since Cinderella so tiny a slipper had never been seen; as plain as shoe could speak, it told a tale of elegance, loveliness, and youth. Vernon picked it up; he had often admired Rosina's singularly small foot, and his first thought was a question whether this little slipper would have fitted it. It was very strange!—it must belong to the Invisible Girl. Then there was a fairy form that kindled that light, a form of such material substance, that its foot needed to be shod; and yet how shod?—with kid so fine, and of shape so exquisite, that it exactly resembled such as Rosina wore! Again the recurrence of the image of the beloved dead came forcibly across him; and a thousand home-felt associations, childish yet sweet, and lover-like though trifling, so filled Vernon's heart, that he threw himself his length on the ground, and wept more bitterly than ever the miserable fate of the sweet orphan.

In the evening the men quitted their work, and Vernon returned with them to the cot where they were to sleep, intending to pursue their voyage, weather permitting, the following morning.

Vernon said nothing of his slipper, but returned with his rough associates. Often he looked back; but the tower rose darkly over the dim waves, and no light appeared. Preparations had been made in the cot for their accommodation, and the only bed in it was offered Vernon; but he refused to deprive his hostess, and spreading his cloak on a heap of dry leaves, endeavoured to give himself up to repose. He slept for some hours; and when he awoke, all was still, save that the hard breathing of the sleepers in the same room with him interrupted the silence. He rose, and going to the window,—looked out over the now placid sea towards the mystic tower; the light burning there, sending its slender rays across the waves. Congratulating himself on a circumstance he had not anticipated, Vernon softly left the cottage, and, wrapping his cloak round him, walked with a swift pace round the bay towards the tower. He reached it; still the light was burning. To enter and restore the maiden her shoe, would be but an act of courtesy; and Vernon intended to do this with such caution, as to come unaware, before its wearer could, with her accustomed arts, withdraw herself from his eyes; but, unluckily, while yet making his way up the narrow pathway, his foot dislodged a loose fragment, that fell with crash and sound down the precipice. He sprung forward, on this, to retrieve by speed the advantage he had lost by this unlucky accident. He reached the door; he entered: all was silent, but also all was dark. He paused in the room below; he felt sure that a slight sound met his ear. He ascended the steps, and entered the upper chamber; but blank obscurity met his penetrating gaze, the starless night admitted not even a twilight glimmer through the only aperture. He closed his eyes, to try, on opening them again, to be able to catch some faint, wandering ray on the visual nerve; but it was in vain. He groped round the room: he stood still, and held his breath; and then, listening intently, he felt sure that another occupied the chamber with him, and that its atmosphere was slightly agitated by another's respiration. He remembered the recess in the staircase; but, before he approached it, he spoke:—he hesitated a moment what to say. "I must believe," he said, "that misfortune alone can cause your seclusion; and if the assistance of a man—of a gentleman—"

An exclamation interrupted him; a voice from the grave spoke his name—the accents of Rosina syllabled, "Henry!—is it indeed Henry whom I hear?"

He rushed forward, directed by the sound, and clasped in his arms the living form of his own lamented girl—his own Invisible Girl he called her; for even yet, as he felt her heart beat near his, and as he entwined her waist with his arm, supporting her as she almost sank to the ground with agitation, he could not see her; and, as her sobs prevented her speech, no sense, but the instinctive one that filled his heart with tumultuous gladness, told him that the slender, wasted form he pressed so fondly was the living shadow of the Hebe beauty he had adored.

The morning saw this pair thus strangely restored to each other on the tranquil sea, sailing with a fair wind for L——, whence they were to proceed to Sir Peter's seat, which, three months before, Rosina had quitted in such agony and terror. The morning light dispelled the shadows that had veiled her, and disclosed the fair person of the Invisible Girl. Altered indeed she was by suffering and woe, but still the same sweet smile played on her lips, and the tender light of her soft blue eyes were all her own. Vernon drew out the slipper, and shoved the cause that had occasioned him to resolve to discover the guardian of the mystic beacon; even now he dared not inquire how she had existed in that desolate spot, or wherefore she had so sedulously avoided observation, when the right thing to have been done was, to have sought him immediately, under whose care, protected by whose love, no danger need be feared. But Rosina shrunk from him as he spoke, and a death-like pallor came over her cheek, as she faintly whispered, "Your father's curse—your father's dreadful threats!" It appeared, indeed, that Sir Peter's violence, and the cruelty of Mrs. Bainbridge, had succeeded in impressing Rosina with wild and unvanquishable terror. She had fled from their house without plan or forethought—driven by frantic horror and overwhelming fear, she had left it with scarcely any money, and there seemed to her no possibility of either returning or proceeding onward. She had no friend except Henry in the wide world; whither could she go?—to have sought Henry would have sealed their fates to misery; for, with an oath, Sir Peter had declared he would rather see them both in their coffins than married. After wandering about, hiding by day, and only venturing forth at night, she had come to this deserted tower, which seemed a place of refuge. How she had lived since then she could hardly tell;—she had lingered in the woods by day, or slept in the vault of the tower, an asylum none were acquainted with or had discovered: by night she burned the pine-cones of the wood, and night was her dearest time; for it seemed to her as if security came with darkness. She was unaware that Sir Peter had left that part of the country, and was terrified lest her hiding-place should be revealed to him. Her only hope was that Henry would return—that Henry would never rest till he had found her. She confessed that the long interval and the approach of winter had visited her with dismay; she feared that, as her strength was failing, and her form wasting to a skeleton, that she might die, and never see her own Henry more.

An illness, indeed, in spite of all his care, followed her restoration to security and the comforts of civilized life; many months went by before the bloom revisiting her cheeks, and her limbs regaining their round-ness, she resembled once more the picture drawn of her in her days of bliss, before any visitation of sorrow. It was a copy of this portrait that decorated the tower, the scene of her suffering, in which I had found shelter. Sir Peter, overjoyed to be relieved from the pangs of remorse, and delighted again to see his orphan-ward, whom he really loved, was now as eager as before he had been averse to bless her union with his son: Mrs. Bainbridge they never saw again. But each year they spent a few months in their Welch mansion, the scene of their early wedded happiness, and the spot where again poor Rosina had awoke to life and joy after her cruel persecutions. Henry's fond care had fitted up the tower, and decorated it as I saw; and often did he come over, with his "Invisible Girl," to renew, in the very scene of its occurrence, the remembrance of all the incidents which had led to their meeting again, during the shades of night, in that sequestered ruin.

THE END

34

1872

CARMILLA

J. Sheridan Le Fanu

Joseph Thomas Sheridan Le Fanu (1814–1873) was one of the best-
known Irish ghost and horror story writers of his time. *Carmilla* was
first serialized in *The Dark Blue* journal in 1871–2 and was then later
published in Le Fanu's short story collection, *In a Glass Darkly*, in
1872. While Bram Stoker's *Dracula* (1897) might be more famous,
Le Fanu's earlier vampire novella is almost equally as influential in
the genre. It is most striking for the fact that it clearly centres on
a vampiric relationship with strong lesbian overtones, which was
unusual for the Victorian period. The story is told to the reader via
the case notes of Dr. Hesselius, an occult/medical detective—one
of the first in literature—who also features throughout the other
tales in *In a Glass Darkly* as a student of psychic phenomena. The
narrative is presented as one of his case studies, which are suggestive
of a form of proto-psychiatric/psychoanalytical analysis, albeit with
a supernatural air. Indeed, *Carmilla* engages with Victorian anxieties
around specific female medical maladies such as hysteria, a condition which had broad wide-ranging symptoms, including fainting,
nervousness, and convulsions, but was often attributed to women
who would not behave and who were sexually deprived or deviant in some form. The erotic nature of the relationship between
the two women has, therefore, been read in various ways: as being

35

representative of repressed sexuality, specifically lesbian desire; as reflecting contemporary fears about sexually voracious women; and as empowering since it renders men powerless, while women become the aggressors and reign supreme.

PROLOGUE

Upon a paper attached to the Narrative which follows, Doctor Hesselius has written a rather elaborate note, which he accompanies with a reference to his Essay on the strange subject which the MS. illuminates.

This mysterious subject he treats, in that Essay, with his usual learning and acumen, and with remarkable directness and condensation. It will form but one volume of the series of that extraordinary man's collected papers.

As I publish the case, in this volume, simply to interest the "laity," I shall forestall the intelligent lady, who relates it, in nothing; and after due consideration, I have determined, therefore, to abstain from presenting any précis of the learned Doctor's reasoning, or extract from his statement on a subject which he describes as "involving, not improbably, some of the profoundest arcana of our dual existence, and its intermediates."

I was anxious on discovering this paper, to reopen the correspondence commenced by Doctor Hesselius, so many years before, with a person so clever and careful as his informant seems to have been. Much to my regret, however, I found that she had died in the interval.

She, probably, could have added little to the Narrative which she communicates in the following pages, with, so far as I can pronounce, such conscientious particularity.

I

An Early Fright

In Styria, we, though by no means magnificent people, inhabit a castle, or schloss. A small income, in that part of the world, goes a great way. Eight or nine hundred a year does wonders. Scantily enough ours would have answered among wealthy people at home. My father is English, and I bear an English name, although I never saw England. But here, in this lonely and primitive place, where everything is so marvellously cheap, I really don't see how ever so much more money would at all materially add to our comforts, or even luxuries.

My father was in the Austrian service, and retired upon a pension and his patrimony, and purchased this feudal residence, and the small estate on which it stands, a bargain.

Nothing can be more picturesque or solitary. It stands on a slight eminence in a forest. The road, very old and narrow, passes in front of its drawbridge, never raised in my time, and its moat, stocked with perch, and sailed over by many swans, and floating on its surface white fleets of water lilies.

Over all this the schloss shows its many-windowed front; its towers, and its Gothic chapel.

The forest opens in an irregular and very picturesque glade before its gate, and at the right a steep Gothic bridge carries the road over a stream that winds in deep shadow through the wood. I have said that this is a very lonely place. Judge whether I say truth. Looking from the hall door towards the road, the forest in which our castle stands extends fifteen miles to the right, and twelve to the left. The nearest inhabited village is about seven of your English miles to the left. The nearest inhabited schloss of any historic associations, is that of old General Spielsdorf, nearly twenty miles away to the right.

I have said "the nearest *inhabited* village," because there is, only three miles westward, that is to say in the direction of General Spielsdorf's schloss, a ruined village, with its quaint little church, now roofless, in the aisle of which are the mouldering tombs of the proud family of Karnstein, now extinct, who once owned the equally desolate chateau which, in the thick of the forest, overlooks the silent ruins of the town.

Respecting the cause of the desertion of this striking and melancholy spot, there is a legend which I shall relate to you another time.

I must tell you now, how very small is the party who constitute the inhabitants of our castle. I don't include servants, or those dependents who occupy rooms in the buildings attached to the schloss. Listen, and wonder! My father, who is the kindest man on earth, but growing old; and I, at the date of my story, only nineteen. Eight years have passed since then.

I and my father constituted the family at the schloss. My mother, a Styrian lady, died in my infancy, but I had a good-natured governess, who had been with me from, I might almost say, my infancy. I could not remember the time when her fat, benignant face was not a familiar picture in my memory.

This was Madame Perrodon, a native of Berne, whose care and good nature now in part supplied to me the loss of my mother, whom I do not even remember, so early I lost her. She made a third at our little dinner party. There was a fourth, Mademoiselle De Lafontaine, a lady such as you term, I believe, a "finishing governess." She spoke French and German, Madame Perrodon French and broken English, to which my father and I added English, which, partly to prevent its becoming a lost language among us, and partly from patriotic motives, we spoke every day. The consequence was a Babel, at which strangers used to laugh, and which I shall make no attempt to reproduce in this narrative. And there were two or three young lady friends besides, pretty nearly of my own age, who were occasional visitors, for longer or shorter terms; and these visits I sometimes returned.

These were our regular social resources; but of course there were chance visits from "neighbours" of only five or six leagues distance. My life was, notwithstanding, rather a solitary one, I can assure you.

My gouvernantes had just so much control over me as you might conjecture such sage persons would have in the case of a rather spoiled girl, whose only parent allowed her pretty nearly her own way in everything.

The first occurrence in my existence, which produced a terrible impression upon my mind, which, in fact, never has been effaced, was one of the very earliest incidents of my life which I can recollect. Some people will think it so trifling that it should not be recorded here. You will see, however, by-and-by, why I mention it. The nursery, as it was called, though I had it all to myself, was a large room in the upper storey of the castle, with a steep oak roof. I can't have been more than six years old, when one night I awoke, and looking round the room from my bed, failed to see the nursery maid. Neither was my nurse there; and I thought myself alone. I was not frightened, for I was one of those happy children who are studiously kept in ignorance of ghost stories, of fairy tales, and of all such lore as makes us cover up our heads when the door cracks suddenly, or the flicker of an expiring candle makes the shadow of a bedpost dance upon the wall, nearer to our faces. I was vexed and insulted at finding myself, as I conceived, neglected, and I began to whimper, preparatory to a hearty bout of roaring; when to my surprise, I saw a solemn, but very pretty face looking at me from the side of the bed. It was that of a young lady who was kneeling, with her hands under the coverlet. I looked at her with a kind of pleased wonder, and ceased whimpering. She caressed me with her hands, and lay down beside me on the bed, and drew me towards her, smiling; I felt immediately delightfully soothed, and fell asleep again. I was wakened by a sensation as if two needles ran into my breast very deep at the same moment, and I cried loudly. The lady started back, with her eyes fixed on me, and then slipped down upon the floor, and, as I thought, hid herself under the bed.

I was now for the first time frightened, and I yelled with all my might and main. Nurse, nursery maid, housekeeper, all came running in, and hearing my story, they made light of it, soothing me all they could meanwhile. But, child as I was, I could perceive that their faces were pale with an unwonted look of anxiety, and I saw them look under the bed, and about the room, and peep under tables and pluck open cupboards; and the housekeeper whispered to the nurse: "Lay your hand along that hollow in the bed; someone *did* lie there, so sure as you did not; the place is still warm."

I remember the nursery maid petting me, and all three examining my chest, where I told them I felt the puncture, and pronouncing that there was no sign visible that any such thing had happened to me.

The housekeeper and the two other servants who were in charge of the nursery, remained sitting up all night; and from that time a servant always sat up in the nursery until I was about fourteen.

I was very nervous for a long time after this. A doctor was called in, he was pallid and elderly. How well I remember his long saturnine face, slightly pitted with smallpox, and his chestnut wig. For a good while, every second day, he came and gave me medicine, which of course I hated.

The morning after I saw this apparition I was in a state of terror, and could not bear to be left alone, daylight though it was, for a moment.

I remember my father coming up and standing at the bedside, and talking cheerfully, and asking the nurse a number of questions, and laughing very heartily at one of the answers; and patting me on the shoulder, and kissing me, and telling me not to be frightened, that it was nothing but a dream and could not hurt me.

But I was not comforted, for I knew the visit of the strange woman was *not* a dream; and I was *awfully* frightened.

I was a little consoled by the nursery maid's assuring me that it was she who had come and looked at me, and lain down beside me in the bed, and that I must have been half-dreaming not to have known her face. But this, though supported by the nurse, did not quite satisfy me.

I remembered, in the course of that day, a venerable old man, in a black cassock, coming into the room with the nurse and housekeeper, and talking a little to them, and very kindly to me; his face was very sweet and gentle, and he told me they were going to pray, and joined my hands together, and desired me to say, softly, while they were praying, "Lord hear all good prayers for us, for Jesus' sake." I think these were the very words, for I often repeated them to myself, and my nurse used for years to make me say them in my prayers.

I remembered so well the thoughtful sweet face of that white-haired old man, in his black cassock, as he stood in that rude, lofty, brown room, with the clumsy furniture of a fashion three hundred years old about him, and the scanty light entering its shadowy atmosphere through the small lattice. He kneeled, and the three women with him, and he prayed aloud with an earnest quavering voice for, what appeared to me, a long time. I forget all my life preceding that event, and for some time after it is all obscure also, but the scenes I have just described stand out vivid as the isolated pictures of the phantasmagoria surrounded by darkness.

II
A Guest

I am now going to tell you something so strange that it will require all your faith in my veracity to believe my story. It is not only true, nevertheless, but truth of which I have been an eyewitness.

It was a sweet summer evening, and my father asked me, as he sometimes did, to take a little ramble with him along that beautiful forest vista which I have mentioned as lying in front of the schloss.

"General Spielsdorf cannot come to us so soon as I had hoped," said my father, as we pursued our walk.

He was to have paid us a visit of some weeks, and we had expected his arrival next day. He was to have brought with him a young lady, his niece and ward, Mademoiselle Rheinfeldt, whom I had never seen, but whom I had heard described as a very charming girl, and in whose society I had promised myself many happy days. I was more disappointed than a young lady living in a town, or a bustling neighbourhood can possibly imagine. This visit, and the new acquaintance it promised, had furnished my day dream for many weeks.

"And how soon does he come?" I asked.

"Not till autumn. Not for two months, I dare say," he answered. "And I am very glad now, dear, that you never knew Mademoiselle Rheinfeldt."

"And why?" I asked, both mortified and curious.

"Because the poor young lady is dead," he replied. "I quite forgot I had not told you, but you were not in the room when I received the General's letter this evening."

I was very much shocked. General Spielsdorf had mentioned in his first letter, six or seven weeks before, that she was not so well as he would wish her, but there was nothing to suggest the remotest suspicion of danger.

"Here is the General's letter," he said, handing it to me. "I am afraid he is in great affliction; the letter appears to me to have been written very nearly in distraction."

We sat down on a rude bench, under a group of magnificent lime trees. The sun was setting with all its melancholy splendour behind the sylvan horizon, and the stream that flows beside our home, and passes under the steep old bridge I have mentioned, wound through many a group of noble trees, almost at our feet, reflecting in its current the fading crimson of the sky. General Spielsdorf's letter was so extraordinary, so vehement, and in some places so self-contradictory, that I read it twice over—the second time aloud to my father—and was still unable to account for it, except by supposing that grief had unsettled his mind.

It said: "I have lost my darling daughter, for as such I loved her. During the last days of dear Bertha's illness I was not able to write to you. Before then I had no idea of her danger. I have lost her, and now learn *all*, too late. She died in the peace of innocence, and in the glorious hope of a blessed futurity. The fiend who betrayed our infatuated hospitality has done it all. I thought I was receiving into my house innocence, gaiety, a charming companion for my lost Bertha. Heavens! what a fool have I been!

I thank God my child died without a suspicion of the cause of her sufferings. She is gone without so much as conjecturing the nature of her illness, and the accursed passion of the agent of all this misery. I devote my remaining days to tracking and extinguishing a monster. I am told I may hope to accomplish my righteous and merciful purpose. At present there is scarcely a gleam of light to guide me. I curse my conceited incredulity, my despicable affectation of superiority, my blindness, my obstinacy—all—too late. I cannot write or talk collectedly now. I am distracted. So soon as I shall have a little recovered, I mean to devote myself for a time to enquiry, which may possibly lead me as far as Vienna. Some time in the autumn, two months hence, or earlier if I live, I will see you—that is, if you permit me; I will then tell you all that I scarce dare put upon paper now. Farewell. Pray for me, dear friend."

In these terms ended this strange letter. Though I had never seen Bertha Rheinfeldt my eyes filled with tears at the sudden intelligence; I was startled, as well as profoundly disappointed.

The sun had now set, and it was twilight by the time I had returned the General's letter to my father.

It was a soft clear evening, and we loitered, speculating upon the possible meanings of the violent and incoherent sentences which I had just been reading. We had nearly a mile to walk before reaching the road that passes the schloss in front, and by that time the moon was shining brilliantly. At the drawbridge we met Madame Perrodon and Mademoiselle De Lafontaine, who had come out, without their bonnets, to enjoy the exquisite moonlight.

We heard their voices gabbling in animated dialogue as we approached. We joined them at the drawbridge, and turned about to admire with them the beautiful scene.

The glade through which we had just walked lay before us. At our left the narrow road wound away under clumps of lordly trees, and was lost to sight amid the thickening forest. At the right the same road crosses the steep and picturesque bridge, near which stands a ruined tower which once guarded that pass; and beyond the bridge an abrupt eminence rises, covered with trees, and showing in the shadows some grey ivy-clustered rocks.

Over the sward and low grounds a thin film of mist was stealing like smoke, marking the distances with a transparent veil; and here and there we could see the river faintly flashing in the moonlight.

No softer, sweeter scene could be imagined. The news I had just heard made it melancholy; but nothing could disturb its character of profound serenity, and the enchanted glory and vagueness of the prospect.

My father, who enjoyed the picturesque, and I, stood looking in silence over the expanse beneath us. The two good governesses, standing a little way behind us, discoursed upon the scene, and were eloquent upon the moon.

Madame Perrodon was fat, middle-aged, and romantic, and talked and sighed poetically. Mademoiselle De Lafontaine—in right of her father who was a German, assumed to be psychological, metaphysical, and something of a mystic—now declared that when the moon shone with a light so intense it was well known that it indicated a special spiritual activity. The effect of the full moon in such a state of brilliancy was manifold. It acted on dreams, it acted on lunacy, it acted on nervous people, it had marvellous physical influences connected with life. Mademoiselle related that her cousin, who was mate of a merchant ship, having taken a nap on deck on such a night, lying on his back, with his face full in the light on the moon, had wakened, after a dream of an old woman clawing him by the cheek, with his features horribly drawn to one side; and his countenance had never quite recovered its equilibrium.

"The moon, this night," she said, "is full of idyllic and magnetic influence—and see, when you look behind you at the front of the schloss how all its windows flash and twinkle with that silvery splendour, as if unseen hands had lighted up the rooms to receive fairy guests."

There are indolent styles of the spirits in which, indisposed to talk ourselves, the talk of others is pleasant to our listless ears; and I gazed on, pleased with the tinkle of the ladies' conversation.

"I have got into one of my moping moods tonight," said my father, after a silence, and quoting Shakespeare, whom, by way of keeping up our English, he used to read aloud, he said:

>"'In truth I know not why I am so sad.
>It wearies me: you say it wearies you;
>But how I got it—came by it.'

"I forget the rest. But I feel as if some great misfortune were hanging over us. I suppose the poor General's afflicted letter has had something to do with it."

At this moment the unwonted sound of carriage wheels and many hoofs upon the road, arrested our attention.

They seemed to be approaching from the high ground overlooking the bridge, and very soon the equipage emerged from that point. Two horsemen first crossed the bridge, then came a carriage drawn by four horses, and two men rode behind.

It seemed to be the travelling carriage of a person of rank; and we were all immediately absorbed in watching that very unusual spectacle. It became, in a few moments, greatly more interesting, for just as the carriage had passed the summit of the steep bridge, one of the leaders, taking fright, communicated his panic to the rest, and after a plunge or two, the whole team broke into a wild gallop together, and dashing between the horsemen who rode in front, came thundering along the road towards us with the speed of a hurricane.

The excitement of the scene was made more painful by the clear, long-drawn screams of a female voice from the carriage window.

We all advanced in curiosity and horror; me rather in silence, the rest with various ejaculations of terror.

Our suspense did not last long. Just before you reach the castle drawbridge, on the route they were coming, there stands by the road-side a magnificent lime tree, on the other stands an ancient stone cross, at sight of which the horses, now going at a pace that was perfectly frightful, swerved so as to bring the wheel over the projecting roots of the tree.

I knew what was coming. I covered my eyes, unable to see it out, and turned my head away; at the same moment I heard a cry from my lady friends, who had gone on a little.

Curiosity opened my eyes, and I saw a scene of utter confusion. Two of the horses were on the ground, the carriage lay upon its side with two wheels in the air; the men were busy removing the traces, and a lady with a commanding air and figure had got out, and stood with clasped hands, raising the handkerchief that was in them every now and then to her eyes.

Through the carriage door was now lifted a young lady, who appeared to be lifeless. My dear old father was already beside the elder lady, with his hat in his hand, evidently tendering his aid and the resources of his schloss. The lady did not appear to hear him, or to have eyes for anything but the slender girl who was being placed against the slope of the bank.

I approached; the young lady was apparently stunned, but she was certainly not dead. My father, who piqued himself on being something of a physician, had just had his fingers on her wrist and assured the lady, who declared herself her mother, that her pulse, though faint and irregular, was undoubtedly still distinguishable. The lady clasped her hands and looked upward, as if in a momentary transport of gratitude; but immediately she broke out again in that theatrical way which is, I believe, natural to some people.

She was what is called a fine-looking woman for her time of life, and must have been handsome; she was tall, but not thin, and dressed in black velvet, and looked rather pale, but with a proud and commanding countenance, though now agitated strangely.

"Who was ever being so born to calamity?" I heard her say, with clasped hands, as I came up. "Here am I, on a journey of life and death, in prosecuting which to lose an hour is possibly to lose all. My child will not have recovered sufficiently to resume her route for who can say how long. I must leave her: I cannot, dare not, delay. How far on, sir, can you tell, is the nearest village? I must leave her there; and shall not see my darling, or even hear of her till my return, three months hence."

I plucked my father by the coat, and whispered earnestly in his ear: "Oh! papa, pray ask her to let her stay with us—it would be so delightful. Do, pray."

"If Madame will entrust her child to the care of my daughter, and of her good gouvernante, Madame Perrodon, and permit her to remain as our guest, under my charge, until her return, it will confer a distinction and an obligation upon us, and we shall treat her with all the care and devotion which so sacred a trust deserves."

"I cannot do that, sir, it would be to task your kindness and chivalry too cruelly," said the lady, distractedly.

"It would, on the contrary, be to confer on us a very great kindness at the moment when we most need it. My daughter has just been disappointed by a cruel misfortune, in a visit from which she had long anticipated a great deal of happiness. If you confide this young lady to our care it will be her best consolation. The nearest village on your route is distant, and affords no such inn as you could think of placing your daughter at; you cannot allow her to continue her journey for any considerable distance without danger. If, as you say, you cannot suspend your journey, you must part with her tonight, and nowhere could you do so with more honest assurances of care and tenderness than here."

There was something in this lady's air and appearance so distinguished and even imposing, and in her manner so engaging, as to impress one, quite apart from the dignity of her equipage, with a conviction that she was a person of consequence.

By this time the carriage was replaced in its upright position, and the horses, quite tractable, in the traces again.

The lady threw on her daughter a glance which I fancied was not quite so affectionate as one might have anticipated from the beginning of the scene; then she beckoned slightly to my father, and withdrew two or three steps with him out of hearing; and talked to him with a fixed and stern countenance, not at all like that with which she had hitherto spoken.

I was filled with wonder that my father did not seem to perceive the change, and also unspeakably curious to learn what it could be that she was speaking, almost in his ear, with so much earnestness and rapidity.

Two or three minutes at most I think she remained thus employed, then she turned, and a few steps brought her to where her daughter lay, supported by Madame Perrodon. She kneeled beside her for a moment and whispered, as Madame supposed, a little benediction in her ear; then hastily kissing her she stepped into her carriage, the door was closed, the footmen in stately liveries jumped up behind, the outriders spurred on, the postilions cracked their whips, the horses plunged and broke suddenly into a furious canter that threatened soon again to become a gallop, and the carriage whirled away, followed at the same rapid pace by the two horsemen in the rear.

III
We Compare Notes

We followed the *cortege* with our eyes until it was swiftly lost to sight in the misty wood; and the very sound of the hoofs and the wheels died away in the silent night air.

Nothing remained to assure us that the adventure had not been an illusion of a moment but the young lady, who just at that moment opened her eyes. I could not see, for her face was turned from me, but she raised her head, evidently looking about her, and I heard a very sweet voice ask complainingly, "Where is mamma?"

Our good Madame Perrodon answered tenderly, and added some comfortable assurances.

I then heard her ask:

"Where am I? What is this place?" and after that she said, "I don't see the carriage; and Matska, where is she?"

Madame answered all her questions in so far as she understood them; and gradually the young lady remembered how the misadventure came about, and was glad to hear that no one in, or in attendance on, the carriage was hurt; and on learning that her mamma had left her here, till her return in about three months, she wept.

I was going to add my consolations to those of Madame Perrodon when Mademoiselle De Lafontaine placed her hand upon my arm, saying:

"Don't approach, one at a time is as much as she can at present converse with; a very little excitement would possibly overpower her now."

As soon as she is comfortably in bed, I thought, I will run up to her room and see her.

My father in the meantime had sent a servant on horseback for the physician, who lived about two leagues away; and a bedroom was being prepared for the young lady's reception.

The stranger now rose, and leaning on Madame's arm, walked slowly over the drawbridge and into the castle gate.

In the hall, servants waited to receive her, and she was conducted forthwith to her room. The room we usually sat in as our drawing room is long, having four windows, that looked over the moat and drawbridge, upon the forest scene I have just described.

It is furnished in old carved oak, with large carved cabinets, and the chairs are cushioned with crimson Utrecht velvet. The walls are covered with tapestry, and surrounded with great gold frames, the figures being as large as life, in ancient and very curious costume, and the subjects represented are hunting, hawking, and generally festive. It is not too stately to be extremely comfortable; and here we had our tea, for with his usual patriotic leanings he insisted that the national beverage should make its appearance regularly with our coffee and chocolate.

We sat here this night, and with candles lighted, were talking over the adventure of the evening.

Madame Perrodon and Mademoiselle De Lafontaine were both of our party. The young stranger had hardly lain down in her bed when she sank into a deep sleep; and those ladies had left her in the care of a servant.

"How do you like our guest?" I asked, as soon as Madame entered. "Tell me all about her?"

"I like her extremely," answered Madame, "she is, I almost think, the prettiest creature I ever saw; about your age, and so gentle and nice."

"She is absolutely beautiful," threw in Mademoiselle, who had peeped for a moment into the stranger's room.

"And such a sweet voice!" added Madame Perrodon.

"Did you remark a woman in the carriage, after it was set up again, who did not get out," inquired Mademoiselle, "but only looked from the window?"

"No, we had not seen her."

Then she described a hideous black woman, with a sort of coloured turban on her head, and who was gazing all the time from the carriage window, nodding and grinning derisively towards the ladies, with gleaming eyes and large white eyeballs, and her teeth set as if in fury.

"Did you remark what an ill-looking pack of men the servants were?" asked Madame.

"Yes," said my father, who had just come in, "ugly, hang-dog looking fellows as ever I beheld in my life. I hope they mayn't rob the poor lady in the forest. They are clever rogues, however; they got everything to rights in a minute."

"I dare say they are worn out with too long travelling," said Madame.

"Besides looking wicked, their faces were so strangely lean, and dark, and sullen. I am very curious, I own; but I dare say the young lady will tell you all about it tomorrow, if she is sufficiently recovered."

"I don't think she will," said my father, with a mysterious smile, and a little nod of his head, as if he knew more about it than he cared to tell us.

This made us all the more inquisitive as to what had passed between him and the lady in the black velvet, in the brief but earnest interview that had immediately preceded her departure.

We were scarcely alone, when I entreated him to tell me. He did not need much pressing.

"There is no particular reason why I should not tell you. She expressed a reluctance to trouble us with the care of her daughter, saying she was in delicate health, and nervous, but not subject to any kind of seizure—she volunteered that—nor to any illusion; being, in fact, perfectly sane."

"How very odd to say all that!" I interpolated. "It was so unnecessary."

"At all events it *was* said," he laughed, "and as you wish to know all that passed, which was indeed very little, I tell you. She then said,

'I am making a long journey of *vital* importance—she emphasized the word—rapid and secret; I shall return for my child in three months; in the meantime, she will be silent as to who we are, whence we come, and whither we are travelling.' That is all she said. She spoke very pure French. When she said the word 'secret,' she paused for a few seconds, looking sternly, her eyes fixed on mine. I fancy she makes a great point of that. You saw how quickly she was gone. I hope I have not done a very foolish thing, in taking charge of the young lady."

For my part, I was delighted. I was longing to see and talk to her; and only waiting till the doctor should give me leave. You, who live in towns, can have no idea how great an event the introduction of a new friend is, in such a solitude as surrounded us.

The doctor did not arrive till nearly one o'clock; but I could no more have gone to my bed and slept, than I could have overtaken, on foot, the carriage in which the princess in black velvet had driven away.

When the physician came down to the drawing room, it was to report very favourably upon his patient. She was now sitting up, her pulse quite regular, apparently perfectly well. She had sustained no injury, and the little shock to her nerves had passed away quite harmlessly. There could be no harm certainly in my seeing her, if we both wished it; and, with this permission I sent, forthwith, to know whether she would allow me to visit her for a few minutes in her room.

The servant returned immediately to say that she desired nothing more.

You may be sure I was not long in availing myself of this permission.

Our visitor lay in one of the handsomest rooms in the schloss. It was, perhaps, a little stately. There was a sombre piece of tapestry opposite the foot of the bed, representing Cleopatra with the asps to her bosom; and other solemn classic scenes were displayed, a little faded, upon the other walls. But there was gold carving, and rich and varied colour enough in the other decorations of the room, to more than redeem the gloom of the old tapestry.

There were candles at the bedside. She was sitting up; her slender pretty figure enveloped in the soft silk dressing gown, embroidered with flowers, and lined with thick quilted silk, which her mother had thrown over her feet as she lay upon the ground.

What was it that, as I reached the bedside and had just begun my little greeting, struck me dumb in a moment, and made me recoil a step or two from before her? I will tell you.

I saw the very face which had visited me in my childhood at night, which remained so fixed in my memory, and on which I had for so many years so often ruminated with horror, when no one suspected of what I was thinking.

It was pretty, even beautiful; and when I first beheld it, wore the same melancholy expression.

But this almost instantly lighted into a strange fixed smile of recognition.

There was a silence of fully a minute, and then at length she spoke; I could not.

"How wonderful!" she exclaimed. "Twelve years ago, I saw your face in a dream, and it has haunted me ever since."

"Wonderful indeed!" I repeated, overcoming with an effort the horror that had for a time suspended my utterances. "Twelve years ago, in vision or reality, I certainly saw you. I could not forget your face. It has remained before my eyes ever since."

Her smile had softened. Whatever I had fancied strange in it, was gone, and it and her dimpling cheeks were now delightfully pretty and intelligent.

I felt reassured, and continued more in the vein which hospitality indicated, to bid her welcome, and to tell her how much pleasure her accidental arrival had given us all, and especially what a happiness it was to me.

I took her hand as I spoke. I was a little shy, as lonely people are, but the situation made me eloquent, and even bold. She pressed my hand, she laid hers upon it, and her eyes glowed, as, looking hastily into mine, she smiled again, and blushed.

She answered my welcome very prettily. I sat down beside her, still wondering; and she said:

"I must tell you my vision about you; it is so very strange that you and I should have had, each of the other so vivid a dream, that each should have seen, I you and you me, looking as we do now, when of course we both were mere children. I was a child, about six years old, and I awoke from a confused and troubled dream, and found myself in a room, unlike my nursery, wainscoted clumsily in some dark wood, and with cupboards and bedsteads, and chairs, and benches placed about it. The beds were, I thought, all empty, and the room itself without anyone but myself in it; and I, after looking about me for some time, and admiring especially an iron candlestick with two branches, which I should certainly know again, crept under one of the beds to reach the window; but as I got from under the bed, I heard someone crying; and looking up, while I was still upon my knees, I saw you—most assuredly you—as I see you now; a beautiful young lady, with golden hair and large blue eyes, and lips—your lips—you as you are here.

"Your looks won me; I climbed on the bed and put my arms about you, and I think we both fell asleep. I was aroused by a scream; you were sitting up screaming. I was frightened, and slipped down upon the ground, and, it seemed to me, lost consciousness for a moment; and when I came to myself, I was again in my nursery at home. Your face I have never forgotten since. I could not be misled by mere resemblance. *You are* the lady whom I saw then."

It was now my turn to relate my corresponding vision, which I did, to the undisguised wonder of my new acquaintance.

"I don't know which should be most afraid of the other," she said, again smiling—"If you were less pretty I think I should be very much afraid of you, but being as you are, and you and I both so young, I feel only that I have made your acquaintance twelve years ago, and have already a right to your intimacy; at all events it does seem as if we were destined, from our earliest childhood, to be friends. I wonder whether you feel as strangely drawn towards me as I do to you; I have never had a friend—shall I find one now?" She sighed, and her fine dark eyes gazed passionately on me.

Now the truth is, I felt rather unaccountably towards the beautiful stranger. I did feel, as she said, "drawn towards her," but there was also something of repulsion. In this ambiguous feeling, however, the sense of attraction immensely prevailed. She interested and won me; she was so beautiful and so indescribably engaging.

I perceived now something of languor and exhaustion stealing over her, and hastened to bid her good night.

"The doctor thinks," I added, "that you ought to have a maid to sit up with you tonight; one of ours is waiting, and you will find her a very useful and quiet creature."

"How kind of you, but I could not sleep, I never could with an attendant in the room. I shan't require any assistance—and, shall I confess my weakness, I am haunted with a terror of robbers. Our house was robbed once, and two servants murdered, so I always lock my door. It has become a habit—and you look so kind I know you will forgive me. I see there is a key in the lock."

She held me close in her pretty arms for a moment and whispered in my ear, "Good night, darling, it is very hard to part with you, but good night; tomorrow, but not early, I shall see you again."

She sank back on the pillow with a sigh, and her fine eyes followed me with a fond and melancholy gaze, and she murmured again "Good night, dear friend."

Young people like, and even love, on impulse. I was flattered by the evident, though as yet undeserved, fondness she showed me. I liked the confidence with which she at once received me. She was determined that we should be very near friends.

Next day came and we met again. I was delighted with my companion; that is to say, in many respects.

Her looks lost nothing in daylight—she was certainly the most beautiful creature I had ever seen, and the unpleasant remembrance of the face presented in my early dream, had lost the effect of the first unexpected recognition.

She confessed that she had experienced a similar shock on seeing me, and precisely the same faint antipathy that had mingled with my admiration of her. We now laughed together over our momentary horrors.

IV
Her Habits—A Saunter

I told you that I was charmed with her in most particulars.

There were some that did not please me so well.

She was above the middle height of women. I shall begin by describing her.

She was slender, and wonderfully graceful. Except that her movements were languid—very languid—indeed, there was nothing in her appearance to indicate an invalid. Her complexion was rich and brilliant; her features were small and beautifully formed; her eyes large, dark, and lustrous; her hair was quite wonderful, I never saw hair so magnificently thick and long when it was down about her shoulders; I have often placed my hands under it, and laughed with wonder at its weight. It was exquisitely fine and soft, and in colour a rich very dark brown, with something of gold. I loved to let it down, tumbling with its own weight, as, in her room, she lay back in her chair talking in her sweet low voice, I used to fold and braid it, and spread it out and play with it. Heavens! If I had but known all!

I said there were particulars which did not please me. I have told you that her confidence won me the first night I saw her; but I found that she exercised with respect to herself, her mother, her history, everything in fact connected with her life, plans, and people, an ever wakeful reserve. I dare say I was unreasonable, perhaps I was wrong; I dare say I ought to have respected the solemn injunction laid upon my father by the stately lady in black velvet. But curiosity is a restless and unscrupulous passion, and no one girl can endure, with patience, that hers should be baffled by another. What harm could it do anyone to tell me what I so ardently desired to know? Had she no trust in my good sense or honour? Why would she not believe me when I assured her, so solemnly, that I would not divulge one syllable of what she told me to any mortal breathing.

There was a coldness, it seemed to me, beyond her years, in her smiling melancholy persistent refusal to afford me the least ray of light.

I cannot say we quarrelled upon this point, for she would not quarrel upon any. It was, of course, very unfair of me to press her, very ill-bred, but I really could not help it; and I might just as well have let it alone.

What she did tell me amounted, in my unconscionable estimation—to nothing.

It was all summed up in three very vague disclosures:

First—Her name was Carmilla.

59

Second—Her family was very ancient and noble.

Third—Her home lay in the direction of the west.

She would not tell me the name of her family, nor their armorial bearings, nor the name of their estate, nor even that of the country they lived in.

You are not to suppose that I worried her incessantly on these subjects. I watched opportunity, and rather insinuated than urged my inquiries. Once or twice, indeed, I did attack her more directly. But no matter what my tactics, utter failure was invariably the result. Reproaches and caresses were all lost upon her. But I must add this, that her evasion was conducted with so pretty a melancholy and deprecation, with so many, and even passionate declarations of her liking for me, and trust in my honour, and with so many promises that I should at last know all, that I could not find it in my heart long to be offended with her.

She used to place her pretty arms about my neck, draw me to her, and laying her cheek to mine, murmur with her lips near my ear, "Dearest, your little heart is wounded; think me not cruel because I obey the irresistible law of my strength and weakness; if your dear heart is wounded, my wild heart bleeds with yours. In the rapture of my enormous humiliation I live in your warm life, and you shall die—die, sweetly die—into mine. I cannot help it; as I draw near to you, you, in your turn, will draw near to others, and learn the rapture of that cruelty, which yet is love; so, for a while, seek to know no more of me and mine, but trust me with all your loving spirit."

And when she had spoken such a rhapsody, she would press me more closely in her trembling embrace, and her lips in soft kisses gently glow upon my cheek.

Her agitations and her language were unintelligible to me.

From these foolish embraces, which were not of very frequent occurrence, I must allow, I used to wish to extricate myself; but my energies seemed to fail me. Her murmured words sounded like a lullaby in my ear, and soothed my resistance into a trance, from which I only seemed to recover myself when she withdrew her arms.

In these mysterious moods I did not like her. I experienced a strange tumultuous excitement that was pleasurable, ever and anon, mingled with a vague sense of fear and disgust. I had no distinct thoughts about her while such scenes lasted, but I was conscious of a love growing into adoration, and also of abhorrence. This I know is paradox, but I can make no other attempt to explain the feeling.

I now write, after an interval of more than ten years, with a trembling hand, with a confused and horrible recollection of certain occurrences and situations, in the ordeal through which I was unconsciously passing; though with a vivid and very sharp remembrance of the main current of my story.

But, I suspect, in all lives there are certain emotional scenes, those in which our passions have been most wildly and terribly roused, that are of all others the most vaguely and dimly remembered.

Sometimes after an hour of apathy, my strange and beautiful companion would take my hand and hold it with a fond pressure, renewed again and again; blushing softly, gazing in my face with languid and burning eyes, and breathing so fast that her dress rose and fell with the tumultuous respiration. It was like the ardour of a lover; it embarrassed me; it was hateful and yet over-powering; and with gloating eyes she drew me to her, and her hot lips travelled along my cheek in kisses; and she would whisper, almost in sobs, "You are mine, you *shall* be mine, you and I are one for ever." Then she had thrown herself back in her chair, with her small hands over her eyes, leaving me trembling.

"Are we related," I used to ask; "what can you mean by all this? I remind you perhaps of someone whom you love; but you must not,

I hate it; I don't know you—I don't know myself when you look so and talk so."

She used to sigh at my vehemence, then turn away and drop my hand.

Respecting these very extraordinary manifestations I strove in vain to form any satisfactory theory—I could not refer them to affectation or trick. It was unmistakably the momentary breaking out of suppressed instinct and emotion. Was she, notwithstanding her mother's volunteered denial, subject to brief visitations of insanity; or was there here a disguise and a romance? I had read in old storybooks of such things. What if a boyish lover had found his way into the house, and sought to prosecute his suit in masquerade, with the assistance of a clever old adventuress. But there were many things against this hypothesis, highly interesting as it was to my vanity.

I could boast of no little attentions such as masculine gallantry delights to offer. Between these passionate moments there were long intervals of commonplace, of gaiety, of brooding melancholy, during which, except that I detected her eyes so full of melancholy fire, following me, at times I might have been as nothing to her. Except in these brief periods of mysterious excitement her ways were girlish; and there was always a languor about her, quite incompatible with a masculine system in a state of health.

In some respects her habits were odd. Perhaps not so singular in the opinion of a town lady like you, as they appeared to us rustic people. She used to come down very late, generally not till one o'clock, she would then take a cup of chocolate, but eat nothing; we then went out for a walk, which was a mere saunter, and she seemed, almost immediately, exhausted, and either returned to the schloss or sat on one of the benches that were placed, here and there, among the trees. This was a bodily languor in which her mind did not sympathize. She was always an animated talker, and very intelligent.

She sometimes alluded for a moment to her own home, or mentioned an adventure or situation, or an early recollection, which indicated a people of strange manners, and described customs of which we knew nothing. I gathered from these chance hints that her native country was much more remote than I had at first fancied.

As we sat thus one afternoon under the trees a funeral passed us by. It was that of a pretty young girl, whom I had often seen, the daughter of one of the rangers of the forest. The poor man was walking behind the coffin of his darling; she was his only child, and he looked quite heartbroken.

Peasants walking two-and-two came behind, they were singing a funeral hymn.

I rose to mark my respect as they passed, and joined in the hymn they were very sweetly singing.

My companion shook me a little roughly, and I turned surprised.

She said brusquely, "Don't you perceive how discordant that is?"

"I think it very sweet, on the contrary," I answered, vexed at the interruption, and very uncomfortable, lest the people who composed the little procession should observe and resent what was passing.

I resumed, therefore, instantly, and was again interrupted. "You pierce my ears," said Carmilla, almost angrily, and stopping her ears with her tiny fingers. "Besides, how can you tell that your religion and mine are the same; your forms wound me, and I hate funerals. What a fuss! Why you must die—*everyone* must die; and all are happier when they do. Come home."

"My father has gone on with the clergyman to the churchyard. I thought you knew she was to be buried today."

"She? I don't trouble my head about peasants. I don't know who she is," answered Carmilla, with a flash from her fine eyes.

"She is the poor girl who fancied she saw a ghost a fortnight ago, and has been dying ever since, till yesterday, when she expired."

"Tell me nothing about ghosts. I shan't sleep tonight if you do."

"I hope there is no plague or fever coming; all this looks very like it," I continued. "The swineherd's young wife died only a week ago, and she thought something seized her by the throat as she lay in her bed, and nearly strangled her. Papa says such horrible fancies do accompany some forms of fever. She was quite well the day before. She sank afterwards, and died before a week."

"Well, *her* funeral is over, I hope, and *her* hymn sung; and our ears shan't be tortured with that discord and jargon. It has made me nervous. Sit down here, beside me; sit close; hold my hand; press it hard-hard-harder."

We had moved a little back, and had come to another seat.

She sat down. Her face underwent a change that alarmed and even terrified me for a moment. It darkened, and became horribly livid; her teeth and hands were clenched, and she frowned and compressed her lips, while she stared down upon the ground at her feet, and trembled all over with a continued shudder as irrepressible as ague. All her energies seemed strained to suppress a fit, with which she was then breathlessly tugging; and at length a low convulsive cry of suffering broke from her, and gradually the hysteria subsided. "There! That comes of strangling people with hymns!" she said at last. "Hold me, hold me still. It is passing away."

And so gradually it did; and perhaps to dissipate the sombre impression which the spectacle had left upon me, she became unusually animated and chatty; and so we got home.

This was the first time I had seen her exhibit any definable symptoms of that delicacy of health which her mother had spoken of. It was the first time, also, I had seen her exhibit anything like temper.

Both passed away like a summer cloud; and never but once afterwards did I witness on her part a momentary sign of anger. I will tell you how it happened.

She and I were looking out of one of the long drawing room windows, when there entered the courtyard, over the drawbridge, a figure of a wanderer whom I knew very well. He used to visit the schloss generally twice a year.

It was the figure of a hunchback, with the sharp lean features that generally accompany deformity. He wore a pointed black beard, and he was smiling from ear to ear, showing his white fangs. He was dressed in buff, black, and scarlet, and crossed with more straps and belts than I could count, from which hung all manner of things. Behind, he carried a magic lantern, and two boxes, which I well knew, in one of which was a salamander, and in the other a mandrake. These monsters used to make my father laugh. They were compounded of parts of monkeys, parrots, squirrels, fish, and hedgehogs, dried and stitched together with great neatness and startling effect. He had a fiddle, a box of conjuring apparatus, a pair of foils and masks attached to his belt, several other mysterious cases dangling about him, and a black staff with copper ferrules in his hand. His companion was a rough spare dog, that followed at his heels, but stopped short, suspiciously at the drawbridge, and in a little while began to howl dismally.

In the meantime, the mountebank, standing in the midst of the courtyard, raised his grotesque hat, and made us a very ceremonious bow, paying his compliments very volubly in execrable French, and German not much better.

Then, disengaging his fiddle, he began to scrape a lively air to which he sang with a merry discord, dancing with ludicrous airs and activity, that made me laugh, in spite of the dog's howling.

Then he advanced to the window with many smiles and salutations, and his hat in his left hand, his fiddle under his arm, and with a fluency that never took breath, he gabbled a long advertisement of all his accomplishments, and the resources of the various arts which he placed at our service, and the curiosities and entertainments which it was in his power, at our bidding, to display.

"Will your ladyships be pleased to buy an amulet against the oupire, which is going like the wolf, I hear, through these woods," he said dropping his hat on the pavement. "They are dying of it right and left and here is a charm that never fails; only pinned to the pillow, and you may laugh in his face."

These charms consisted of oblong slips of vellum, with cabalistic ciphers and diagrams upon them.

Carmilla instantly purchased one, and so did I.

He was looking up, and we were smiling down upon him, amused; at least, I can answer for myself. His piercing black eye, as he looked up in our faces, seemed to detect something that fixed for a moment his curiosity.

In an instant he unrolled a leather case, full of all manner of odd little steel instruments.

"See here, my lady," he said, displaying it, and addressing me, "I profess, among other things less useful, the art of dentistry. Plague take the dog!" he interpolated. "Silence, beast! He howls so that your ladyships can scarcely hear a word. Your noble friend, the young lady at your right, has the sharpest tooth,—long, thin, pointed, like an awl, like a needle; ha, ha! With my sharp and long sight, as I look up, I have seen it distinctly; now if it happens to hurt the young lady, and I think it must, here am I, here are my file, my punch, my nippers; I will make it round and blunt, if her ladyship pleases; no longer the tooth of a fish, but of a beautiful young lady as she is. Hey? Is the young lady displeased? Have I been too bold? Have I offended her?"

The young lady, indeed, looked very angry as she drew back from the window.

"How dares that mountebank insult us so? Where is your father? I shall demand redress from him. My father would have had the wretch

66

tied up to the pump, and flogged with a cart whip, and burnt to the bones with the cattle brand!"

She retired from the window a step or two, and sat down, and had hardly lost sight of the offender, when her wrath subsided as suddenly as it had risen, and she gradually recovered her usual tone, and seemed to forget the little hunchback and his follies.

My father was out of spirits that evening. On coming in he told us that there had been another case very similar to the two fatal ones which had lately occurred. The sister of a young peasant on his estate, only a mile away, was very ill, had been, as she described it, attacked very nearly in the same way, and was now slowly but steadily sinking.

"All this," said my father, "is strictly referable to natural causes. These poor people infect one another with their superstitions, and so repeat in imagination the images of terror that have infested their neighbours."

"But that very circumstance frightens one horribly," said Carmilla.

"How so?" inquired my father.

"I am so afraid of fancying I see such things; I think it would be as bad as reality."

"We are in God's hands: nothing can happen without his permission, and all will end well for those who love him. He is our faithful creator; He has made us all, and will take care of us."

"Creator! *Nature!*" said the young lady in answer to my gentle father. "And this disease that invades the country is natural. Nature. All things proceed from Nature—don't they? All things in the heaven, in the earth, and under the earth, act and live as Nature ordains? I think so."

"The doctor said he would come here today," said my father, after a silence. "I want to know what he thinks about it, and what he thinks we had better do."

"Doctors never did me any good," said Carmilla.

"Then you have been ill?" I asked.

"More ill than ever you were," she answered.

"Long ago?"

"Yes, a long time. I suffered from this very illness; but I forget all but my pain and weakness, and they were not so bad as are suffered in other diseases."

"You were very young then?"

"I dare say, let us talk no more of it. You would not wound a friend?"

She looked languidly in my eyes, and passed her arm round my waist lovingly, and led me out of the room. My father was busy over some papers near the window.

"Why does your papa like to frighten us?" said the pretty girl with a sigh and a little shudder.

"He doesn't, dear Carmilla, it is the very furthest thing from his mind."

"Are you afraid, dearest?"

"I should be very much if I fancied there was any real danger of my being attacked as those poor people were."

"You are afraid to die?"

"Yes, every one is."

"But to die as lovers may—to die together, so that they may live together. Girls are caterpillars while they live in the world, to be finally butterflies when the summer comes; but in the meantime there are grubs and larvae, don't you see—each with their peculiar propensities, necessities and structure. So says Monsieur Buffon, in his big book, in the next room."

Later in the day the doctor came, and was closeted with papa for some time.

He was a skilful man, of sixty and upwards, he wore powder, and shaved his pale face as smooth as a pumpkin. He and papa emerged from the room together, and I heard papa laugh, and say as they came out:

"Well, I do wonder at a wise man like you. What do you say to hippogriffs and dragons?"

The doctor was smiling, and made answer, shaking his head—

"Nevertheless life and death are mysterious states, and we know little of the resources of either."

And so they walked on, and I heard no more. I did not then know what the doctor had been broaching, but I think I guess it now.

V

A Wonderful Likeness

This evening there arrived from Gratz the grave, dark-faced son of the picture cleaner, with a horse and cart laden with two large packing cases, having many pictures in each. It was a journey of ten leagues, and whenever a messenger arrived at the schloss from our little capital of Gratz, we used to crowd about him in the hall, to hear the news.

This arrival created in our secluded quarters quite a sensation. The cases remained in the hall, and the messenger was taken charge of by the servants till he had eaten his supper. Then with assistants, and armed with hammer, ripping chisel, and turnscrew, he met us in the hall, where we had assembled to witness the unpacking of the cases.

Carmilla sat looking listlessly on, while one after the other the old pictures, nearly all portraits, which had undergone the process of renovation, were brought to light. My mother was of an old Hungarian family, and most of these pictures, which were about to be restored to their places, had come to us through her.

My father had a list in his hand, from which he read, as the artist rummaged out the corresponding numbers. I don't know that the pictures were very good, but they were, undoubtedly, very old, and some of them very curious also. They had, for the most part, the merit of being now seen by me, I may say, for the first time; for the smoke and dust of time had all but obliterated them.

"There is a picture that I have not seen yet," said my father. "In one corner, at the top of it, is the name, as well as I could read, 'Marcia Karnstein,' and the date '1698'; and I am curious to see how it has turned out."

I remembered it; it was a small picture, about a foot and a half high, and nearly square, without a frame; but it was so blackened by age that I could not make it out.

The artist now produced it, with evident pride. It was quite beautiful; it was startling; it seemed to live. It was the effigy of Carmilla!

"Carmilla, dear, here is an absolute miracle. Here you are, living, smiling, ready to speak, in this picture. Isn't it beautiful, Papa? And see, even the little mole on her throat."

My father laughed, and said, "Certainly it is a wonderful likeness," but he looked away, and to my surprise seemed but little struck by it, and went on talking to the picture cleaner, who was also something of an artist, and discoursed with intelligence about the portraits or other works, which his art had just brought into light and colour, while I was more and more lost in wonder the more I looked at the picture.

"Will you let me hang this picture in my room, papa?" I asked.

"Certainly, dear," said he, smiling, "I'm very glad you think it so like. It must be prettier even than I thought it, if it is."

The young lady did not acknowledge this pretty speech, did not seem to hear it. She was leaning back in her seat, her fine eyes under their long lashes gazing on me in contemplation, and she smiled in a kind of rapture.

"And now you can read quite plainly the name that is written in the corner. It is not Marcia; it looks as if it was done in gold. The name is Mircalla, Countess Karnstein, and this is a little coronet over and underneath A.D. 1698. I am descended from the Karnsteins; that is, mamma was."

"Ah!" said the lady, languidly, "so am I, I think, a very long descent, very ancient. Are there any Karnsteins living now?"

"None who bear the name, I believe. The family were ruined, I believe, in some civil wars, long ago, but the ruins of the castle are only about three miles away."

"How interesting!" she said, languidly. "But see what beautiful moonlight!" She glanced through the hall door, which stood a little open. "Suppose you take a little ramble round the court, and look down at the road and river."

"It is so like the night you came to us," I said.

She sighed; smiling.

She rose, and each with her arm about the other's waist, we walked out upon the pavement.

In silence, slowly we walked down to the drawbridge, where the beautiful landscape opened before us.

"And so you were thinking of the night I came here?" she almost whispered.

"Are you glad I came?"

"Delighted, dear Carmilla," I answered.

"And you asked for the picture you think like me, to hang in your room," she murmured with a sigh, as she drew her arm closer about my waist, and let her pretty head sink upon my shoulder. "How romantic you are, Carmilla," I said. "Whenever you tell me your story, it will be made up chiefly of some one great romance."

She kissed me silently.

"I am sure, Carmilla, you have been in love; that there is, at this moment, an affair of the heart going on."

"I have been in love with no one, and never shall," she whispered, "unless it should be with you."

How beautiful she looked in the moonlight!

Shy and strange was the look with which she quickly hid her face in my neck and hair, with tumultuous sighs, that seemed almost to sob, and pressed in mine a hand that trembled.

Her soft cheek was glowing against mine. "Darling, darling," she murmured, "I live in you; and you would die for me, I love you so."

I started from her.

She was gazing on me with eyes from which all fire, all meaning had flown, and a face colourless and apathetic.

"Is there a chill in the air, dear?" she said drowsily. "I almost shiver; have I been dreaming? Let us come in. Come; come; come in."

"You look ill, Carmilla; a little faint. You certainly must take some wine," I said.

"Yes. I will. I'm better now. I shall be quite well in a few minutes. Yes, do give me a little wine," answered Carmilla, as we approached the door.

"Let us look again for a moment; it is the last time, perhaps, I shall see the moonlight with you."

"How do you feel now, dear Carmilla? Are you really better?" I asked.

I was beginning to take alarm, lest she should have been stricken with the strange epidemic that they said had invaded the country about us.

"Papa would be grieved beyond measure," I added, "if he thought you were ever so little ill, without immediately letting us know. We have a very skilful doctor near us, the physician who was with papa today."

"I'm sure he is. I know how kind you all are; but, dear child, I am quite well again. There is nothing ever wrong with me, but a little weakness. People say I am languid; I am incapable of exertion; I can scarcely walk as far as a child of three years old: and every now and then the little strength I have falters, and I become as you have just seen me. But after all I am very easily set up again; in a moment I am perfectly myself. See how I have recovered."

So, indeed, she had; and she and I talked a great deal, and very animated she was; and the remainder of that evening passed without any recurrence of what I called her infatuations. I mean her crazy talk and looks, which embarrassed, and even frightened me.

But there occurred that night an event which gave my thoughts quite a new turn, and seemed to startle even Carmilla's languid nature into momentary energy.

VI

A Very Strange Agony

When we got into the drawing room, and had sat down to our coffee and chocolate, although Carmilla did not take any, she seemed quite herself again, and Madame, and Mademoiselle De Lafontaine, joined us, and made a little card party, in the course of which papa came in for what he called his "dish of tea."

When the game was over he sat down beside Carmilla on the sofa, and asked her, a little anxiously, whether she had heard from her mother since her arrival.

She answered "No."

He then asked whether she knew where a letter would reach her at present.

"I cannot tell," she answered ambiguously, "but I have been thinking of leaving you; you have been already too hospitable and too kind to me. I have given you an infinity of trouble, and I should wish to take a carriage tomorrow, and post in pursuit of her; I know where I shall ultimately find her, although I dare not yet tell you."

"But you must not dream of any such thing," exclaimed my father, to my great relief. "We can't afford to lose you so, and I won't consent to your leaving us, except under the care of your mother, who was so good as to consent to your remaining with us till she should herself return. I should be quite happy if I knew that you heard from her: but this evening the accounts of the progress of the mysterious disease that has invaded our neighbourhood, grow even more alarming; and my beautiful guest, I do feel the responsibility, unaided by advice from your mother, very much. But I shall do my best; and one thing is certain, that you must not think of leaving us without her distinct direction to that effect. We should suffer too much in parting from you to consent to it easily."

"Thank you, sir, a thousand times for your hospitality," she answered, smiling bashfully. "You have all been too kind to me; I have seldom been so happy in all my life before, as in your beautiful chateau, under your care, and in the society of your dear daughter."

So he gallantly, in his old-fashioned way, kissed her hand, smiling and pleased at her little speech.

I accompanied Carmilla as usual to her room, and sat and chatted with her while she was preparing for bed.

"Do you think," I said at length, "that you will ever confide fully in me?"

She turned round smiling, but made no answer, only continued to smile on me.

"You won't answer that?" I said. "You can't answer pleasantly; I ought not to have asked you."

"You were quite right to ask me that, or anything. You do not know how dear you are to me, or you could not think any confidence too great to look for. But I am under vows, no nun half so awfully, and I dare not tell my story yet, even to you. The time is very near when you shall know everything. You will think me cruel, very selfish, but love is always selfish; the more ardent the more selfish. How jealous I am you cannot know. You must come with me, loving me, to death; or else hate me and still come with me, and *hating* me through death and after. There is no such word as indifference in my apathetic nature."

"Now, Carmilla, you are going to talk your wild nonsense again," I said hastily.

"Not I, silly little fool as I am, and full of whims and fancies; for your sake I'll talk like a sage. Were you ever at a ball?"

"No; how you do run on. What is it like? How charming it must be."

"I almost forget, it is years ago."

I laughed.

"You are not so old. Your first ball can hardly be forgotten yet."

"I remember everything about it—with an effort. I see it all, as divers see what is going on above them, through a medium, dense, rippling, but transparent. There occurred that night what has confused the picture, and made its colours faint. I was all but assassinated in my bed, wounded here," she touched her breast, "and never was the same since."

"Were you near dying?"

"Yes, very—a cruel love—strange love, that would have taken my life. Love will have its sacrifices. No sacrifice without blood. Let us go to sleep now; I feel so lazy. How can I get up just now and lock my door?"

She was lying with her tiny hands buried in her rich wavy hair, under her cheek, her little head upon the pillow, and her glittering eyes followed me wherever I moved, with a kind of shy smile that I could not decipher.

I bid her good night, and crept from the room with an uncomfortable sensation.

I often wondered whether our pretty guest ever said her prayers. I certainly had never seen her upon her knees. In the morning she never came down until long after our family prayers were over, and at night she never left the drawing room to attend our brief evening prayers in the hall.

If it had not been that it had casually come out in one of our careless talks that she had been baptized, I should have doubted her being a Christian. Religion was a subject on which I had never heard her speak a word. If I had known the world better, this particular neglect or antipathy would not have so much surprised me.

The precautions of nervous people are infectious, and persons of a like temperament are pretty sure, after a time, to imitate them. I had adopted Carmilla's habit of locking her bedroom door, having taken into my head all her whimsical alarms about midnight invaders and prowling assassins. I had also adopted her precaution of making a brief search through her room, to satisfy herself that no lurking assassin or robber was "ensconced."

These wise measures taken, I got into my bed and fell asleep. A light was burning in my room. This was an old habit, of very early date, and which nothing could have tempted me to dispense with.

Thus fortified I might take my rest in peace. But dreams come through stone walls, light up dark rooms, or darken light ones, and their persons make their exits and their entrances as they please, and laugh at locksmiths.

I had a dream that night that was the beginning of a very strange agony.

I cannot call it a nightmare, for I was quite conscious of being asleep.

But I was equally conscious of being in my room, and lying in bed, precisely as I actually was. I saw, or fancied I saw, the room and its furniture just as I had seen it last, except that it was very dark, and I saw something moving round the foot of the bed, which at first I could not accurately distinguish. But I soon saw that it was a sooty-black animal that resembled a monstrous cat. It appeared to me about four or five feet long for it measured fully the length of the hearthrug as it passed over it; and it continued to-ing and fro-ing with the lithe, sinister restlessness of a beast in a cage. I could not cry out, although as you may suppose, I was terrified. Its pace was growing faster, and the room rapidly darker and darker, and at length so dark that I could no longer see anything of it but its eyes. I felt it spring lightly on the bed. The two broad eyes approached my face, and suddenly I felt a stinging pain as if two large needles darted, an inch or two apart, deep into my breast. I waked with a scream. The room was lighted by the candle that burnt there all through the night, and I saw a female figure standing at the foot of the bed, a little at the right side. It was in a dark loose dress, and its hair was down and covered its shoulders. A block of stone could not have been more still. There was not the slightest stir of respiration. As I stared at it, the figure appeared to have changed its place, and was now nearer the door; then, close to it, the door opened, and it passed out.

I was now relieved, and able to breathe and move. My first thought was that Carmilla had been playing me a trick, and that I had forgotten to secure my door. I hastened to it, and found it locked as usual on the inside. I was afraid to open it—I was horrified. I sprang into my bed and covered my head up in the bedclothes, and lay there more dead than alive till morning.

VII
Descending

It would be vain my attempting to tell you the horror with which, even now, I recall the occurrence of that night. It was no such transitory terror as a dream leaves behind it. It seemed to deepen by time, and communicated itself to the room and the very furniture that had encompassed the apparition.

I could not bear next day to be alone for a moment. I should have told papa, but for two opposite reasons. At one time I thought he would laugh at my story, and I could not bear its being treated as a jest; and at another I thought he might fancy that I had been attacked by the mysterious complaint which had invaded our neighbourhood. I had myself no misgiving of the kind, and as he had been rather an invalid for some time, I was afraid of alarming him.

I was comfortable enough with my good-natured companions, Madame Perrodon, and the vivacious Mademoiselle Lafontaine. They both perceived that I was out of spirits and nervous, and at length I told them what lay so heavy at my heart.

Mademoiselle laughed, but I fancied that Madame Perrodon looked anxious.

"By-the-by," said Mademoiselle, laughing, "the long lime tree walk, behind Carmilla's bedroom window, is haunted!"

"Nonsense!" exclaimed Madame, who probably thought the theme rather inopportune, "and who tells that story, my dear?"

"Martin says that he came up twice, when the old yard gate was being repaired, before sunrise, and twice saw the same female figure walking down the lime tree avenue."

"So he well might, as long as there are cows to milk in the river fields," said Madame.

"I daresay; but Martin chooses to be frightened, and never did I see fool more frightened."

"You must not say a word about it to Carmilla, because she can see down that walk from her room window," I interposed, "and she is, if possible, a greater coward than I."

Carmilla came down rather later than usual that day.

"I was so frightened last night," she said, so soon as we were together, "and I am sure I should have seen something dreadful if it had not been for that charm I bought from the poor little hunchback whom I called such hard names. I had a dream of something black coming round my bed, and I awoke in a perfect horror, and I really thought, for some seconds, I saw a dark figure near the chimneypiece, but I felt under my pillow for my charm, and the moment my fingers touched it, the figure disappeared, and I felt quite certain, only that I had it by me, that something frightful would have made its appearance, and, perhaps, throttled me, as it did those poor people we heard of."

"Well, listen to me," I began, and recounted my adventure, at the recital of which she appeared horrified.

"And had you the charm near you?" she asked, earnestly.

"No, I had dropped it into a china vase in the drawing room, but I shall certainly take it with me tonight, as you have so much faith in it."

At this distance of time I cannot tell you, or even understand, how I overcame my horror so effectually as to lie alone in my room that night. I remember distinctly that I pinned the charm to my pillow. I fell asleep almost immediately, and slept even more soundly than usual all night.

Next night I passed as well. My sleep was delightfully deep and dreamless.

But I wakened with a sense of lassitude and melancholy, which, however, did not exceed a degree that was almost luxurious.

"Well, I told you so," said Carmilla, when I described my quiet sleep, "I had such delightful sleep myself last night; I pinned the charm to the breast of my nightdress. It was too far away the night before. I am quite sure it was all fancy, except the dreams. I used to think that evil spirits made dreams, but our doctor told me it is no such thing. Only a fever passing by, or some other malady, as they often do, he said, knocks at the door, and not being able to get in, passes on, with that alarm."

"And what do you think the charm is?" said I.

"It has been fumigated or immersed in some drug, and is an antidote against the malaria," she answered.

"Then it acts only on the body?"

"Certainly; you don't suppose that evil spirits are frightened by bits of ribbon, or the perfumes of a druggist's shop? No, these complaints, wandering in the air, begin by trying the nerves, and so infect the brain, but before they can seize upon you, the antidote repels them. That I am sure is what the charm has done for us. It is nothing magical, it is simply natural."

I should have been happier if I could have quite agreed with Carmilla, but I did my best, and the impression was a little losing its force.

For some nights I slept profoundly; but still every morning I felt the same lassitude, and a languor weighed upon me all day. I felt myself a changed girl. A strange melancholy was stealing over me, a melancholy that I would not have interrupted. Dim thoughts of death began to open, and an idea that I was slowly sinking took gentle, and, somehow, not unwelcome, possession of me. If it was sad, the tone of mind which this induced was also sweet.

Whatever it might be, my soul acquiesced in it.

I would not admit that I was ill, I would not consent to tell my papa, or to have the doctor sent for.

Carmilla became more devoted to me than ever, and her strange paroxysms of languid adoration more frequent. She used to gloat on me with increasing ardour the more my strength and spirits waned. This always shocked me like a momentary glare of insanity.

Without knowing it, I was now in a pretty advanced stage of the strangest illness under which mortal ever suffered. There was an unaccountable fascination in its earlier symptoms that more than reconciled me to the incapacitating effect of that stage of the malady. This fascination increased for a time, until it reached a certain point, when gradually a sense of the horrible mingled itself with it, deepening, as you shall hear, until it discoloured and perverted the whole state of my life.

The first change I experienced was rather agreeable. It was very near the turning point from which began the descent of Avernus.

Certain vague and strange sensations visited me in my sleep. The prevailing one was of that pleasant, peculiar cold thrill which we feel in bathing, when we move against the current of a river. This was soon accompanied by dreams that seemed interminable, and were so vague that I could never recollect their scenery and persons, or any one connected portion of their action. But they left an awful impression, and a sense of exhaustion, as if I had passed through a long period of great mental exertion and danger.

After all these dreams there remained on waking a remembrance of having been in a place very nearly dark, and of having spoken to people whom I could not see; and especially of one clear voice, of a female's, very deep, that spoke as if at a distance, slowly, and producing always the same sensation of indescribable solemnity and fear. Sometimes there came a sensation as if a hand was drawn softly along my cheek and neck. Sometimes it was as if warm lips kissed me, and longer and longer and more lovingly as they reached my throat, but there the caress fixed itself. My heart beat faster, my breathing rose and fell rapidly and full drawn; a sobbing, that rose into a sense of strangulation, supervened, and turned into a dreadful convulsion, in which my senses left me and I became unconscious.

It was now three weeks since the commencement of this unaccountable state.

My sufferings had, during the last week, told upon my appearance. I had grown pale, my eyes were dilated and darkened underneath, and the languor which I had long felt began to display itself in my countenance.

My father asked me often whether I was ill; but, with an obstinacy which now seems to me unaccountable, I persisted in assuring him that I was quite well.

In a sense this was true. I had no pain, I could complain of no bodily derangement. My complaint seemed to be one of the imagination, or the nerves, and, horrible as my sufferings were, I kept them, with a morbid reserve, very nearly to myself.

It could not be that terrible complaint which the peasants called the oupire, for I had now been suffering for three weeks, and they were seldom ill for much more than three days, when death put an end to their miseries.

Carmilla complained of dreams and feverish sensations, but by no means of so alarming a kind as mine. I say that mine were extremely alarming. Had I been capable of comprehending my condition, I would have invoked aid and advice on my knees. The narcotic of an unsuspected influence was acting upon me, and my perceptions were benumbed.

I am going to tell you now of a dream that led immediately to an odd discovery.

One night, instead of the voice I was accustomed to hear in the dark, I heard one, sweet and tender, and at the same time terrible, which said,

"Your mother warns you to beware of the assassin." At the same time a light unexpectedly sprang up, and I saw Carmilla, standing, near the foot of my bed, in her white nightdress, bathed, from her chin to her feet, in one great stain of blood.

I wakened with a shriek, possessed with the one idea that Carmilla was being murdered. I remember springing from my bed, and my next recollection is that of standing on the lobby, crying for help.

Madame and Mademoiselle came scurrying out of their rooms in alarm; a lamp burned always on the lobby, and seeing me, they soon learned the cause of my terror.

I insisted on our knocking at Carmilla's door. Our knocking was unanswered.

It soon became a pounding and an uproar. We shrieked her name, but all was vain.

We all grew frightened, for the door was locked. We hurried back, in panic, to my room. There we rang the bell long and furiously. If my father's room had been at that side of the house, we would have called him up at once to our aid. But, alas! he was quite out of hearing, and to reach him involved an excursion for which we none of us had courage.

Servants, however, soon came running up the stairs; I had got on my dressing gown and slippers meanwhile, and my companions were already similarly furnished. Recognizing the voices of the servants on the lobby, we sallied out together; and having renewed, as fruitlessly, our summons at Carmilla's door, I ordered the men to force the lock. They did so, and we stood, holding our lights aloft, in the doorway, and so stared into the room.

We called her by name; but there was still no reply. We looked round the room. Everything was undisturbed. It was exactly in the state in which I had left it on bidding her good night. But Carmilla was gone.

CARMILLA

VIII
Search

At sight of the room, perfectly undisturbed except for our violent entrance, we began to cool a little, and soon recovered our senses sufficiently to dismiss the men. It had struck Mademoiselle that possibly Carmilla had been wakened by the uproar at her door, and in her first panic had jumped from her bed, and hid herself in a press, or behind a curtain, from which she could not, of course, emerge until the majordomo and his myrmidons had withdrawn. We now recommenced our search, and began to call her name again.

It was all to no purpose. Our perplexity and agitation increased. We examined the windows, but they were secured. I implored of Carmilla, if she had concealed herself, to play this cruel trick no longer—to come out and to end our anxieties. It was all useless. I was by this time convinced that she was not in the room, nor in the dressing room, the door of which was still locked on this side. She could not have passed it. I was utterly puzzled. Had Carmilla discovered one of those secret passages which the old housekeeper said were known to exist in the schloss, although the tradition of their exact situation had been lost? A little time would, no doubt, explain all—utterly perplexed as, for the present, we were.

It was past four o'clock, and I preferred passing the remaining hours of darkness in Madame's room. Daylight brought no solution of the difficulty.

The whole household, with my father at its head, was in a state of agitation next morning. Every part of the chateau was searched. The grounds were explored. No trace of the missing lady could be discovered. The stream was about to be dragged; my father was in distraction; what a tale to have to tell the poor girl's mother on her

84

return. I, too, was almost beside myself, though my grief was quite of a different kind.

The morning was passed in alarm and excitement. It was now one o'clock, and still no tidings. I ran up to Carmilla's room, and found her standing at her dressing table. I was astounded. I could not believe my eyes. She beckoned me to her with her pretty finger, in silence. Her face expressed extreme fear.

I ran to her in an ecstasy of joy; I kissed and embraced her again and again. I ran to the bell and rang it vehemently, to bring others to the spot who might at once relieve my father's anxiety.

"Dear Carmilla, what has become of you all this time? We have been in agonies of anxiety about you," I exclaimed. "Where have you been? How did you come back?"

"Last night has been a night of wonders," she said.

"For mercy's sake, explain all you can."

"It was past two last night," she said, "when I went to sleep as usual in my bed, with my doors locked, that of the dressing room, and that opening upon the gallery. My sleep was uninterrupted, and, so far as I know, dreamless; but I woke just now on the sofa in the dressing room there, and I found the door between the rooms open, and the other door forced. How could all this have happened without my being wakened? It must have been accompanied with a great deal of noise, and I am particularly easily wakened; and how could I have been carried out of my bed without my sleep having been interrupted, I whom the slightest stir startles?"

By this time, Madame, Mademoiselle, my father, and a number of the servants were in the room. Carmilla was, of course, overwhelmed with inquiries, congratulations, and welcomes. She had but one story to tell, and seemed the least able of all the party to suggest any way of accounting for what had happened.

My father took a turn up and down the room, thinking. I saw Carmilla's eye follow him for a moment with a sly, dark glance.

When my father had sent the servants away, Mademoiselle having gone in search of a little bottle of valerian and sal volatile, and there being no one now in the room with Carmilla, except my father, Madame, and myself, he came to her thoughtfully, took her hand very kindly, led her to the sofa, and sat down beside her.

"Will you forgive me, my dear, if I risk a conjecture, and ask a question?"

"Who can have a better right?" she said. "Ask what you please, and I will tell you everything. But my story is simply one of bewilderment and darkness. I know absolutely nothing. Put any question you please, but you know, of course, the limitations mamma has placed me under."

"Perfectly, my dear child. I need not approach the topics on which she desires our silence. Now, the marvel of last night consists in your having been removed from your bed and your room, without being wakened, and this removal having occurred apparently while the windows were still secured, and the two doors locked upon the inside. I will tell you my theory and ask you a question."

Carmilla was leaning on her hand dejectedly; Madame and I were listening breathlessly.

"Now, my question is this. Have you ever been suspected of walking in your sleep?"

"Never, since I was very young indeed."

"But you did walk in your sleep when you were young?"

"Yes; I know I did. I have been told so often by my old nurse."

My father smiled and nodded.

"Well, what has happened is this. You got up in your sleep, unlocked the door, not leaving the key, as usual, in the lock, but taking it out and locking it on the outside; you again took the key out, and carried it away with you to some one of the five-and-twenty rooms on this floor, or perhaps upstairs or downstairs. There are so many rooms and closets, so much heavy furniture, and such accumulations of lumber, that it would require a week to search this old house thoroughly. Do you see, now, what I mean?"

"I do, but not all," she answered.

"And how, papa, do you account for her finding herself on the sofa in the dressing room, which we had searched so carefully?"

"She came there after you had searched it, still in her sleep, and at last awoke spontaneously, and was as much surprised to find herself where she was as any one else. I wish all mysteries were as easily and innocently explained as yours, Carmilla," he said, laughing. "And so we may congratulate ourselves on the certainty that the most natural explanation of the occurrence is one that involves no drugging, no tampering with locks, no burglars, or poisoners, or witches—nothing that need alarm Carmilla, or anyone else, for our safety."

Carmilla was looking charmingly. Nothing could be more beautiful than her tints. Her beauty was, I think, enhanced by that graceful languor that was peculiar to her. I think my father was silently contrasting her looks with mine, for he said:

"I wish my poor Laura was looking more like herself"; and he sighed.

So our alarms were happily ended, and Carmilla restored to her friends.

IX
The Doctor

As Carmilla would not hear of an attendant sleeping in her room, my father arranged that a servant should sleep outside her door, so that she would not attempt to make another such excursion without being arrested at her own door.

That night passed quietly; and next morning early, the doctor, whom my father had sent for without telling me a word about it, arrived to see me.

Madame accompanied me to the library; and there the grave little doctor, with white hair and spectacles, whom I mentioned before, was waiting to receive me.

I told him my story, and as I proceeded he grew graver and graver.

We were standing, he and I, in the recess of one of the windows, facing one another. When my statement was over, he leaned with his shoulders against the wall, and with his eyes fixed on me earnestly, with an interest in which was a dash of horror.

After a minute's reflection, he asked Madame if he could see my father.

He was sent for accordingly, and as he entered, smiling, he said:

"I dare say, doctor, you are going to tell me that I am an old fool for having brought you here; I hope I am."

But his smile faded into shadow as the doctor, with a very grave face, beckoned him to him.

He and the doctor talked for some time in the same recess where I had just conferred with the physician. It seemed an earnest and argumentative conversation. The room is very large, and I and Madame stood together, burning with curiosity, at the farther end. Not a word could we hear, however, for they spoke in a very low tone, and the deep recess of the window quite concealed the doctor from view, and very nearly my father, whose foot, arm, and shoulder only could we see; and the voices were, I suppose, all the less audible for the sort of closet which the thick wall and window formed.

After a time my father's face looked into the room; it was pale, thoughtful, and, I fancied, agitated.

"Laura, dear, come here for a moment. Madame, we shan't trouble you, the doctor says, at present."

Accordingly I approached, for the first time a little alarmed; for, although I felt very weak, I did not feel ill; and strength, one always fancies, is a thing that may be picked up when we please.

My father held out his hand to me, as I drew near, but he was looking at the doctor, and he said:

"It certainly is very odd; I don't understand it quite. Laura, come here, dear; now attend to Doctor Spielsberg, and recollect yourself."

"You mentioned a sensation like that of two needles piercing the skin, somewhere about your neck, on the night when you experienced your first horrible dream. Is there still any soreness?"

"None at all," I answered.

"Can you indicate with your finger about the point at which you think this occurred?"

"Very little below my throat—here," I answered.

I wore a morning dress, which covered the place I pointed to.

"Now you can satisfy yourself," said the doctor. "You won't mind your papa's lowering your dress a very little. It is necessary, to detect a symptom of the complaint under which you have been suffering."

I acquiesced. It was only an inch or two below the edge of my collar.

"God bless me!—so it is," exclaimed my father, growing pale.

"You see it now with your own eyes," said the doctor, with a gloomy triumph.

"What is it?" I exclaimed, beginning to be frightened.

"Nothing, my dear young lady, but a small blue spot, about the size of the tip of your little finger; and now," he continued, turning to papa, "the question is what is best to be done?"

"Is there any danger?" I urged, in great trepidation.

"I trust not, my dear," answered the doctor. "I don't see why you should not recover. I don't see why you should not begin immediately to get better. That is the point at which the sense of strangulation begins?"

"Yes," I answered.

"And—recollect as well as you can—the same point was a kind of centre of that thrill which you described just now, like the current of a cold stream running against you?"

"It may have been; I think it was."

"Ay, you see?" he added, turning to my father. "Shall I say a word to Madame?"

"Certainly," said my father.

He called Madame to him, and said:

"I find my young friend here far from well. It won't be of any great consequence, I hope; but it will be necessary that some steps be taken, which I will explain by-and-by; but in the meantime, Madame, you will be so good as not to let Miss Laura be alone for one moment. That is the only direction I need give for the present. It is indispensable."

"We may rely upon your kindness, Madame, I know," added my father.

Madame satisfied him eagerly.

"And you, dear Laura, I know you will observe the doctor's direction."

"I shall have to ask your opinion upon another patient, whose symptoms slightly resemble those of my daughter, that have just been detailed to you—very much milder in degree, but I believe quite of the same sort. She is a young lady—our guest; but as you say you will be passing this way again this evening, you can't do better than take your supper here, and you can then see her. She does not come down till the afternoon."

"I thank you," said the doctor. "I shall be with you, then, at about seven this evening."

And then they repeated their directions to me and to Madame, and with this parting charge my father left us, and walked out with the doctor; and I saw them pacing together up and down between the road and the moat, on the grassy platform in front of the castle, evidently absorbed in earnest conversation.

The doctor did not return. I saw him mount his horse there, take his leave, and ride away eastward through the forest.

Nearly at the same time I saw the man arrive from Dranfield with the letters, and dismount and hand the bag to my father.

In the meantime, Madame and I were both busy, lost in conjecture as to the reasons of the singular and earnest direction which the doctor and my father had concurred in imposing. Madame, as she afterwards told me, was afraid the doctor apprehended a sudden seizure, and that, without prompt assistance, I might either lose my life in a fit, or at least be seriously hurt.

The interpretation did not strike me; and I fancied, perhaps luckily for my nerves, that the arrangement was prescribed simply to secure a companion, who would prevent my taking too much exercise, or eating unripe fruit, or doing any of the fifty foolish things to which young people are supposed to be prone.

About half an hour after my father came in—he had a letter in his hand—and said:

"This letter had been delayed; it is from General Spielsdorf. He might have been here yesterday, he may not come till tomorrow or he may be here today."

He put the open letter into my hand; but he did not look pleased, as he used when a guest, especially one so much loved as the General, was coming.

On the contrary, he looked as if he wished him at the bottom of the Red Sea. There was plainly something on his mind which he did not choose to divulge.

"Papa, darling, will you tell me this?" said I, suddenly laying my hand on his arm, and looking, I am sure, imploringly in his face.

"Perhaps," he answered, smoothing my hair caressingly over my eyes.

"Does the doctor think me very ill?"

"No, dear; he thinks, if right steps are taken, you will be quite well again, at least, on the high road to a complete recovery, in a day or two," he answered, a little dryly. "I wish our good friend, the General, had chosen any other time; that is, I wish you had been perfectly well to receive him."

"But do tell me, papa," I insisted, "what does he think is the matter with me?"

"Nothing; you must not plague me with questions," he answered, with more irritation than I ever remember him to have displayed before; and seeing that I looked wounded, I suppose, he kissed me, and added, "You shall know all about it in a day or two; that is, all that I know. In the meantime you are not to trouble your head about it."

He turned and left the room, but came back before I had done wondering and puzzling over the oddity of all this; it was merely to say that he was going to Karnstein, and had ordered the carriage to be ready at twelve, and that I and Madame should accompany him; he was going to see the priest who lived near those picturesque grounds, upon business, and as Carmilla had never seen them, she could follow, when she came down, with Mademoiselle, who would bring materials for what you call a picnic, which might be laid for us in the ruined castle.

At twelve o'clock, accordingly, I was ready, and not long after, my father, Madame and I set out upon our projected drive.

Passing the drawbridge we turn to the right, and follow the road over the steep Gothic bridge, westward, to reach the deserted village and ruined castle of Karnstein.

No sylvan drive can be fancied prettier. The ground breaks into gentle hills and hollows, all clothed with beautiful wood, totally destitute of the comparative formality which artificial planting and early culture and pruning impart.

The irregularities of the ground often lead the road out of its course, and cause it to wind beautifully round the sides of broken hollows and the steeper sides of the hills, among varieties of ground almost inexhaustible.

Turning one of these points, we suddenly encountered our old friend, the General, riding towards us, attended by a mounted servant. His portmanteaus were following in a hired wagon, such as we term a cart.

The General dismounted as we pulled up, and, after the usual greetings, was easily persuaded to accept the vacant seat in the carriage and send his horse on with his servant to the schloss.

X

Bereaved

It was about ten months since we had last seen him: but that time had sufficed to make an alteration of years in his appearance. He had grown thinner; something of gloom and anxiety had taken the place of that cordial serenity which used to characterize his features. His dark blue eyes, always penetrating, now gleamed with a sterner light from under his shaggy grey eyebrows. It was not such a change as grief alone usually induces, and angrier passions seemed to have had their share in bringing it about.

We had not long resumed our drive, when the General began to talk, with his usual soldierly directness, of the bereavement, as he termed it, which he had sustained in the death of his beloved niece and ward; and he then broke out in a tone of intense bitterness and fury, inveighing against the "hellish arts" to which she had fallen a victim, and expressing, with more exasperation than piety, his wonder that Heaven should tolerate so monstrous an indulgence of the lusts and malignity of hell.

My father, who saw at once that something very extraordinary had befallen, asked him, if not too painful to him, to detail the circumstances which he thought justified the strong terms in which he expressed himself.

"I should tell you all with pleasure," said the General, "but you would not believe me."

"Why should I not?" he asked.

"Because," he answered testily, "you believe in nothing but what consists with your own prejudices and illusions. I remember when I was like you, but I have learned better."

"Try me," said my father; "I am not such a dogmatist as you suppose. Besides which, I very well know that you generally require proof for what you believe, and am, therefore, very strongly predisposed to respect your conclusions."

"You are right in supposing that I have not been led lightly into a belief in the marvellous—for what I have experienced is marvellous—and I have been forced by extraordinary evidence to credit that which ran counter, diametrically, to all my theories. I have been made the dupe of a preternatural conspiracy."

Notwithstanding his professions of confidence in the General's penetration, I saw my father, at this point, glance at the General, with, as I thought, a marked suspicion of his sanity.

The General did not see it, luckily. He was looking gloomily and curiously into the glades and vistas of the woods that were opening before us.

"You are going to the Ruins of Karnstein?" he said. "Yes, it is a lucky coincidence; do you know I was going to ask you to bring me there to inspect them. I have a special object in exploring. There is a ruined chapel, ain't there, with a great many tombs of that extinct family?"

"So there are—highly interesting," said my father. "I hope you are thinking of claiming the title and estates?"

My father said this gaily, but the General did not recollect the laugh, or even the smile, which courtesy exacts for a friend's joke; on the contrary, he looked grave and even fierce, ruminating on a matter that stirred his anger and horror.

"Something very different," he said, gruffly. "I mean to unearth some of those fine people. I hope, by God's blessing, to accomplish a pious sacrilege here, which will relieve our earth of certain monsters, and enable honest people to sleep in their beds without being assailed by murderers. I have strange things to tell you, my dear friend, such as I myself would have scouted as incredible a few months since."

My father looked at him again, but this time not with a glance of suspicion—with an eye, rather, of keen intelligence and alarm.

"The house of Karnstein," he said, "has been long extinct: a hundred years at least. My dear wife was maternally descended from the Karnsteins. But the name and title have long ceased to exist. The castle is a ruin; the very village is deserted; it is fifty years since the smoke of a chimney was seen there; not a roof left."

"Quite true. I have heard a great deal about that since I last saw you; a great deal that will astonish you. But I had better relate everything in the order in which it occurred," said the General. "You saw my dear ward—my child, I may call her. No creature could have been more beautiful, and only three months ago none more blooming."

"Yes, poor thing! when I saw her last she certainly was quite lovely," said my father. "I was grieved and shocked more than I can tell you, my dear friend; I knew what a blow it was to you."

He took the General's hand, and they exchanged a kind pressure. Tears gathered in the old soldier's eyes. He did not seek to conceal them. He said:

"We have been very old friends; I knew you would feel for me, childless as I am. She had become an object of very near interest to me, and repaid my care by an affection that cheered my home and made my life happy. That is all gone. The years that remain to me on earth may not be very long; but by God's mercy I hope to accomplish a service to mankind before I die, and to subserve the vengeance of Heaven upon the fiends who have murdered my poor child in the spring of her hopes and beauty!"

"You said, just now, that you intended relating everything as it occurred," said my father. "Pray do; I assure you that it is not mere curiosity that prompts me."

By this time we had reached the point at which the Drunstall road, by which the General had come, diverges from the road which we were travelling to Karnstein.

"How far is it to the ruins?" inquired the General, looking anxiously forward.

"About half a league," answered my father. "Pray let us hear the story you were so good as to promise."

XI
The Story

"With all my heart," said the General, with an effort; and after a short pause in which to arrange his subject, he commenced one of the strangest narratives I ever heard.

"My dear child was looking forward with great pleasure to the visit you had been so good as to arrange for her to your charming daughter." Here he made me a gallant but melancholy bow. "In the meantime we had an invitation to my old friend the Count Carlsfeld, whose schloss is about six leagues to the other side of Karnstein. It was to attend the series of fetes which, you remember, were given by him in honour of his illustrious visitor, the Grand Duke Charles."

"Yes; and very splendid, I believe, they were," said my father.

"Princely! But then his hospitalities are quite regal. He has Aladdin's lamp. The night from which my sorrow dates was devoted to a magnificent masquerade. The grounds were thrown open, the trees hung with coloured lamps. There was such a display of fireworks as Paris itself had never witnessed. And such music—music, you know, is my weakness—such ravishing music! The finest instrumental band, perhaps, in the world, and the finest singers who could be collected from all the great operas in Europe. As you wandered through these fantastically illuminated grounds, the moon-lighted chateau throwing a rosy light from its long rows of windows, you would suddenly hear these ravishing voices stealing from the silence of some grove, or rising from boats upon the lake. I felt myself, as I looked and listened, carried back into the romance and poetry of my early youth.

"When the fireworks were ended, and the ball beginning, we returned to the noble suite of rooms that were thrown open to the dancers. A masked ball, you know, is a beautiful sight; but so brilliant a spectacle of the kind I never saw before.

"It was a very aristocratic assembly. I was myself almost the only 'nobody' present.

"My dear child was looking quite beautiful. She wore no mask. Her excitement and delight added an unspeakable charm to her features, always lovely. I remarked a young lady, dressed magnificently, but wearing a mask, who appeared to me to be observing my ward with extraordinary interest. I had seen her, earlier in the evening, in the great hall, and again, for a few minutes, walking near us, on the terrace under the castle windows, similarly employed. A lady, also masked, richly and gravely dressed, and with a stately air, like a person of rank, accompanied her as a chaperon. Had the young lady not worn a mask, I could, of course, have been much more certain upon the question whether she was really watching my poor darling. I am now well assured that she was.

"We were now in one of the salons. My poor dear child had been dancing, and was resting a little in one of the chairs near the door; I was standing near. The two ladies I have mentioned had approached and the younger took the chair next my ward; while her companion stood beside me, and for a little time addressed herself, in a low tone, to her charge.

"Availing herself of the privilege of her mask, she turned to me, and in the tone of an old friend, and calling me by my name, opened a conversation with me, which piqued my curiosity a good deal. She referred to many scenes where she had met me—at Court, and at distinguished houses. She alluded to little incidents which I had long ceased to think of, but which, I found, had only lain in abeyance in my memory, for they instantly started into life at her touch.

"I became more and more curious to ascertain who she was, every moment. She parried my attempts to discover very adroitly and pleasantly. The knowledge she showed of many passages in my life seemed to me all but unaccountable; and she appeared to take a not unnatural pleasure in foiling my curiosity, and in seeing me flounder in my eager perplexity, from one conjecture to another.

"In the meantime the young lady, whom her mother called by the odd name of Millarca, when she once or twice addressed her, had, with the same ease and grace, got into conversation with my ward.

"She introduced herself by saying that her mother was a very old acquaintance of mine. She spoke of the agreeable audacity which a mask rendered practicable; she talked like a friend; she admired her dress, and insinuated very prettily her admiration of her beauty. She amused her with laughing criticisms upon the people who crowded the ballroom, and laughed at my poor child's fun. She was very witty and lively when she pleased, and after a time they had grown very good friends, and the young stranger lowered her mask, displaying a remarkably beautiful face. I had never seen it before, neither had my dear child. But though it was new to us, the features were so engaging, as well as lovely, that it was impossible not to feel the attraction powerfully. My poor girl did so. I never saw anyone more taken with another at first sight, unless, indeed, it was the stranger herself, who seemed quite to have lost her heart to her.

"In the meantime, availing myself of the license of a masquerade, I put not a few questions to the elder lady.

"'You have puzzled me utterly,' I said, laughing. 'Is that not enough? Won't you, now, consent to stand on equal terms, and do me the kindness to remove your mask?'

"'Can any request be more unreasonable?' she replied. 'Ask a lady to yield an advantage! Beside, how do you know you should recognize me? Years make changes.'

"'As you see,' I said, with a bow, and, I suppose, a rather melancholy little laugh.

"'As philosophers tell us,' she said; 'and how do you know that a sight of my face would help you?'

"'I should take chance for that,' I answered. 'It is vain trying to make yourself out an old woman; your figure betrays you.'

"'Years, nevertheless, have passed since I saw you, rather since you saw me, for that is what I am considering. Millarca, there, is my daughter; I cannot then be young, even in the opinion of people whom time has taught to be indulgent, and I may not like to be compared with what you remember me. You have no mask to remove. You can offer me nothing in exchange.'

"'My petition is to your pity, to remove it.'

"'And mine to yours, to let it stay where it is,' she replied.

"'Well, then, at least you will tell me whether you are French or German; you speak both languages so perfectly.'

"'I don't think I shall tell you that, General; you intend a surprise, and are meditating the particular point of attack.'

"'At all events, you won't deny this,' I said, 'that being honoured by your permission to converse, I ought to know how to address you. Shall I say Madame la Comtesse?'

"She laughed, and she would, no doubt, have met me with another evasion—if, indeed, I can treat any occurrence in an interview every circumstance of which was prearranged, as I now believe, with the profoundest cunning, as liable to be modified by accident.

"'As to that,' she began; but she was interrupted, almost as she opened her lips, by a gentleman, dressed in black, who looked particularly elegant and distinguished, with this drawback, that his face was the most deadly pale I ever saw, except in death. He was in no masquerade—in the plain evening dress of a gentleman; and he said, without a smile, but with a courtly and unusually low bow:—

"'Will Madame la Comtesse permit me to say a very few words which may interest her?'

"The lady turned quickly to him, and touched her lip in token of silence; she then said to me, 'Keep my place for me, General; I shall return when I have said a few words.'

"And with this injunction, playfully given, she walked a little aside with the gentleman in black, and talked for some minutes, apparently very earnestly. They then walked away slowly together in the crowd, and I lost them for some minutes.

"I spent the interval in cudgelling my brains for a conjecture as to the identity of the lady who seemed to remember me so kindly, and I was thinking of turning about and joining in the conversation between my pretty ward and the Countess's daughter, and trying whether, by the time she returned, I might not have a surprise in store for her, by having her name, title, chateau, and estates at my fingers' ends. But at this moment she returned, accompanied by the pale man in black, who said:

"'I shall return and inform Madame la Comtesse when her carriage is at the door.'

"He withdrew with a bow."

XII
A Petition

"'Then we are to lose Madame la Comtesse, but I hope only for a few hours,' I said, with a low bow.

"'It may be that only, or it may be a few weeks. It was very unlucky his speaking to me just now as he did. Do you now know me?'

"I assured her I did not.

"'You shall know me,' she said, 'but not at present. We are older and better friends than, perhaps, you suspect. I cannot yet declare myself. I shall in three weeks pass your beautiful schloss, about which I have been making enquiries. I shall then look in upon you for an hour or two, and renew a friendship which I never think of without a thousand pleasant recollections. This moment a piece of news has reached me like a thunderbolt. I must set out now, and travel by a devious route, nearly a hundred miles, with all the dispatch I can possibly make. My perplexities multiply. I am only deterred by the compulsory reserve I practise as to my name from making a very singular request of you. My poor child has not quite recovered her strength. Her horse fell with her, at a hunt which she had ridden out to witness, her nerves have not yet recovered the shock, and our physician says that she must on no account exert herself for some time to come. We came here, in consequence, by very easy stages—hardly six leagues a day. I must now travel day and night, on a mission of life and death—a mission the critical and momentous nature of which I shall be able to explain to you when we meet, as I hope we shall, in a few weeks, without the necessity of any concealment.'

"She went on to make her petition, and it was in the tone of a person from whom such a request amounted to conferring, rather than seeking a favour.

This was only in manner, and, as it seemed, quite unconsciously. Than the terms in which it was expressed, nothing could be more deprecatory. It was simply that I would consent to take charge of her daughter during her absence.

"This was, all things considered, a strange, not to say, an audacious request. She in some sort disarmed me, by stating and admitting everything that could be urged against it, and throwing herself entirely upon my chivalry. At the same moment, by a fatality that seems to have predetermined all that happened, my poor child came to my side, and, in an undertone, besought me to invite her new friend, Millarca, to pay us a visit. She had just been sounding her, and thought, if her mamma would allow her, she would like it extremely.

"At another time I should have told her to wait a little, until, at least, we knew who they were. But I had not a moment to think in. The two ladies assailed me together, and I must confess the refined and beautiful face of the young lady, about which there was something extremely engaging, as well as the elegance and fire of high birth, determined me; and, quite overpowered, I submitted, and undertook, too easily, the care of the young lady, whom her mother called Millarca.

"The Countess beckoned to her daughter, who listened with grave attention while she told her, in general terms, how suddenly and peremptorily she had been summoned, and also of the arrangement she had made for her under my care, adding that I was one of her earliest and most valued friends.

"I made, of course, such speeches as the case seemed to call for, and found myself, on reflection, in a position which I did not half like.

"The gentleman in black returned, and very ceremoniously conducted the lady from the room.

"The demeanour of this gentleman was such as to impress me with the conviction that the Countess was a lady of very much more importance than her modest title alone might have led me to assume.

"Her last charge to me was that no attempt was to be made to learn more about her than I might have already guessed, until her return. Our distinguished host, whose guest she was, knew her reasons.

"'But here,' she said, 'neither I nor my daughter could safely remain for more than a day. I removed my mask imprudently for a moment, about an hour ago, and, too late, I fancied you saw me. So I resolved to seek an opportunity of talking a little to you. Had I found that you had seen me, I would have thrown myself on your high sense of honour to keep my secret some weeks. As it is, I am satisfied that you did not see me; but if you now suspect, or, on reflection, should suspect, who I am, I commit myself, in like manner, entirely to your honour. My daughter will observe the same secrecy, and I well know that you will, from time to time, remind her, lest she should thoughtlessly disclose it.'

"She whispered a few words to her daughter, kissed her hurriedly twice, and went away, accompanied by the pale gentleman in black, and disappeared in the crowd.

"'In the next room,' said Millarca, 'there is a window that looks upon the hall door. I should like to see the last of mamma, and to kiss my hand to her.'

"We assented, of course, and accompanied her to the window. We looked out, and saw a handsome old-fashioned carriage, with a troop of couriers and footmen. We saw the slim figure of the pale gentleman in black, as he held a thick velvet cloak, and placed it about her shoulders and threw the hood over her head. She nodded to him, and just touched his hand with hers. He bowed low repeatedly as the door closed, and the carriage began to move.

"'She is gone,' said Millarca, with a sigh.

"'She is gone,' I repeated to myself, for the first time—in the hurried moments that had elapsed since my consent—reflecting upon the folly of my act.

"'She did not look up,' said the young lady, plaintively.

"'The Countess had taken off her mask, perhaps, and did not care to show her face,' I said; 'and she could not know that you were in the window.'

"She sighed, and looked in my face. She was so beautiful that I relented. I was sorry I had for a moment repented of my hospitality, and I determined to make her amends for the unavowed churlishness of my reception.

"The young lady, replacing her mask, joined my ward in persuading me to return to the grounds, where the concert was soon to be renewed. We did so, and walked up and down the terrace that lies under the castle windows.

"Millarca became very intimate with us, and amused us with lively descriptions and stories of most of the great people whom we saw upon the terrace. I liked her more and more every minute. Her gossip without being ill-natured, was extremely diverting to me, who had been so long out of the great world. I thought what life she would give to our sometimes lonely evenings at home.

"This ball was not over until the morning sun had almost reached the horizon. It pleased the Grand Duke to dance till then, so loyal people could not go away, or think of bed.

"We had just got through a crowded saloon, when my ward asked me what had become of Millarca. I thought she had been by her side, and she fancied she was by mine. The fact was, we had lost her.

"All my efforts to find her were vain. I feared that she had mistaken, in the confusion of a momentary separation from us, other people for her new friends, and had, possibly, pursued and lost them in the extensive grounds which were thrown open to us.

"Now, in its full force, I recognized a new folly in my having undertaken the charge of a young lady without so much as knowing her name; and fettered as I was by promises, of the reasons for imposing which I knew nothing, I could not even point my inquiries by saying that the missing young lady was the daughter of the Countess who had taken her departure a few hours before.

"Morning broke. It was clear daylight before I gave up my search. It was not till near two o'clock next day that we heard anything of my missing charge.

"At about that time a servant knocked at my niece's door, to say that he had been earnestly requested by a young lady, who appeared to be in great distress, to make out where she could find the General Baron Spielsdorf and the young lady his daughter, in whose charge she had been left by her mother.

"There could be no doubt, notwithstanding the slight inaccuracy, that our young friend had turned up; and so she had. Would to heaven we had lost her!

"She told my poor child a story to account for her having failed to recover us for so long. Very late, she said, she had got to the house-keeper's bedroom in despair of finding us, and had then fallen into a deep sleep which, long as it was, had hardly sufficed to recruit her strength after the fatigues of the ball.

"That day Millarca came home with us. I was only too happy, after all, to have secured so charming a companion for my dear girl."

XIII
The Woodman

"There soon, however, appeared some drawbacks. In the first place, Millarca complained of extreme languor—the weakness that remained after her late illness—and she never emerged from her room till the afternoon was pretty far advanced. In the next place, it was accidentally discovered, although she always locked her door on the inside, and never disturbed the key from its place till she admitted the maid to assist at her toilet, that she was undoubtedly sometimes absent from her room in the very early morning, and at various times later in the day, before she wished it to be understood that she was stirring. She was repeatedly seen from the windows of the schloss, in the first faint grey of the morning, walking through the trees, in an easterly direction, and looking like a person in a trance. This convinced me that she walked in her sleep. But this hypothesis did not solve the puzzle. How did she pass out from her room, leaving the door locked on the inside? How did she escape from the house without unbarring door or window?

"In the midst of my perplexities, an anxiety of a far more urgent kind presented itself.

"My dear child began to lose her looks and health, and that in a manner so mysterious, and even horrible, that I became thoroughly frightened.

"She was at first visited by appalling dreams; then, as she fancied, by a spectre, sometimes resembling Millarca, sometimes in the shape of a beast, indistinctly seen, walking round the foot of her bed, from side to side. Lastly came sensations. One, not unpleasant, but very peculiar, she said, resembled the flow of an icy stream against her breast. At a later time, she felt something like a pair of large needles pierce her, a little below the throat, with a very sharp pain. A few nights after, followed a gradual and convulsive sense of strangulation; then came unconsciousness."

I could hear distinctly every word the kind old General was saying, because by this time we were driving upon the short grass that spreads on either side of the road as you approach the roofless village which had not shown the smoke of a chimney for more than half a century.

You may guess how strangely I felt as I heard my own symptoms so exactly described in those which had been experienced by the poor girl who, but for the catastrophe which followed, would have been at that moment a visitor at my father's chateau. You may suppose, also, how I felt as I heard him detail habits and mysterious peculiarities which were, in fact, those of our beautiful guest, Carmilla!

A vista opened in the forest; we were on a sudden under the chimneys and gables of the ruined village, and the towers and battlements of the dismantled castle, round which gigantic trees are grouped, overhung us from a slight eminence.

In a frightened dream I got down from the carriage, and in silence, for we had each abundant matter for thinking; we soon mounted the ascent, and were among the spacious chambers, winding stairs, and dark corridors of the castle.

"And this was once the palatial residence of the Karnsteins!" said the old General at length, as from a great window he looked out across the village, and saw the wide, undulating expanse of forest. "It was a bad family, and here its bloodstained annals were written," he continued. "It is hard that they should, after death, continue to plague the human race with their atrocious lusts. That is the chapel of the Karnsteins, down there."

He pointed down to the grey walls of the Gothic building partly visible through the foliage, a little way down the steep. "And I hear the axe of a woodman," he added, "busy among the trees that surround it; he possibly may give us the information of which I am in search, and point out the grave of Mircalla, Countess of Karnstein. These rustics preserve the local traditions of great families, whose stories die out among the rich and titled so soon as the families themselves become extinct."

"We have a portrait, at home, of Mircalla, the Countess Karnstein; should you like to see it?" asked my father.

"Time enough, dear friend," replied the General. "I believe that I have seen the original; and one motive which has led me to you earlier than I at first intended, was to explore the chapel which we are now approaching."

"What! see the Countess Mircalla," exclaimed my father; "why, she has been dead more than a century!"

"Not so dead as you fancy, I am told," answered the General.

"I confess, General, you puzzle me utterly," replied my father, looking at him, I fancied, for a moment with a return of the suspicion I detected before. But although there was anger and detestation, at times, in the old General's manner, there was nothing flighty.

"There remains to me," he said, as we passed under the heavy arch of the Gothic church—for its dimensions would have justified its being so styled—"but one object which can interest me during the few years that remain to me on earth, and that is to wreak on her the vengeance which, I thank God, may still be accomplished by a mortal arm."

"What vengeance can you mean?" asked my father, in increasing amazement.

"I mean, to decapitate the monster," he answered, with a fierce flush, and a stamp that echoed mournfully through the hollow ruin, and his clenched hand was at the same moment raised, as if it grasped the handle of an axe, while he shook it ferociously in the air.

"What?" exclaimed my father, more than ever bewildered.

"To strike her head off."

"Cut her head off!"

"Aye, with a hatchet, with a spade, or with anything that can cleave through her murderous throat. You shall hear," he answered, trembling with rage. And hurrying forward he said:

"That beam will answer for a seat; your dear child is fatigued; let her be seated, and I will, in a few sentences, close my dreadful story."

The squared block of wood, which lay on the grass-grown pavement of the chapel, formed a bench on which I was very glad to seat myself, and in the meantime the General called to the woodman, who had been removing some boughs which leaned upon the old walls; and, axe in hand, the hardy old fellow stood before us.

He could not tell us anything of these monuments; but there was an old man, he said, a ranger of this forest, at present sojourning in the house of the priest, about two miles away, who could point out every monument of the old Karnstein family; and, for a trifle, he undertook to bring him back with him, if we would lend him one of our horses, in little more than half an hour.

"Have you been long employed about this forest?" asked my father of the old man.

"I have been a woodman here," he answered in his patois, "under the forester, all my days; so has my father before me, and so on, as many generations as I can count up. I could show you the very house in the village here, in which my ancestors lived."

"How came the village to be deserted?" asked the General.

"It was troubled by revenants, sir; several were tracked to their graves, there detected by the usual tests, and extinguished in the usual way, by decapitation, by the stake, and by burning; but not until many of the villagers were killed.

"But after all these proceedings according to law," he continued—"so many graves opened, and so many vampires deprived of their horrible animation—the village was not relieved. But a Moravian nobleman, who happened to be travelling this way, heard how matters were, and being skilled—as many people are in his country—in such affairs, he offered to deliver the village from its tormentor. He did so thus: There being a bright moon that night, he ascended, shortly after sunset, the towers of the chapel here, from whence he could distinctly see the churchyard beneath him; you can see it from that window. From this point he watched until he saw the vampire come out of his grave, and place near it the linen clothes in which he had been folded, and then glide away towards the village to plague its inhabitants.

"The stranger, having seen all this, came down from the steeple, took the linen wrappings of the vampire, and carried them up to the top of the tower, which he again mounted. When the vampire returned from his prowlings and missed his clothes, he cried furiously to the Moravian, whom he saw at the summit of the tower, and who, in reply, beckoned him to ascend and take them. Whereupon the vampire, accepting his invitation, began to climb the steeple, and so soon as he had reached the battlements, the Moravian, with a stroke of his sword, clove his skull in twain, hurling him down to the churchyard, whither, descending by the winding stairs, the stranger followed and cut his head off, and next day delivered it and the body to the villagers, who duly impaled and burnt them.

"This Moravian nobleman had authority from the then head of the family to remove the tomb of Mircalla, Countess Karnstein, which he did effectually, so that in a little while its site was quite forgotten."

"Can you point out where it stood?" asked the General, eagerly.

The forester shook his head, and smiled.

"Not a soul living could tell you that now," he said; "besides, they say her body was removed; but no one is sure of that either."

Having thus spoken, as time pressed, he dropped his axe and departed, leaving us to hear the remainder of the General's strange story.

XIV
The Meeting

"My beloved child," he resumed, "was now growing rapidly worse. The physician who attended her had failed to produce the slightest impression on her disease, for such I then supposed it to be. He saw my alarm, and suggested a consultation. I called in an abler physician, from Gratz. Several days elapsed before he arrived. He was a good and pious, as well as a learned man. Having seen my poor ward together, they withdrew to my library to confer and discuss. I, from the adjoining room, where I awaited their summons, heard these two gentlemen's voices raised in something sharper than a strictly philosophical discussion. I knocked at the door and entered. I found the old physician from Gratz maintaining his theory. His rival was combating it with undisguised ridicule, accompanied with bursts of laughter. This unseemly manifestation subsided and the altercation ended on my entrance.

"'Sir,' said my first physician,' my learned brother seems to think that you want a conjuror, and not a doctor.'

"'Pardon me,' said the old physician from Gratz, looking displeased, 'I shall state my own view of the case in my own way another time. I grieve, Monsieur le General, that by my skill and science I can be of no use. Before I go I shall do myself the honour to suggest something to you.'

"He seemed thoughtful, and sat down at a table and began to write. Profoundly disappointed, I made my bow, and as I turned to go, the other doctor pointed over his shoulder to his companion who was writing, and then, with a shrug, significantly touched his forehead.

"This consultation, then, left me precisely where I was. I walked out into the grounds, all but distracted. The doctor from Gratz, in ten or fifteen minutes, overtook me. He apologized for having followed me, but said that he could not conscientiously take his leave without a few words more. He told me that he could not be mistaken; no natural disease exhibited the same symptoms; and that death was already very near. There remained, however, a day, or possibly two, of life.

If the fatal seizure were at once arrested, with great care and skill her strength might possibly return. But all hung now upon the confines of the irrevocable. One more assault might extinguish the last spark of vitality which is, every moment, ready to die.

"'And what is the nature of the seizure you speak of?' I entreated.

"'I have stated all fully in this note, which I place in your hands upon the distinct condition that you send for the nearest clergyman, and open my letter in his presence, and on no account read it till he is with you; you would despise it else, and it is a matter of life and death. Should the priest fail you, then, indeed, you may read it.'

"He asked me, before taking his leave finally, whether I would wish to see a man curiously learned upon the very subject, which, after I had read his letter, would probably interest me above all others, and he urged me earnestly to invite him to visit him there; and so took his leave.

"The ecclesiastic was absent, and I read the letter by myself. At another time, or in another case, it might have excited my ridicule. But into what quackeries will not people rush for a last chance, where all accustomed means have failed, and the life of a beloved object is at stake?

"Nothing, you will say, could be more absurd than the learned man's letter. It was monstrous enough to have consigned him to a madhouse. He said that the patient was suffering from the visits of a vampire! The punctures which she described as having occurred near the throat, were, he insisted, the insertion of those two long, thin, and sharp teeth which, it is well known, are peculiar to vampires; and there could be no doubt, he added, as to the well-defined presence of the small livid mark which all concurred in describing as that induced by the demon's lips, and every symptom described by the sufferer was in exact conformity with those recorded in every case of a similar visitation.

"Being myself wholly sceptical as to the existence of any such portent as the vampire, the supernatural theory of the good doctor furnished, in my opinion, but another instance of learning and intelligence oddly associated with some one hallucination. I was so miserable, however, that, rather than try nothing, I acted upon the instructions of the letter.

"I concealed myself in the dark dressing room, that opened upon the poor patient's room, in which a candle was burning, and watched there till she was fast asleep. I stood at the door, peeping through the small crevice, my sword laid on the table beside me, as my directions prescribed, until, a little after one, I saw a large black object, very ill-defined, crawl, as it seemed to me, over the foot of the bed, and swiftly spread itself up to the poor girl's throat, where it swelled, in a moment, into a great, palpitating mass.

"For a few moments I had stood petrified. I now sprang forward, with my sword in my hand. The black creature suddenly contracted towards the foot of the bed, glided over it, and, standing on the floor about a yard below the foot of the bed, with a glare of skulking ferocity and horror fixed on me, I saw Millarca. Speculating I know not what, I struck at her instantly with my sword; but I saw her standing near the door, unscathed. Horrified, I pursued, and struck again. She was gone; and my sword flew to shivers against the door.

"I can't describe to you all that passed on that horrible night. The whole house was up and stirring. The spectre Millarca was gone. But her victim was sinking fast, and before the morning dawned, she died."

The old General was agitated. We did not speak to him. My father walked to some little distance, and began reading the inscriptions on the tombstones; and thus occupied, he strolled into the door of a side chapel to prosecute his researches. The General leaned against the wall, dried his eyes, and sighed heavily. I was relieved on hearing the voices of Carmilla and Madame, who were at that moment approaching. The voices died away.

In this solitude, having just listened to so strange a story, connected, as it was, with the great and titled dead, whose monuments were mouldering among the dust and ivy round us, and every incident of which bore so awfully upon my own mysterious case—in this haunted spot, darkened by the towering foliage that rose on every side, dense and high above its noiseless walls—a horror began to steal over me, and my heart sank as I thought that my friends were, after all, not about to enter and disturb this triste and ominous scene.

The old General's eyes were fixed on the ground, as he leaned with his hand upon the basement of a shattered monument.

Under a narrow, arched doorway, surmounted by one of those demoniacal grotesques in which the cynical and ghastly fancy of old Gothic carving delights, I saw very gladly the beautiful face and figure of Carmilla enter the shadowy chapel.

I was just about to rise and speak, and nodded smiling, in answer to her peculiarly engaging smile; when with a cry, the old man by my side caught up the woodman's hatchet, and started forward. On seeing him a brutalized change came over her features. It was an instantaneous and horrible transformation, as she made a crouching step backwards. Before I could utter a scream, he struck at her with all his force, but she dived under his blow, and unscathed, caught him in her tiny grasp by the wrist. He struggled for a moment to release his arm, but his hand opened, the axe fell to the ground, and the girl was gone.

He staggered against the wall. His grey hair stood upon his head, and a moisture shone over his face, as if he were at the point of death.

The frightful scene had passed in a moment. The first thing I recollect after, is Madame standing before me, and impatiently repeating again and again, the question, "Where is Mademoiselle Carmilla?"

I answered at length, "I don't know—I can't tell—she went there," and I pointed to the door through which Madame had just entered; "only a minute or two since."

"But I have been standing there, in the passage, ever since Mademoiselle Carmilla entered; and she did not return."

She then began to call "Carmilla," through every door and passage and from the windows, but no answer came.

"She called herself Carmilla?" asked the General, still agitated.

"Carmilla, yes," I answered.

"Aye," he said; "that is Millarca. That is the same person who long ago was called Mircalla, Countess Karnstein. Depart from this accursed ground, my poor child, as quickly as you can. Drive to the clergyman's house, and stay there till we come. Begone! May you never behold Carmilla more; you will not find her here."

XV

Ordeal and Execution

As he spoke one of the strangest-looking men I ever beheld entered the chapel at the door through which Carmilla had made her entrance and her exit. He was tall, narrow-chested, stooping, with high shoulders, and dressed in black. His face was brown and dried in with deep furrows; he wore an oddly shaped hat with a broad leaf. His hair, long and grizzled, hung on his shoulders. He wore a pair of gold spectacles, and walked slowly, with an odd shambling gait, with his face sometimes turned up to the sky, and sometimes bowed down towards the ground, seemed to wear a perpetual smile; his long thin arms were swinging, and his lank hands, in old black gloves ever so much too wide for them, waving and gesticulating in utter abstraction.

"The very man!" exclaimed the General, advancing with manifest delight. "My dear Baron, how happy I am to see you, I had no hope of meeting you so soon." He signed to my father, who had by this time returned, and leading the fantastic old gentleman, whom he called the Baron to meet him. He introduced him formally, and they at once entered into earnest conversation. The stranger took a roll of paper from his pocket, and spread it on the worn surface of a tomb that stood by. He had a pencil case in his fingers, with which he traced imaginary lines from point to point on the paper, which from their often glancing from it, together, at certain points of the building, I concluded to be a plan of the chapel. He accompanied, what I may term, his lecture, with occasional readings from a dirty little book, whose yellow leaves were closely written over.

They sauntered together down the side aisle, opposite to the spot where I was standing, conversing as they went; then they began measuring distances by paces, and finally they all stood together, facing a piece of the sidewall, which they began to examine with great minuteness; pulling off the ivy that clung over it, and rapping the plaster with the ends of their sticks, scraping here, and knocking there. At length they ascertained the existence of a broad marble tablet, with letters carved in relief upon it.

With the assistance of the woodman, who soon returned, a monumental inscription, and carved escutcheon, were disclosed. They proved to be those of the long lost monument of Mircalla, Countess Karnstein.

The old General, though not I fear given to the praying mood, raised his hands and eyes to heaven, in mute thanksgiving for some moments.

"Tomorrow," I heard him say; "the commissioner will be here, and the Inquisition will be held according to law."

Then turning to the old man with the gold spectacles, whom I have described, he shook him warmly by both hands and said:

"Baron, how can I thank you? How can we all thank you? You will have delivered this region from a plague that has scourged its inhabitants for more than a century. The horrible enemy, thank God, is at last tracked."

My father led the stranger aside, and the General followed. I know that he had led them out of hearing, that he might relate my case, and I saw them glance often quickly at me, as the discussion proceeded.

My father came to me, kissed me again and again, and leading me from the chapel, said:

"It is time to return, but before we go home, we must add to our party the good priest, who lives but a little way from this; and persuade him to accompany us to the schloss."

In this quest we were successful: and I was glad, being unspeakably fatigued when we reached home. But my satisfaction was changed to dismay, on discovering that there were no tidings of Carmilla. Of the scene that had occurred in the ruined chapel, no explanation was offered to me, and it was clear that it was a secret which my father for the present determined to keep from me.

The sinister absence of Carmilla made the remembrance of the scene more horrible to me. The arrangements for the night were singular. Two servants, and Madame were to sit up in my room that night; and the ecclesiastic with my father kept watch in the adjoining dressing room.

The priest had performed certain solemn rites that night, the purport of which I did not understand any more than I comprehended the reason of this extraordinary precaution taken for my safety during sleep.

I saw all clearly a few days later.

The disappearance of Carmilla was followed by the discontinuance of my nightly sufferings.

You have heard, no doubt, of the appalling superstition that prevails in Upper and Lower Styria, in Moravia, Silesia, in Turkish Serbia, in Poland, even in Russia; the superstition, so we must call it, of the Vampire.

If human testimony, taken with every care and solemnity, judicially, before commissions innumerable, each consisting of many members, all chosen for integrity and intelligence, and constituting reports more voluminous perhaps than exist upon any one other class of cases, is worth anything, it is difficult to deny, or even to doubt the existence of such a phenomenon as the Vampire.

For my part I have heard no theory by which to explain what I myself have witnessed and experienced, other than that supplied by the ancient and well-attested belief of the country.

The next day the formal proceedings took place in the Chapel of Karnstein.

The grave of the Countess Mircalla was opened; and the General and my father recognized each his perfidious and beautiful guest, in the face now disclosed to view. The features, though a hundred and fifty years had passed since her funeral, were tinted with the warmth of life. Her eyes were open; no cadaverous smell exhaled from the coffin. The two medical men, one officially present, the other on the part of the promoter of the inquiry, attested the marvellous fact that there was a faint but appreciable respiration, and a corresponding action of the heart. The limbs were perfectly flexible, the flesh elastic; and the leaden coffin floated with blood, in which to a depth of seven inches, the body lay immersed.

Here then, were all the admitted signs and proofs of vampirism. The body, therefore, in accordance with the ancient practice, was raised, and a sharp stake driven through the heart of the vampire, who uttered a piercing shriek at the moment, in all respects such as might escape from a living person in the last agony. Then the head was struck off, and a torrent of blood flowed from the severed neck. The body and head was next placed on a pile of wood, and reduced to ashes, which were thrown upon the river and borne away, and that territory has never since been plagued by the visits of a vampire.

My father has a copy of the report of the Imperial Commission, with the signatures of all who were present at these proceedings, attached in verification of the statement. It is from this official paper that I have summarized my account of this last shocking scene.

XVI
Conclusion

I write all this you suppose with composure. But far from it; I cannot think of it without agitation. Nothing but your earnest desire so repeatedly expressed, could have induced me to sit down to a task that has unstrung my nerves for months to come, and reinduced a shadow of the unspeakable horror which years after my deliverance continued to make my days and nights dreadful, and solitude insupportably terrific.

Let me add a word or two about that quaint Baron Vordenburg, to whose curious lore we were indebted for the discovery of the Countess Mircalla's grave.

He had taken up his abode in Gratz, where, living upon a mere pittance, which was all that remained to him of the once princely estates of his family, in Upper Styria, he devoted himself to the minute and laborious investigation of the marvellously authenticated tradition of

Vampirism. He had at his fingers' ends all the great and little works upon the subject.

"Magia Posthuma," "Phlegon de Mirabilibus," "Augustinus de cura pro Mortuis," "Philosophicae et Christianae Cogitationes de Vampiris," by John Christofer Herenberg; and a thousand others, among which I remember only a few of those which he lent to my father. He had a voluminous digest of all the judicial cases, from which he had extracted a system of principles that appear to govern—some always, and others occasionally only—the condition of the vampire. I may mention, in passing, that the deadly pallor attributed to that sort of revenants, is a mere melodramatic fiction. They present, in the grave, and when they show themselves in human society, the appearance of healthy life. When disclosed to light in their coffins, they exhibit all the symptoms that are enumerated as those which proved the vampire-life of the long-dead Countess Karnstein.

How they escape from their graves and return to them for certain hours every day, without displacing the clay or leaving any trace of disturbance in the state of the coffin or the cerements, has always been admitted to be utterly inexplicable. The amphibious existence of the vampire is sustained by daily renewed slumber in the grave. Its horrible lust for living blood supplies the vigour of its waking existence. The vampire is prone to be fascinated with an engrossing vehemence, resembling the passion of love, by particular persons. In pursuit of these it will exercise inexhaustible patience and stratagem, for access to a particular object may be obstructed in a hundred ways. It will never desist until it has satiated its passion, and drained the very life of its coveted victim. But it will, in these cases, husband and protract its murderous enjoyment with the refinement of an epicure, and heighten it by the gradual approaches of an artful courtship. In these cases it seems to yearn for something like sympathy and consent. In ordinary ones it goes direct to its object, overpowers with violence, and strangles and exhausts often at a single feast.

The vampire is, apparently, subject, in certain situations, to special conditions. In the particular instance of which I have given you a relation, Mircalla seemed to be limited to a name which, if not her real one, should at least reproduce, without the omission or addition of a single letter, those, as we say, anagrammatically, which compose it.

Carmilla did this; so did Millarca.

My father related to the Baron Vordenburg, who remained with us for two or three weeks after the expulsion of Carmilla, the story about the Moravian nobleman and the vampire at Karnstein churchyard, and then he asked the Baron how he had discovered the exact position of the long-concealed tomb of the Countess Mircalla? The Baron's grotesque features puckered up into a mysterious smile; he looked down, still smiling on his worn spectacle case and fumbled with it. Then looking up, he said:

"I have many journals, and other papers, written by that remarkable man; the most curious among them is one treating of the visit of which you speak, to Karnstein. The tradition, of course, discolours and distorts a little. He might have been termed a Moravian nobleman, for he had changed his abode to that territory, and was, beside, a noble. But he was, in truth, a native of Upper Styria. It is enough to say that in very early youth he had been a passionate and favoured lover of the beautiful Mircalla, Countess Karnstein. Her early death plunged him into inconsolable grief. It is the nature of vampires to increase and multiply, but according to an ascertained and ghostly law.

"Assume, at starting, a territory perfectly free from that pest. How does it begin, and how does it multiply itself? I will tell you. A person, more or less wicked, puts an end to himself. A suicide, under certain circumstances, becomes a vampire. That spectre visits living people in their slumbers; they die, and almost invariably, in the grave, develop into vampires. This happened in the case of the beautiful Mircalla, who was haunted by one of those demons. My ancestor, Vordenburg, whose title I still bear, soon discovered this, and in the course of the studies to which he devoted himself, learned a great deal more.

"Among other things, he concluded that suspicion of vampirism would probably fall, sooner or later, upon the dead Countess, who in life had been his idol. He conceived a horror, be she what she might, of her remains being profaned by the outrage of a posthumous execution. He has left a curious paper to prove that the vampire, on its expulsion from its amphibious existence, is projected into a far more horrible life; and he resolved to save his once beloved Mircalla from this.

"He adopted the stratagem of a journey here, a pretended removal of her remains, and a real obliteration of her monument. When age had stolen upon him, and from the vale of years, he looked back on the scenes he was leaving, he considered, in a different spirit, what he had done, and a horror took possession of him. He made the tracings and notes which have guided me to the very spot, and drew up a confession of the deception that he had practised. If he had intended any further action in this matter, death prevented him; and the hand of a remote descendant has, too late for many, directed the pursuit to the lair of the beast."

We talked a little more, and among other things he said was this:

"One sign of the vampire is the power of the hand. The slender hand of Mircalla closed like a vice of steel on the General's wrist when he raised the hatchet to strike. But its power is not confined to its grasp; it leaves a numbness in the limb it seizes, which is slowly, if ever, recovered from."

The following Spring my father took me a tour through Italy. We remained away for more than a year. It was long before the terror of recent events subsided; and to this hour the image of Carmilla returns to memory with ambiguous alternations—sometimes the playful, languid, beautiful girl; sometimes the writhing fiend I saw in the ruined church; and often from a reverie I have started, fancying I heard the light step of Carmilla at the drawing room door.

MR. CAPTAIN AND THE NYMPH

Wilkie Collins

Wilkie Collins (1824–1889) is the godfather of Sensation Fiction. This form of writing exploded in the 1860s, "the decade of sensation", and its pages were rife with bigamy plots, cliffhangers, sex scandals, and good old-fashioned murder. It is no wonder that these novels attracted much condemnation. In 1860, Henry L. Mansel famously worried that Sensation novels as a genre were "indications of a widespread corruption, of which they are in part both the effect and the cause; called into existence to supply the cravings of a diseased appetite, and contributing themselves to foster the disease and to stimulate the want that they supply".* Meanwhile the writer Margaret Oliphant felt that they were distasteful given that they were filled with "Women driven wild with love for the man who leads them into desperation [...] Women who marry their grooms in fits of sensual passion [...] who pray their lovers to carry them off from husbands and homes they hate [...] who give and receive burning kisses and frantic embraces, and live in a voluptuous dream [...] the dreaming maiden waits. She waits now from flesh and muscles, for strong arms that seize her and warm breath that thrills her through and a host of other physical attractions. [...] [But] this eagerness of physical sensation is offered to [English girls] not only as the portrait of their own state of mind, but as their amusement

* Mansel, Henry L., "Sensation Novels", *Quarterly Review*, April 1863.

and mental food".* These fears of disease, addiction, corruption, and sexual misbehaviour did not put the public off, and they consumed these stories in vast quantities. "Mr. Captain and the Nymph" is a tale of forbidden passions and colonial anxieties. It was first published as "The Captain's Last Love" as one of the Christmas stories for the New York sporting periodical *Spirit of the Times* in 1876. It was then republished in *Belgravia* in January 1877. It later underwent a change of title and minor alterations when it was anthologized in Collins's collection of short stories *Little Novels* (1887). In it, we encounter transgressive sexuality—the Captain is vain, perfumed, and suspiciously feminine— while the Nymph represents the dangers of inappropriate desire. This ghastly story acts as a warning to would-be conquerors, lest they be the ones conquered.

* Oliphant, Margaret, "Sensational Novels", *Blackwood's Magazine*, May 1862.

"The Captain is still in the prime of life," the widow remarked. "He has given up his ship; he possesses a sufficient income, and he has nobody to live with him. I should like to know why he doesn't marry."

"The Captain was excessively rude to Me," the widow's younger sister added, on her side. "When we took leave of him in London, I asked if there was any chance of his joining us at Brighton this season. He turned his back on me as if I had mortally offended him; and he made me this extraordinary answer: 'Miss! I hate the sight of the sea.' The man has been a sailor all his life. What does he mean by saying that he hates the sight of the sea?"

These questions were addressed to a third person present—and the person was a man. He was entirely at the mercy of the widow and the widow's sister. The other ladies of the family—who might have taken him under their protection—had gone to an evening concert. He was known to be the Captain's friend, and to be well acquainted with events in the Captain's life. As it happened, he had reasons for hesitating to revive associations connected with those events. But what polite alternative was left to him? He must either inflict disappointment, and, worse still, aggravate curiosity—or he must resign himself to circumstances, and tell the ladies why the Captain would never marry, and why (sailor as he was) he hated the sight of the sea. They were both young women and handsome women—and the person to whom they had appealed (being a man) followed the example of submission to the sex, first set in the garden of Eden. He enlightened the ladies, in the terms that follow:

II

The British merchantman, *Fortuna*, sailed from the port of Liverpool (at a date which it is not necessary to specify) with the morning tide. She was bound for certain islands in the Pacific Ocean, in search of a cargo of sandal-wood—a commodity which, in those days, found a ready and profitable market in the Chinese Empire.

A large discretion was reposed in the Captain by the owners, who knew him to be not only trustworthy, but a man of rare ability, carefully cultivated during the leisure hours of a seafaring life. Devoted heart and soul to his professional duties, he was a hard reader and an excellent linguist as well. Having had considerable experience among the inhabitants of the Pacific Islands, he had attentively studied their characters, and had mastered their language in more than one of its many dialects. Thanks to the valuable information thus obtained, the Captain was never at a loss to conciliate the islanders. He had more than once succeeded in finding a cargo under circumstances in which other captains had failed.

Possessing these merits, he had also his fair share of human defects. For instance, he was a little too conscious of his own good looks—of his bright chestnut hair and whiskers, of his beautiful blue eyes, of his fair white skin, which many a woman had looked at with the admiration that is akin to envy. His shapely hands were protected by gloves; a broad-brimmed hat sheltered his complexion in fine weather from the sun. He was nice in the choice of his perfumes; he never drank spirits, and the smell of tobacco was abhorrent to him. New men among his officers and his crew, seeing him in his cabin, perfectly dressed, washed, and brushed until he was an object speckless to look upon—a merchant-captain soft of voice, careful in his choice of words, devoted to study in his leisure hours—were apt to conclude that they had trusted themselves at sea under a commander who was an anomalous mixture of a schoolmaster and a dandy. But if the slightest infraction of discipline took place, or if the storm rose and the vessel proved to be in peril, it was soon discovered that the gloved hands held a rod of iron; that the soft voice could make itself heard through wind and sea from one end of the deck to the other; and that it issued orders which the greatest fool on board discovered to be orders that had saved the ship. Throughout his professional life, the general impression that this variously gifted man produced on the little world about him was always the same. Some few liked him; everybody respected him; nobody understood him. The Captain accepted these results. He persisted in reading his books and protecting his complexion, with this result: his owners shook hands with him, and put up with his gloves.

The *Fortuna* touched at Rio for water, and for supplies of food which might prove useful in case of scurvy. In due time the ship rounded Cape Horn, favoured by the finest weather ever known in those latitudes by the oldest hand on board. The mate—one Mr. Duncalf—a boozing, wheezing, self-confident old sea-dog, with a flaming face and a vast vocabulary of oaths, swore that he didn't like it. "The foul weather's coming, my lads," said Mr. Duncalf. "Mark my words, there'll be wind enough to take the curl out of the Captain's whiskers before we are many days older!"

For one uneventful week, the ship cruised in search of the islands to which the owners had directed her. At the end of that time the wind took the predicted liberties with the Captain's whiskers; and

Mr. Duncalf stood revealed to an admiring crew in the character of a true prophet.

For three days and three nights the *Fortuna* ran before the storm, at the mercy of wind and sea. On the fourth morning the gale blew itself out, the sun appeared again toward noon, and the Captain was able to take an observation. The result informed him that he was in a part of the Pacific Ocean with which he was entirely unacquainted. Thereupon, the officers were called to a council in the cabin.

Mr. Duncalf, as became his rank, was consulted first. His opinion possessed the merit of brevity. "My lads, this ship's bewitched. Take my word for it, we shall wish ourselves back in our own latitudes before we are many days older." Which, being interpreted, meant that Mr. Duncalf was lost, like his superior officer, in a part of the ocean of which he knew nothing.

The remaining members of the council having no suggestions to offer, left the Captain to take his own way. He decided (the weather being fine again) to stand on under an easy press of sail for four-and-twenty hours more, and to see if anything came of it.

Soon after nightfall, something did come of it. The lookout forward hailed the quarter-deck with the dread cry, "Breakers ahead!" In less than a minute more, everybody heard the crash of the broken water. The *Fortuna* was put about, and came round slowly in the light wind. Thanks to the timely alarm and the fine weather, the safety of the vessel was easily provided for. They kept her under a short sail; and they waited for the morning.

The dawn showed them in the distance a glorious green island, not marked in the ship's charts—an island girt about by a coral-reef, and having in its midst a high-peaked mountain which looked, through the telescope, like a mountain of volcanic origin. Mr. Duncalf, taking his morning draught of rum and water, shook his groggy old head and said (and swore): "My lads, I don't like the look of that island." The Captain was of a different opinion. He had one of the ship's boats put into the water; he armed himself and four of his crew who accompanied him; and away he went in the morning sunlight to visit the island.

Skirting round the coral reef, they found a natural breach, which proved to be broad enough and deep enough not only for the passage of the boat, but of the ship herself if needful. Crossing the broad inner belt of smooth water, they approached the golden sands of the island, strewed with magnificent shells, and crowded by the dusky islanders—men, women, and children, all waiting in breathless astonishment to see the strangers land.

The Captain kept the boat off, and examined the islanders carefully. The innocent, simple people danced, and sang, and ran into the water, imploring their wonderful white visitors by gestures to come on shore. Not a creature among them carried arms of any sort; a hospitable curiosity animated the entire population. The men cried out, in their smooth musical language, "Come and eat!" and the plump black-eyed women, all laughing together, added their own invitation, "Come and be kissed!" Was it in mortals to resist such temptations as these? The Captain led the way on shore, and the women surrounded him in an instant, and screamed for joy at the glorious spectacle of his whiskers, his complexion, and his gloves. So the mariners from the far north were welcomed to the newly-discovered island.

III

The morning wore on. Mr. Duncalf, in charge of the ship, cursing the island over his rum and water, as a "beastly green strip of a place, not laid down in any Christian chart," was kept waiting four mortal hours before the Captain returned to his command, and reported himself to his officers as follows:

He had found his knowledge of the Polynesian dialects sufficient to make himself in some degree understood by the natives of the new island. Under the guidance of the chief he had made a first journey of exploration, and had seen for himself that the place was a marvel of natural beauty and fertility. The one barren spot in it was the peak of the volcanic mountain, composed of crumbling rock; originally no doubt lava and ashes, which had cooled and consolidated with the lapse of time. So far as he could see, the crater at the top was now an extinct crater. But, if he had understood rightly, the chief had spoken of earthquakes and eruptions at certain bygone periods, some of which lay within his own earliest recollections of the place.

Adverting next to considerations of practical utility, the Captain announced that he had seen sandal-wood enough on the island to load a dozen ships, and that the natives were willing to part with it for a few toys and trinkets generally distributed among them. To the mate's disgust, the *Fortuna* was taken inside the reef that day, and was anchored before sunset in a natural harbour. Twelve hours of recreation, beginning with the next morning, were granted to the men, under the wise restrictions in such cases established by the Captain. That interval over, the work of cutting the precious wood and loading the ship was to be unremittingly pursued.

Mr. Duncalf had the first watch after the *Fortuna* had been made snug. He took the boatswain aside (an ancient sea-dog like himself), and he said in a gruff whisper: "My lad, this here ain't the island laid down in our sailing orders. See if mischief don't come of disobeying orders before we are many days older."

Nothing in the shape of mischief happened that night. But at sunrise the next morning a suspicious circumstance occurred; and Mr. Duncalf whispered to the boatswain: "What did I tell you?" The Captain and the chief of the islanders held a private conference in the cabin, and the Captain, after first forbidding any communication with the shore until his return, suddenly left the ship, alone with the chief, in the chief's own canoe.

What did this strange disappearance mean? The Captain himself, when he took his seat in the canoe, would have been puzzled to answer that question. He asked, in the nearest approach that his knowledge could make to the language used in the island, whether he would be a long time or a short time absent from his ship.

The chief answered mysteriously (as the Captain understood him) in these words: "Long time or short time, your life depends on it, and the lives of your men."

Paddling his light little boat in silence over the smooth water inside the reef, the chief took his visitor ashore at a part of the island which was quite new to the Captain. The two crossed a ravine, and ascended an eminence beyond. There the chief stopped, and silently pointed out to sea.

The Captain looked in the direction indicated to him, and discovered a second and a smaller island, lying away to the southwest. Taking out his telescope from the case by which it was slung at his back, he narrowly examined the place. Two of the native canoes were lying off the shore of the new island; and the men in them appeared to be all kneeling or crouching in curiously chosen attitudes. Shifting the range of his glass, he next beheld a white-robed figure, tall and solitary—the one inhabitant of the island whom he could discover. The man was standing on the highest point of a rocky cape. A fire was burning at his feet. Now he lifted his arms solemnly to the sky; now he dropped some invisible fuel into the fire, which made a blue smoke; and now he cast other invisible objects into the canoes floating beneath him, which the islanders reverently received with bodies that crouched in abject submission. Lowering his telescope, the Captain looked round at the chief for an explanation. The chief gave the explanation readily. His language was interpreted by the English stranger in these terms:

"Wonderful white man! the island you see yonder is a Holy Island. As such it is *Taboo*—an island sanctified and set apart. The honourable person whom you notice on the rock is an all-powerful favourite of the gods. He is by vocation a Sorcerer, and by rank a Priest. You now see him casting charms and blessings into the canoes of our fishermen, who kneel to him for fine weather and great plenty of fish. If any profane person, native or stranger, presumes to set foot on that island, my otherwise peaceful subjects will (in the performance of a religious duty) put that person to death. Mention this to your men. They will be fed by my male people, and fondled by my female people, so long as they keep clear of the Holy Isle. As they value their lives, let them respect this prohibition. Is it understood between us? Wonderful white man! my canoe is waiting for you. Let us go back."

Understanding enough of the chief's language (illustrated by his gestures) to receive in the right spirit the communication thus addressed to him, the Captain repeated the warning to the ship's company in the plainest possible English. The officers and men then took their holiday on shore, with the exception of Mr. Duncalf, who positively refused to leave the ship. For twelve delightful hours they were fed by the male people, and fondled by the female people, and then they were mercilessly torn from the flesh-pots and the arms of their new friends, and set to work on the sandal-wood in good earnest. Mr. Duncalf superintended the loading, and waited for the mischief that was to come of disobeying the owners' orders with a confidence worthy of a better cause.

IV

Strangely enough, chance once more declared itself in favour of the mate's point of view. The mischief did actually come; and the chosen instrument of it was a handsome young islander, who was one of the sons of the chief.

The Captain had taken a fancy to the sweet-tempered, intelligent lad. Pursuing his studies in the dialect of the island, at leisure hours, he had made the chief's son his tutor, and had instructed the youth in English by way of return. More than a month had passed in this intercourse, and the ship's lading was being rapidly completed—when, in an evil hour, the talk between the two turned on the subject of the Holy Island.

"Does nobody live on the island but the Priest?" the Captain asked.

The chief's son looked round him suspiciously. "Promise me you won't tell anybody!" he began very earnestly.

The Captain gave his promise.

"There is one other person on the island," the lad whispered; "a person to feast your eyes upon, if you could only see her! She is the Priest's daughter. Removed to the island in her infancy, she has never left it since. In that sacred solitude she has only looked on two human beings—her father and her mother. I once saw her from my canoe, taking care not to attract her notice, or to approach too near the holy soil. Oh, so young, dear master, and, oh, so beautiful!" The chief's son completed the description by kissing his own hands as an expression of rapture.

The Captain's fine blue eyes sparkled. He asked no more questions; but, later on that day, he took his telescope with him, and paid a secret visit to the eminence which overlooked the Holy Island. The next day, and the next, he privately returned to the same place. On the fourth day, fatal Destiny favoured him. He discovered the nymph of the island.

Standing alone upon the cape on which he had already seen her father, she was feeding some tame birds which looked like turtle-doves. The glass showed the Captain her white robe, fluttering in the sea-breeze; her long black hair falling to her feet; her slim and supple young figure; her simple grace of attitude, as she turned this way and that, attending to the wants of her birds. Before her was the blue ocean; behind her rose the lustrous green of the island forest. He looked and looked until his eyes and arms ached. When she disappeared among the trees, followed by her favourite birds, the Captain shut up his telescope with a sigh, and said to himself: "I have seen an angel!"

From that hour he became an altered man; he was languid, silent, interested in nothing. General opinion, on board his ship, decided that he was going to be taken ill.

A week more elapsed, and the officers and crew began to talk of the voyage to their market in China. The Captain refused to fix a day for sailing. He even took offence at being asked to decide. Instead of sleeping in his cabin, he went ashore for the night.

Not many hours afterward (just before daybreak), Mr. Duncalf, snoring in his cabin on deck, was aroused by a hand laid on his shoulder. The swinging lamp, still alight, showed him the dusky face of the chief's son, convulsed with terror. By wild signs, by disconnected words in the little English which he had learned, the lad tried to make the mate understand him. Dense Mr. Duncalf, understanding nothing, hailed the second officer, on the opposite side of the deck. The second officer was young and intelligent; he rightly interpreted the terrible news that had come to the ship.

The Captain had broken his own rules. Watching his opportunity, under cover of the night, he had taken a canoe, and had secretly crossed the channel to the Holy Island. No one had been near him at the time but the chief's son. The lad had vainly tried to induce him to abandon his desperate enterprise, and had vainly waited on the shore in the hope of hearing the sound of the paddle announcing his return. Beyond all reasonable doubt, the infatuated man had set foot on the shores of the tabooed island.

The one chance for his life was to conceal what he had done, until the ship could be got out of the harbour, and then (if no harm had come to him in the interval) to rescue him after nightfall. It was decided to spread the report that he had really been taken ill, and that he was confined to his cabin. The chief's son, whose heart the Captain's kindness had won, could be trusted to do this, and to keep the secret faithfully for his good friend's sake.

Toward noon, the next day, they attempted to take the ship to sea, and failed for want of wind. Hour by hour, the heat grew more oppressive. As the day declined, there were ominous appearances in the western heaven. The natives, who had given some trouble during the day by their anxiety to see the Captain, and by their curiosity to know the cause of the sudden preparations for the ship's departure, all went ashore together, looking suspiciously at the sky, and reappeared no more. Just at midnight, the ship (still in her snug berth inside the reef) suddenly trembled from her keel to her uppermost masts. Mr. Duncalf, surrounded by the startled crew, shook his knotty fist at the island as if he could see it in the dark. "My lads, what did I tell you? That was a shock of earthquake."

With the morning the threatening aspect of the weather unexpectedly disappeared. A faint hot breeze from the land, just enough to give the ship steerage-way, offered Mr. Duncalf a chance of getting to sea. Slowly the *Fortuna*, with the mate himself at the wheel, half sailed, half drifted into the open ocean. At a distance of barely two miles from the island the breeze was felt no more, and the vessel lay becalmed for the rest of the day.

At night the men waited their orders, expecting to be sent after their Captain in one of the boats. The intense darkness, the airless heat, and a second shock of earthquake (faintly felt in the ship at her present distance from the land) warned the mate to be cautious. "I smell mischief in the air," said Mr. Duncalf. "The Captain must wait till I am surer of the weather."

Still no change came with the new day. The dead calm continued, and the airless heat. As the day declined, another ominous appearance became visible. A thin line of smoke was discovered through the telescope, ascending from the topmost peak of the mountain on the main island. Was the volcano threatening an eruption? The mate, for one, entertained no doubt of it. "By the Lord, the place is going to burst up!" said Mr. Duncalf. "Come what may of it, we must find the Captain tonight!"

V

What was the Captain doing? and what chance had the crew of finding him that night?

He had committed himself to his desperate adventure, without forming any plan for the preservation of his own safety; without giving even a momentary consideration to the consequences which might follow the risk that he had run. The charming figure that he had seen haunted him night and day. The image of the innocent creature, secluded from humanity in her island solitude, was the one image that filled his mind. A man, passing a woman in the street, acts on the impulse to turn and follow her, and in that one thoughtless moment shapes the destiny of his future life. The Captain had acted on a similar impulse, when he took the first canoe he had found on the beach, and shaped his reckless course for the tabooed island.

Reaching the shore while it was still dark, he did one sensible thing—he hid the canoe so that it might not betray him when the daylight came. That done, he waited for the morning on the outskirts of the forest.

The trembling light of dawn revealed the mysterious solitude around him. Following the outer limits of the trees, first in one direction, then in another, and finding no trace of any living creature, he decided on penetrating to the interior of the island. He entered the forest.

An hour of walking brought him to rising ground. Continuing the ascent, he got clear of the trees, and stood on the grassy top of a broad cliff which overlooked the sea. An open hut was on the cliff. He cautiously looked in, and discovered that it was empty. The few household utensils left about, and the simple bed of leaves in a corner, were covered with fine sandy dust. Night-birds flew blundering out of the inner cavities of the roof, and took refuge in the shadows of the forest below. It was plain that the hut had not been inhabited for some time past.

Standing at the open doorway and considering what he should do next, the Captain saw a bird flying toward him out of the forest. It was a turtle-dove, so tame that it fluttered close up to him. At the same moment the sound of sweet laughter became audible among the trees. His heart beat fast; he advanced a few steps and stopped. In a moment more the nymph of the island appeared, in her white robe, ascending the cliff in pursuit of her truant bird. She saw the strange man, and suddenly stood still; struck motionless by the amazing discovery that had burst upon her. The Captain approached, smiling and holding out his hand. She never moved; she stood before him in helpless wonderment—her lovely black eyes fixed spellbound on his face; her dusky bosom palpitating above the fallen folds of her robe; her rich red lips parted in mute astonishment. Feasting his eyes on her beauty in silence, the Captain after a while ventured to speak to her in the language of the main island. The sound of his voice, addressing her in the words that she understood, roused the lovely creature to action. She started, stepped close up to him, and dropped on her knees at his feet.

"My father worships invisible deities," she said, softly. "Are you a visible deity? Has my mother sent you?" She pointed as she spoke to the deserted hut behind them. "You appear," she went on, "in the place where my mother died. Is it for her sake that you show yourself to her child? Beautiful deity, come to the Temple—come to my father!"

The Captain gently raised her from the ground. If her father saw him, he was a doomed man.

Infatuated as he was, he had sense enough left to announce himself plainly in his own character, as a mortal creature arriving from a distant land. The girl instantly drew back from him with a look of terror.

"He is not like my father," she said to herself; "he is not like me. Is he the lying demon of the prophecy? Is he the predestined destroyer of our island?"

The Captain's experience of the sex showed him the only sure way out of the awkward position in which he was now placed. He appealed to his personal appearance.

"Do I look like a demon?" he asked.

Her eyes met his eyes; a faint smile trembled on her lips. He ventured on asking what she meant by the predestined destruction of the island. She held up her hand solemnly, and repeated the prophecy.

The Holy Island was threatened with destruction by an evil being, who would one day appear on its shores. To avert the fatality the place had been sanctified and set apart, under the protection of the gods and their priest. Here was the reason for the taboo, and for the extraordinary rigour with which it was enforced. Listening to her with the deepest interest, the Captain took her hand and pressed it gently.

"Do I feel like a demon?" he whispered.

Her slim brown fingers closed frankly on his hand. "You feel soft and friendly," she said with the fearless candour of a child. "Squeeze me again. I like it!"

The next moment she snatched her hand away from him; the sense of his danger had suddenly forced itself on her mind. "If my father sees you," she said, "he will light the signal fire at the Temple, and the people from the other island will come here and put you to death. Where is your canoe? No! It is daylight. My father may see you on the water." She considered a little, and, approaching him, laid her hands on his shoulders. "Stay here till nightfall," she resumed. "My father never comes this way. The sight of the place where my mother died is horrible to him. You are safe here. Promise to stay where you are till night-time."

The Captain gave his promise.

Freed from anxiety so far, the girl's mobile temperament recovered its native cheerfulness, its sweet gayety and spirit. She admired the beautiful stranger as she might have admired a new bird that had flown to her to be fondled with the rest. She patted his fair white skin, and wished she had a skin like it. She lifted the great glossy folds of her long black hair, and compared it with the Captain's bright curly locks, and longed to change colours with him from the bottom of her heart. His dress was a wonder to her; his watch was a new revelation. She rested her head on his shoulder to listen delightedly to the ticking, as he held the watch to her ear. Her fragrant breath played on his face, her warm, supple figure rested against him softly. The Captain's arm stole round her waist, and the Captain's lips gently touched her cheek. She lifted her head with a look of pleased surprise. "Thank you," said the child of Nature, simply. "Kiss me again; I like it. May I kiss you?" The tame turtle-dove perched on her shoulder as she gave the Captain her first kiss, and diverted her thoughts to the pets that she had left, in pursuit of the truant dove. "Come," she said, "and see my birds. I keep them on this side of the forest. There is no danger, so long as you don't show yourself on the other side. My name is Aimata. Aimata will take care of you. Oh, what a beautiful white neck you have!" She put her arm admiringly round his neck. The Captain's arm held her tenderly to him. Slowly the two descended the cliff, and were lost in the leafy solitudes of the forest. And the tame dove fluttered before them, a winged messenger of love, cooing to his mate.

VI

The night had come, and the Captain had not left the island.

Aimata's resolution to send him away in the darkness was a forgotten resolution already. She had let him persuade her that he was in no danger, so long as he remained in the hut on the cliff; and she had promised, at parting, to return to him while the Priest was still sleeping, at the dawn of day.

He was alone in the hut. The thought of the innocent creature whom he loved was sorrowfully as well as tenderly present to his mind. He almost regretted his rash visit to the island. "I will take her with me to England," he said to himself. "What does a sailor care for the opinion of the world? Aimata shall be my wife."

The intense heat oppressed him. He stepped out on the cliff, toward midnight, in search of a breath of air.

At that moment, the first shock of earthquake (felt in the ship while she was inside the reef) shook the ground he stood on. He instantly thought of the volcano on the main island. Had he been mistaken in supposing the crater to be extinct? Was the shock that he had just felt a warning from the volcano, communicated through a submarine connection between the two islands? He waited and watched through the hours of darkness, with a vague sense of apprehension, which was not to be reasoned away. With the first light of daybreak he descended into the forest, and saw the lovely being whose safety was already precious to him as his own, hurrying to meet him through the trees.

She waved her hand distractedly as she approached him. "Go!" she cried; "go away in your canoe before our island is destroyed!"

He did his best to quiet her alarm. Was it the shock of earthquake that had frightened her? No: it was more than the shock of earthquake—it was something terrible which had followed the shock. There was a lake near the Temple, the waters of which were supposed to be heated by subterranean fires. The lake had risen with the earthquake, had bubbled furiously, and had then melted away into the earth and been lost. Her father, viewing the portent with horror, had gone to the cape to watch the volcano on the main island, and to implore by prayers and sacrifices the protection of the gods. Hearing this, the Captain entreated Aimata to let him see the emptied lake, in the absence of the Priest. She hesitated; but his influence was all-powerful. He prevailed on her to turn back with him through the forest.

Reaching the furthest limit of the trees, they came out upon open rocky ground which sloped gently downward toward the centre of the island. Having crossed this space, they arrived at a natural amphitheatre of rock. On one side of it the Temple appeared, partly excavated, partly formed by a natural cavern. In one of the lateral branches of the cavern was the dwelling of the Priest and his daughter. The mouth of it looked out on the rocky basin of the lake. Stooping over the edge, the Captain discovered, far down in the empty depths, a light cloud of steam. Not a drop of water was visible, look where he might.

Aimata pointed to the abyss, and hid her face on his bosom. "My father says," she whispered, "that it is your doing."

The Captain started. "Does your father know that I am on the island?"

She looked up at him with a quick glance of reproach. "Do you think I would tell him, and put your life in peril?" she asked. "My father felt the destroyer of the island in the earthquake; my father saw the coming destruction in the disappearance of the lake." Her eyes rested on him with a loving languor. "Are you indeed the demon of the prophecy?" she said, winding his hair round her finger. "I am not afraid of you, if you are. I am a creature bewitched; I love the demon." She kissed him passionately. "I don't care if I die," she whispered between the kisses, "if I only die with you!"

The Captain made no attempt to reason with her. He took the wiser way—he appealed to her feelings.

"You will come and live with me happily in my own country," he said. "My ship is waiting for us. I will take you home with me, and you shall be my wife."

She clapped her hands for joy. Then she thought of her father, and drew back from him in tears.

The Captain understood her. "Let us leave this dreary place," he suggested. "We will talk about it in the cool glades of the forest, where you first said you loved me."

She gave him her hand. "Where I first said I loved you!" she repeated, smiling tenderly as she looked at him. They left the lake together.

VII

The darkness had fallen again; and the ship was still becalmed at sea.

Mr. Duncalf came on deck after his supper. The thin line of smoke, seen rising from the peak of the mountain that evening, was now succeeded by ominous flashes of fire from the same quarter, intermittently visible. The faint hot breeze from the land was felt once more. "There's just an air of wind," Mr. Duncalf remarked. "I'll try for the Captain while I have the chance."

One of the boats was lowered into the water—under command of the second mate, who had already taken the bearings of the tabooed island by daylight. Four of the men were to go with him, and they were all to be well armed. Mr. Duncalf addressed his final instructions to the officer in the boat.

"You will keep a lookout, sir, with a lantern in the bows. If the natives annoy you, you know what to do. Always shoot natives. When you get anigh the island, you will fire a gun and sing out for the Captain."

"Quite needless," interposed a voice from the sea. "The Captain is here!"

Without taking the slightest notice of the astonishment that he had caused, the commander of the *Fortuna* paddled his canoe to the side of the ship. Instead of ascending to the deck, he stepped into the boat, waiting alongside. "Lend me your pistols," he said quietly to the second officer, "and oblige me by taking your men back to their duties on board." He looked up at Mr. Duncalf and gave some further directions. "If there is any change in the weather, keep the ship standing off and on, at a safe distance from the land, and throw up a rocket from time to time to show your position. Expect me on board again by sunrise."

"What!" cried the mate. "Do you mean to say you are going back to the island—in that boat—all by yourself?"

"I am going back to the island," answered the Captain, as quietly as ever; "in this boat—all by myself." He pushed off from the ship, and hoisted the sail as he spoke.

"You're deserting your duty!" the old sea-dog shouted, with one of his loudest oaths.

"Attend to my directions," the Captain shouted back, as he drifted away into the darkness.

Mr. Duncalf—violently agitated for the first time in his life—took leave of his superior officer, with a singular mixture of solemnity and politeness, in these words:

"The Lord have mercy on your soul! I wish you good-evening."

VIII

Alone in the boat, the Captain looked with a misgiving mind at the flashing of the volcano on the main island.

If events had favoured him, he would have removed Aimata to the shelter of the ship on the day when he saw the emptied basin on the lake. But the smoke of the Priest's sacrifice had been discovered by the chief; and he had dispatched two canoes with instructions to make inquiries. One of the canoes had returned; the other was kept in waiting off the cape, to place a means of communicating with the main island at the disposal of the Priest. The second shock of earthquake had naturally increased the alarm of the chief. He had sent messages to the Priest, entreating him to leave the island, and other messages to Aimata suggesting that she should exert her influence over her father, if he hesitated. The Priest refused to leave the Temple. He trusted in his gods and his sacrifices—he believed they might avert the fatality that threatened his sanctuary.

Yielding to the holy man, the chief sent re-enforcements of canoes to take their turn at keeping watch off the headland. Assisted by torches, the islanders were on the alert (in superstitious terror of the demon of the prophecy) by night as well as by day. The Captain had no alternative but to keep in hiding, and to watch his opportunity of approaching the place in which he had concealed his canoe. It was only after Aimata had left him as usual, to return to her father at the close of evening, that the chances declared themselves in his favour. The fire-flashes from the mountain, visible when the night came, had struck terror into the hearts of the men on the watch. They thought of their wives, their children, and their possessions on the main island, and they one and all deserted their Priest. The Captain seized the opportunity of communicating with the ship, and of exchanging a frail canoe which he was ill able to manage, for a swift-sailing boat capable of keeping the sea in the event of stormy weather.

As he now neared the land, certain small sparks of red, moving on the distant water, informed him that the canoes of the sentinels had been ordered back to their duty.

Carefully avoiding the lights, he reached his own side of the island without accident, and, guided by the boat's lantern, anchored under the cliff. He climbed the rocks, advanced to the door of the hut, and was met, to his delight and astonishment, by Aimata on the threshold.

"I dreamed that some dreadful misfortune had parted us forever," she said; "and I came here to see if my dream was true. You have taught me what it is to be miserable; I never felt my heart ache till I looked into the hut and found that you had gone. Now I have seen you, I am satisfied. No! you must not go back with me. My father may be out looking for me. It is you that are in danger, not I. I know the forest as well by dark as by daylight."

The Captain detained her when she tried to leave him.

"Now you *are* here," he said, "why should I not place you at once in safety? I have been to the ship; I have brought back one of the boats. The darkness will befriend us—let us embark while we can."

She shrank away as he took her hand. "You forget my father!" she said.

"Your father is in no danger, my love. The canoes are waiting for him at the cape; I saw the lights as I passed."

With that reply he drew her out of the hut and led her toward the sea. Not a breath of the breeze was now to be felt. The dead calm had returned—and the boat was too large to be easily managed by one man alone at the oars.

"The breeze may come again," he said. "Wait here, my angel, for the chance."

As he spoke, the deep silence of the forest below them was broken by a sound. A harsh wailing voice was heard, calling:

"Aimata! Aimata!"

"My father!" she whispered; "he has missed me. If he comes here you are lost."

She kissed him with passionate fervour; she held him to her for a moment with all her strength.

"Expect me at daybreak," she said, and disappeared down the landward slope of the cliff.

He listened, anxious for her safety. The voices of the father and daughter just reached him from among the trees. The Priest spoke in no angry tones; she had apparently found an acceptable excuse for her absence. Little by little, the failing sound of their voices told him that they were on their way back together to the Temple.

The silence fell again. Not a ripple broke on the beach. Not a leaf rustled in the forest. Nothing moved but the reflected flashes of the volcano on the main island over the black sky. It was an airless and an awful calm.

He went into the hut, and laid down on his bed of leaves—not to sleep, but to rest. All his energies might be required to meet the coming events of the morning. After the voyage to and from the ship, and the long watching that had preceded it, strong as he was he stood in need of repose.

For some little time he kept awake, thinking. Insensibly the oppression of the intense heat, aided in its influence by his own fatigue, treacherously closed his eyes. In spite of himself, the weary man fell into a deep sleep.

He was awakened by a roar like the explosion of a park of artillery. The volcano on the main island had burst into a state of eruption. Smoky flame-light overspread the sky, and flashed through the open doorway of the hut. He sprang from his bed—and found himself up to his knees in water.

Had the sea overflowed the land?

He waded out of the hut, and the water rose to his middle. He looked round him by the lurid light of the eruption. The one visible object within the range of view was the sea, stained by reflections from the blood-red sky, swirling and rippling strangely in the dead calm. In a moment more, he became conscious that the earth on which he stood was sinking under his feet. The water rose to his neck; the last vestige of the roof of the hut disappeared.

He looked round again, and the truth burst on him. The island was sinking—slowly, slowly sinking into volcanic depths, below even the depth of the sea! The highest object was the hut, and that had dropped inch by inch under water before his own eyes. Thrown up to the surface by occult volcanic influences, the island had sunk back, under the same influences, to the obscurity from which it had emerged!

A black shadowy object, turning in a wide circle, came slowly near him as the all-destroying ocean washed its bitter waters into his mouth. The buoyant boat, rising as the sea rose, had dragged its anchor, and was floating round in the vortex made by the slowly sinking island. With a last desperate hope that Aimata might have been saved as *he* had been saved, he swam to the boat, seized the heavy oars with the strength of a giant, and made for the place (so far as he could guess at it now) where the lake and the Temple had once been.

He looked round and round him; he strained his eyes in the vain attempt to penetrate below the surface of the seething dimpling sea. Had the panic-stricken watchers in the canoes saved themselves, without an effort to preserve the father and daughter? Or had they both been suffocated before they could make an attempt to escape? He called to her in his misery, as if she could hear him out of the fathomless depths: "Aimata! Aimata!" The roar of the distant eruption answered him. The mounting fires lit the solitary sea far and near over the sinking island. The boat turned slowly and more slowly in the lessening vortex. Never again would those gentle eyes look at him with unutterable love! Never again would those fresh lips touch his lips with their fervent kiss! Alone, amid the savage forces of Nature in conflict, the miserable mortal lifted his hands in frantic supplication—and the burning sky glared down on him in its pitiless grandeur, and struck him to his knees in the boat. His reason sank with his sinking limbs. In the merciful frenzy that succeeded the shock, he saw afar off, in her white robe, an angel poised on the waters, beckoning him to follow her to the brighter and the better world. He loosened the sail, he seized the oars; and the faster he pursued it, the faster the mocking vision fled from him over the empty and endless sea.

IX

The boat was discovered, on the next morning, from the ship.

All that the devotion of the officers of the *Fortuna* could do for their unhappy commander was done on the homeward voyage. Restored to his own country, and to skilled medical help, the Captain's mind by slow degrees recovered its balance. He has taken his place in society again—he lives and moves and manages his affairs like the rest of us. But his heart is dead to all new emotions; nothing remains in it but the sacred remembrance of his lost love. He neither courts nor avoids the society of women. Their sympathy finds him grateful, but their attractions seem to be lost on him; they pass from his mind as they pass from his eyes—they stir nothing in him but the memory of Aimata.

"Now you know, ladies, why the Captain will never marry, and why (sailor as he is) he hates the sight of the sea."

THE LITTLE WOMAN IN BLACK

Mary Elizabeth Braddon

Mary Elizabeth Braddon (1835–1915) was another Sensation Fiction writer. She was extremely prolific, writing more than ninety novels and one hundred and fifty short stories, as well as many plays and articles. Her most famous novel is *Lady Audley's Secret* (1862) which, like much of her writing, responded to the cruelties inflicted from male-biased marriage laws by creating a heroine who is so scheming she threatens the very fabric of society. In 1857, the Matrimonial Clauses Act had made it easier to divorce in one way as it removed the need for an Act of Parliament to sanction the separation. However, women still remained at a disadvantage as, if they wanted a divorce, they had to prove that their husband had been adulterous, and that he had treated her with cruelty, deserted her, or committed incest. A man just had to prove that his wife had been unfaithful. This Act also moved private martial disputes into the public arena as it created a new Court of Divorce and Matrimonial Causes where the dirty linen of the higher classes was turned into public spectacle in the periodicals and in the new Sensation Fiction devoured by a gossip-hungry public. "The Little Woman in Black" is one of Braddon's least-known ghostly tales. It takes place in part on the stage, an environment that was familiar to her as she spent several years supporting herself as an actress prior to becoming an author. While it is set in the past, its themes of romantic shame and fears of public gossip speak very much to its original Victorian audience.

There was hardly anything talked about in the clubs and the coffee-houses that November of 1753, but the approaching marriage of Miss Sarah Pawlett and Lord Bellenden. My lord was one of the finest gentlemen in England, a statesman and a diplomatist, a man of great learning, eight-and-thirty years of age, honoured and favoured at Court, on terms of friendly intimacy at Strawberry Hill and Marble Hill, where Lady Suffolk swore he was the one honest man in his Majesty's dominions. He was owner of a splendid estate in Hertfordshire, and a fine house in St. James's Park; he had a castle in Ireland, and a deer forest in North Britain. In a word, he was the best match in all London.

Had the beautiful Sarah been about to marry some lordling of the fribble and fop tribe, instead of this splendid gentleman, the town would doubtless have had a good deal to say about her promotion; for it is not an every-day incident for an actress to be raised to the peerage, albeit Polly Peacham, after more than twenty years of probation, had lately been made Duchess of Bolton; but for the Covent Garden actress to carry off the finest gentleman in London was another matter, and folks were greatly amazed at her high fortune. She herself bore her success calmly, was said, indeed, to have a somewhat melancholy air when she showed herself in her coach in the park, or attended a fashionable auction to bid for some old delft jar or Indian monster. But a pensive air best became that statuesque loveliness of hers, and rollicking and blithsome as she was in a comedy part, she had ever in society the look of a tearless Niobe, pale as marble, and with large violet eyes full of a strange pathos.

"She had not always that doleful air," said little Tom Squatt, the critic, an early admirer of Sarah's; "I remember the time when she was as gay as a bird—ready to jump over the moon—and that was when she was not always sure of her dinner."

"Ah, that was before she took the town," said another literary gentleman at the Little Hell Fire Club, a room over a tavern in Covent Garden, where a choice of circle of garretteers and hireling wits met every night after the play. "Success sobers 'em all. They begin to think of saving money, and turn religious. Besides, that was before she fell in love with Ned Langley."

At this time there was much head-shaking and elevation of eyebrows in the little assembly, and divers pinches of snuff were taken with an air and a shoulder-shrug, as who should say, "We could, an' if we would," and so on. Yet scandal had hardly breathed its venom over the young actress's fair frame. She had never left the wing of the old half-pay Major, her father, who had fought with King George at Dettingen, and who was punctiliousness itself upon all points of honour; and she was known to have supported a brood of younger sisters, down at heel slatterns, with pretty faces and towzled heads, out of her earnings as an actress.

True! But she was also known to have been for at least one brief season—the girl's dream-land time—over head and ears in love with handsome Ned Langley. Langley the irresistible, the beau-ideal lover and reprobate of the dead old reprobate-drama, the Wildair, the Lovelace, the Mirabel, the Ranger of fashionable comedy; polished, elegant, supple, villainous, bewitching.

Ned could hardly help carrying some of his comedy characteristics into real life. The town would not have had him otherwise. Society began by giving him his diabolical reputation, and poor Ned had to live up to it. He must be Don Juan or nothing. His fashion would have waned in a season had it been hinted that he lived soberly and had ceased to intrigue with women of quality. In dress, and manner, and morals, he must needs be as the heroes of Wycherley and Vanburgh, if he would keep his vogue. And Ned was vain, and loved to be the fashion; and he deemed it his first duty to himself and society to ruin the peace of any beautiful woman who came within his ken.

Sarah Pawlett came into Covent Garden Theatre innocent, fresh, warm-hearted, pure-minded, pious even, in an age when unbelief was the last fashion. She came from her humble training in booths and barns, and queer little provincial theatres, and took the town by storm. Her beauty, her youth, her buoyancy came upon the jaded London playgoer as a surprise. It was long since so bright and spontaneous a being had flashed and sparkled on those boards. She seemed the very spirit of comedy; and to see her act a love scene—half sentiment, half mockery—with Ned Langley, was to see the very perfection of acting.

The town flocked to hear these two interchange the joyous banter of Wycherley or Congreve, charmed with their sparkle and fire, their dash and exuberance.

Of course, stage-lovers so delightful must be lovers off the stage and in earnest. The tumultuous love scenes of that broad, bright comedy must find their counterpart off the stage in a deeper and more fatal love. This is the universal belief of the playgoer.

For once in a way the audience were right in their guess-work. Those stage-lovers had not wooed and bantered each other in the shine of the oil lamps for half a year before they had fallen deeper in love than ever Wycherley or Congreve dreamed of in their gamut of passion. She gave up heart and soul to the gallant lover, surrendered her young fresh lips to his stage-kisses, melted in his arms, heart beating against heart, sweetest eyes lifted confidingly to his, while the audience applauded and cried, "How exquisite, how natural!"

She was to be his wife. No shadow of any other thought had ever crossed the unsullied surface of her mind. As yet there had been no word spoken of their marriage. They two had been but seldom alone together. The old Major was at his post behind the scenes every night, and carried his daughter off to their lodgings in Holborn directly after the performance. He attended rehearsals, took snuff with the actors and actresses, and bored them exceedingly with his prosy old stories of Dettingen, or the forty-five. He had been stationed at Derby when the young Pretender turned back with his rabble army. He was a Hanoverian to the marrow.

No, there had been no word of marriage. The wooing had been all stage-wooing—tender embraces, eyes entangling themselves in eyes, swooning sighs, impassioned kisses, hearts beating to suffocation, but all stage-play. If the Major complained that these love scenes were too natural the town was enraptured, and greeted those two young lovers as if the pair had made but one perfect whole. Applause given to her was sweetest laudation for him. He looked down at her fondly, proudly, as they stood hand in hand at the fall of the curtain. He was much more experienced in stage-craft than she; and it may be that he fancied he had taught her to act. Those who know genius when they see it, knew that with her acting was as the gift of song to the bird, God-given, spontaneous.

After that first half-year of stage courtship there came a time when little hints and faint breathings of venom began to be heard in the side-scenes and green-room; shrugs, innuendoes, a suggestion that the prosy old Major was being hoodwinked by those fiery spirits; that the lovely girl who walked off to her dingy lodging so meekly every midnight, muffled and hooded, and clinging to her father's arm, had begun to be experienced in the ruses by which ladies of quality over-reach a tyrannical parent or a jealous husband; that the frank smile and the sparkling eye now served to mask a secret.

"Why don't they marry?" asked the comic old man.

"The old Major would never consent to throw away his clever, beautiful daughter upon an extravagant wretch like Langley," answered the lady who played the heavy mothers. "Why, her salary has to keep the whole family—yes, feed and clothe all those hulking sisters, and find the old man in grog. She is the milch-cow; and if she were to marry Langley they must all starve."

"If Ned were a man of spirit he would run away with her," said the actor; "or get himself spliced by one of your May Fair parsons."

"Ned has too many strings to his bow," answered the lady, with her tragic air; "half the women of quality in London are in love with him. He has the *ton* at his beck and call. Ned would be a fool to marry."

"Not to marry Sarah Pawlett, my good soul. That girl is a fortune in herself. She is a genius, madam, a genius. Ned must be a man of snow if he can resist such charms, such graces. When she comes on the stage it is like the sun breaking through a cloud. The whole scene—nay, the whole theatre brightens."

But time went on, and there was no hint of marriage between those two ideal lovers. The old Major was laid up with gout, and unable to haunt the side-scenes as of old; but he was represented by a duenna of Irish extraction—an old servant who had nursed all the towzle-haired girls, including Sarah herself. This dragon was of a mild nature, and the lovers enjoyed each other's society very freely while the demon Podagra laid the old soldier by the heels. They seemed to move in a paradise of their own, regardless of those around them, thoughtless of the morrow, forgetful of yesterday, infinitely happy in the present hour.

Their careless joy gave occasion for more shoulder-shrugging among their worldly-wise comrades. There were some who gave the lovely Sally over for lost, some who denounced the handsome Ned as an arrant scoundrel—behind his back, mark you; but if this beautiful butterfly creature were hovering on the brink of precipice, there was no hand stretched forth to hold her back from the abyss.

Suddenly the stream of gossip was turned into a new channel, and the only talk of wings and green-room, club and coffee-house, was of the wonderful conquest Sarah Pawlett had made in my lord Bellenden—no light-minded haunter of play-houses and French taverns, but one of the magnates of the land, a gentleman of the purest water, a gem without a flaw, white and perfect as the Regent's diamond. While Ned Langley had trifled and fooled, this most estimable gentleman had stooped from his high estate to make the actress an honourable offer of marriage.

Old Major Pawlett was on his legs again by the time this happened. His gout had fled before the magic wand of supreme good luck. He proudly accepted his lordship's generous offer. The girl was but a child—not nineteen until next April—and she had all a child's way-wardness. Yet she could not be otherwise than deeply grateful, moved and melted to her heart's core by his lordship's generosity.

The girl herself said nothing of gratitude, or any other feeling. She stood up in the midst of the shabby lodging-house parlour, thin and straight and pale, like a tall white lily, and allowed herself to be given away to this stately nobleman as if she had been a chattel.

He looked down at her with his grave, grand face, smiling calmly; confident in his power to hold that which he won, strong in past triumphs over the heart of women, strong in the consciousness of his own worth. He put a diamond hoop on the third finger of the cold, unresisting hand—so cold albeit so yielding.

"Let our wedding bells sound as soon as may be, dear one," he said; "we have nothing to wait for."

"Oh, not too soon, not too soon," she pleaded piteously; "your lordship is almost a stranger to me."

"Never again lordship, and not long a stranger," he answered gently.

He saw that look of anguish in the lovely face, and knew that her heart was not his; but he saw the pure and candid soul shining out of the sorrowful eyes; and he told himself that such a heart was worth winning.

There was a painful scene between Sally and her old father as soon as the nobleman's back was turned. The girl grovelled at the Major's feet, vowed with passionate sobs that she would do anything for her father and her sisters, except this one thing that was wanted of her. She would work like a pack-horse. She would bring them every guinea she earned—she would wear one old grogram gown from year's end to year's end. She would live on bread and cheese. But the Major upbraided her with basest ingratitude to him and to Providence—to Providence for having given her such a lover as Lord Bellenden, to her father for his having been clever enough to bring such a lover to honourable proposals.

"Do you suppose if I had been anything else other than an officer and a gentleman, and a man of the world to boot, his lordship would have offered you marriage?" he demanded indignantly. "Nay," answered the girl, with a touch of pride that ennobled her—pride in the man who loved her, albeit she could not return his love, "his lordship is a man of honour, and would not have made dishonourable proposals to the lowliest orphan in the land. He is like King Cophetua in the old ballad."

"I wonder you have the impudence to praise him after the fuss you have been making," said the old man angrily, and he emphasized his speech with sundry forcible epithets common to the conversation of military men in those days.

He watched his daughter like a lynx that night at the theatre. Not a word could Ned Langley and she say to each other in the green-room or at the side-scenes; but there was one opportunity on the stage when they two were standing together at the back of the scene, while the low comedian and the comic old woman were fooling in front of the foot-lights.

She told him what had happened, clasping his hands in hers, looking up at him with divine love and confidence.

"You must marry me, and quickly too," she said. "There is no other way out of it. If you don't I shall be married to Lord Bellenden, willy nilly. My father's heart is set upon it, and all the girls were in tears this afternoon beseeching me. If you love me, Ned, as you have sworn you do, ah, so often—so often, you must make me your wife without a day's delay."

He looked at her with passionate earnestness, betwixt love and pain. "My dearest, it can't be," he said, "it can't be."

"But, why not?"

"Don't ask me, love, it can't be—and only reflect, sweet one, what a chance you are throwing away. Such a match as Lord Bellenden is not offered to an actress twice in a century. You would be doing better than either of those Gunning girls about whom we have all heard so much—and indeed you are handsomer than either; and what," he whispered in her ear, drawing close to her as the serpent to Eve, "what is to prevent us loving each other till the end of the chapter, even if you *are* Lady Bellenden?"

Her hands grew cold as death, and she wrenched them from his, as she would have snatched them out of a fiery furnace. She recoiled from him, stood apart from him for the rest of the scene, neither looked at him nor spoke to him, save when the business of the stage compelled her.

Three days afterwards Ned Langley went over to the enemy, accepted an engagement at the rival house, and the manager was left in despair.

"What the plague am I to do?" he asked piteously, with his wig pushed on one side, from sheer vexation. "There is no comedian like him in London—not in the world, perhaps—in spite of their talk of those frog-eating jackanapeses in the Rue St. Honoré."

"Play tragedy," said Sarah, "and then you won't miss him. You have Mr. Deloraine, who took the town in Romeo. I am dying to act tragedy."

"What, you, Mrs. Madcap? Do you think that you, who have kept the town laughing so long, will ever set them crying?"

"Try me!" she answered, fixing him with those beautiful eyes of her, so large, so limpid in their exquisite azure. "I can cry myself, mark you, sir; and that's half the battle."

She stood a little way from him, threw her head slightly backward, and lifted up her eyes to heaven, in a Carlo Dolci attitude. Slowly, gradually, the beautiful eyes filled, and slowly overflowed. Pearly drops chased each other down the delicate cheeks; not a contortion disfigured the chiselled features; no flush disturbed the pure pallor of that ivory skin.

"Yes, you will do it," cried the manager. "What a face to prelude Juliet's potion scene, when mother and nurse have left her, and she stands alone, like Niobe, fixed in despair. Yes, you shall play Juliet next week. Deloraine is at his best in Romeo, and at forty looks an admirable twenty-five."

The manager kept his word, and mistress Sarah's Juliet was the mode for a month. The town was all agog about her matrimonial engagement, and flocked to see her act with ever increasing fervour. She had refused to leave the stage till the eve of her wedding; refused with a charming feminine obstinacy which delighted her lover, though he would have had it otherwise. A man so deep in love is all the more smitten by having his very wish denied. Sarah was the coyest, proudest, most tormenting of mistresses; and there was that shadow of sadness, which came and went like the clouds that drift across the moon on a windy autumn night, and only made her more beautiful.

Mr. Deloraine was plain and pock-marked, and lacked all the graces of handsome Ned Langley; but he contrived to make himself handsome on the stage, by the aid of white lead and ceruse, and he was a highly respectable gentleman, who paid his way and went to church on Sundays. He had a dull wife and eleven children, so Lord Bellenden had no cause for jealousy about this Romeo, even when he saw Juliet in his arms at the passionate hour of parting, what time the lark carolled above the olive woods beyond Verona.

Little by little—by infinitesimal stages of days and hours—Sarah learnt, first to honour, and then to love her noble wooer. He was a man worthy to be loved—generous, chivalrous as that lover in the old ballad which Sarah knew by heart—nobler than the ideal of her girlish dreams. She surrendered her heart to him almost unwillingly, deeming herself unworthy to be loved by him, unworthy even to love him; but she could not withhold her love. He commanded her affection, as he had first commanded her respect.

She loved him, and in a few weeks she was to be married to him. The most fashionable mantua-maker at the West End was busy with her gowns and falbalas: the Bellenden diamonds were being remounted for her: a chariot of the newest shape and style was being built for her: and ladies of the highest *ton* stood up in their carriages to stare at her as she drove through the Park in a hired Berlin with her father.

With all this she was not happy, and she had more than one reason for her unhappiness. First, there was the thought of Ned Langley's treachery, and the love she had wasted upon him. This rankled like a green wound. Then there was the stinging memory of certain girlish half-mad letter she had written to him, when she had believed him noble as a Greek god. Thirdly, there was the haunting presence of a little woman in black, who dogged her in the street by day, now following her, now lurking at corners to watch her, and who sat on the same bench, in the same spot—the third seat from the end near the door on the prompt side, in the second row of the pit—every night.

At first, Sarah had been interested, amused, flattered by the lady's constant attendance. She had pointed her out to Ned Langley, solitary, silent, intent upon the play; evidently a friendless creature, alone in the desert of the town, with no amusement but the play-house.

"She looks a poor little shabby-genteel creature, but a lady all the same," Sarah had said to Langley, "and how she watches you and me, and hangs upon every word we utter. I am quite taken with the poor harmless soul. I wish you would find out who she is?"

"Impossible, child! a stranger from the country, most likely. A waif thrown up by the ocean of change—a widow who has lost her fortune and her husband, and has come to London to seek new ones."

On another occasion, when Sarah talked of the little woman in black, Ned had a vexed air.

"I believe she is a political spy," he said; "the Government is still suspicious of dealings with the Pretender, and has all sorts of agents."

And now, when she and Ned Langley were strangers for evermore, Sarah found herself watched more closely than ever by the little woman in shabby black—a pale, sharp-featured little woman, who might, per-chance, have been pretty in girlhood, but who had lost all her beauty at five-and-thirty, which was about the age Sarah gave her. She had a restless, lynx-eyed look, as of one who had worn herself out with watching other people.

One night that the Major had stayed late at a convivial party, Sarah, walking home with her maid, was overtaken by a pair of lightly-tripping feet in Lincoln's Inn Fields, and was startled by the tap of a hand on her shoulder.

She turned and fronted the little woman in black, whose pale, pinched face seemed ghostly in the dim light of the oil-lamp overhead. They had just turned the corner by his Grace of Newcastle's big stone mansion.

"What do you want, woman?" asked Sarah haughtily.

"Five minutes' conversation with you, madam; and it is for your welfare that you should grant me the interview."

"You can fall a little in the rear, Margaret," said Sarah to the old servant. "This lady wishes to talk to me in private."

The Irishwoman looked doubtful, and fell back only a few paces. The woman in black seemed too small a person to be dangerous. Her head hardly reached the queenly Sarah's shoulder.

"You are going to make a great match, madam," said the stranger; "all the town is full of your good fortune."

"I hope you have not stopped me so solemnly in order to tell me that!" retorted the actress. "I have noted you in the pit many an evening, madam, and as you seem an admirer of the drama I should be sorry to deem you crazy."

"No, madam, I am not crazy, though I have had more than enough to make me so. A father's anger, aye, and the loss of every friend I had in youth, a fortune forfeited, and, for a crowning mercy, an unfaithful husband—yes, unfaithful—though it was for him I sacrificed father and fortune, friends and position. I was the only daughter of a bishop, madam, and kept the best company before I was married."

"Those facts are interesting, madam, to yourself or your personal friends, but hardly so to me. I wish you good-night," said Sarah hastily, assured that the lady was a lunatic. But the little woman pressed upon her steps.

"I shall find mean to awaken your interest presently, madam," she said. "You are about to be married to the best match in London, as I was saying, and your fortune is to be envied by all your sex. I have heard wagers in the pit as to whether the marriage would or would not come off."

"The people who made such wagers were monstrously insolent."

"No doubt, madam; but insolence is the order of the day. Now, I myself would not mind wagering that your engagement with Lord Bellenden would be off tomorrow if he knew as much as I do; and if he were favoured with the perusal of certain letters which you wrote—and by the dozen—to handsome Ned Langley, your stage-lover, madam, and your very earnest lover off the stage."

"My letters!" cried Sarah, aghast. "What do you know of my letters?"

She was utterly unskilled in deceit, unpractised in denial, and admitted her folly as freely as a child would have done.

"What do I know of them? They are my daily reading; they are my morning service. I know them by heart, madam. Yes, and I know of your meetings, too; your stolen kisses in the old house by the river—among the rats and the spiders, and the ghosts, madam—yes, the ghosts. You were scared by a ghost once, I think, when you and Ned were standing side by side in the twilight in that empty house which you chose for your *rendezvous*."

"Yes," cried Sarah, "there was a figure flitted by—noiseless—shadowy. It turned my blood to ice—a figure in black. It was *you*!"

She stood gazing at the little woman in the moonlight—so pale, so attenuated. Yes, that was the form which had flitted past on the shadowy landing by the open door of the room in which she and Ned were standing, hand clasped in hand, pouring out their tale of love.

She had taken the little black figure for a visitant from the other world; and now she knew that it was even worse than a ghost—a woman, mad, or it might be, only jealous—a woman with a bitter, unscrupulous tongue bent on doing her mischief.

This creature would betray her to her lord, whom she reverenced, whom she loved. It was of Bellenden she thought as she faced her foe in the corner of the square by the turn-stile, the moon shining down upon them, the shadows of the houses making great bolts of darkness here and there.

She had done this foolish thing, she, Sarah Pawlett, whom Lord Bellenden deemed the purest of women. She had compromised herself deeply for that false lover of hers, consenting to stolen meetings in an old empty house by the river, between the Temple and Blackfriars, a house that had been in Chancery for fifty years, and which was supposed to be haunted. Ned Langley had procured a key somehow; and here they had met with impunity between the morning rehearsal and the evening performance. When Sally was late in returning to the family dinner or the family tea, she had but to say that the rehearsal had been longer than usual.

There had not been many such meetings, a dozen at most, and the *rendezvous* had been of a perfectly innocent character; but the mere fact of such secret stolen interviews would have been quite enough to compromise or to condemn Sarah in the opinion of such a man as Lord Bellenden.

Her letters were full of allusions to these meetings; she had dwelt with all a girl's romantic fondness upon the delight of being alone with her idol; of touching his soft silken locks, of looking up into his eyes. The letters were written with all the self-abandonment of a young heart, written to one who was to be the writer's husband, who was her all in all, the beginning and end of her universe; written to one whom she would no more have suspected of falsehood or other meanness than she would have doubted the purity of the blue ether far away above the common earth, in a region where defilement cometh not. She had not asked for the return of her letters, for, until that never-to-be-forgotten night when she had told Ned Langley that the time had come for their marriage, she had lived in the assurance that she was to be his wife. He had not definitely spoken of their union, but it had seemed to her a thing of course from the hour in which they confessed their mutual love. What else had they to live for, either of them, but to love and wed? they who seemed made to be mated; like two flowers on one stem, turning to each other naturally as the wind of fate blew them.

After that bitter moment in which her lover had revealed his worth-lessness, Sarah had been too proud in her deep anger to approach him, or communicate with him in any form, even for the sake of regaining her letters. She had hardly thought of those letters, indeed; thinking of the whole love story as a chapter in her life that was closed for ever; a vault sealed and secret, in which lay the dead corpse of her first passionate love.

And now she was learning that there might be a second love, sweeter even than the first; graver, deeper, truer; less romantic, but more ennobling; she was learning this and forgetting everything else, when this new trouble came upon her. Those letters, those foolish, wildly sentimental letters, were in the keeping of this strange woman.

"How came you by my letter, madam?" she asked indignantly. "Are you a thief?"

"No, madam. I am a much-injured woman; and you ought to take it kindly that I have borne my wrongs so patiently, and not disgraced you in your theatre, where you are like a queen. But stage queens have had mud thrown in their faces before today."

"*You* disgrace me! you?"

"Yes, I, madam; Ned Langley's wife."

"Ned—Langley's—wife!"

Sarah repeated the words slowly, almost in a whisper.

"Oh! he did not tell you that he was a married man, did he? he never does. You are not the first he has deluded. He does worse than that, for he tells villainous lies about me; he tells his fellow-actors that the poor little crack-brained woman at his lodgings is not his wife, but his mistress—a young lady of quality whom he ran away with, and who has been a burden to him ever since. *That's* what he tells his friends, madam; because that story leaves him at liberty to make love to the last fashionable actress, and to promise her marriage. And I am fool enough to stay with him and to slave for him, knowing all this; to warm his slippers of a night before he comes home, and mix his grog for him, and bear with him when he staggers home drunk from his Hell Fire Club, and hear his boasts of women of *ton* who are over head and ears in love with him. It was one night when he was in liquor that I found the first of your letters in his pocket; and after that I watched him, and picked them up everywhere. You've no notion how careless he is of such letters; and, madam, the women all write alike, and lovers get tired of so much honey. I've heard him say, 'More of their precious scribble.' We wives have the best of it, perhaps, with such fellows; for at least, we are behind the scenes, and we see them with their masks off."

"And you have my letters—all of them?"

"Three-and-twenty, madam. I doubt that's all, for I ransack every corner in quest of such things. I know my gentleman's ways!"

"Will you give them me back, tonight?" asked Sarah, eagerly.

"No, madam, neither tonight nor tomorrow. I will not give them back to Sarah Pawlett; I will only return them to Lady Bellenden. When you are his lordship's wife, madam, the letters shall be yours."

"I see," said Sarah, gloomily, "it is the old story. I have heard of such things. You mean to keep the letters, and hold them over me as a continual threat after I am married. You will make me pay you to be silent about them."

"Pay me! No, madam, I am not so base as that. I have no grudge against you. I cannot even blame your conduct, though it was somewhat imprudent. You are but one of many whom handsome Ned Langley has deluded. I am not a double-dealer. The letters shall be yours when you are Lady Bellenden. On your wedding-day, if you like."

"Why wait till then? Give me the letters tomorrow, and I shall be your grateful debtor for life. There is nothing in my power, as an honest woman, that I would not do for you."

"You promise fair, madam, but I have my fancy. I will only surrender those letters to Lord Bellenden's wife."

"But you must have your price—you must want something of me."

"Well perhaps I do. Yes, every man has his price, and I suppose every woman has hers too. I shall tell you mine when I give you back your letters on your wedding-day."

Sarah tried, even with tears, to argue Ned Langley's wife out of this rigid determination. The three women—Irish Margaret in the rear—walked round Lincoln's Inn Fields twice in the moonlight, Sarah pleading—the little woman as firm as a rock.

"On your wedding-day, madam, and no sooner," she said at parting; "I shall be in the church, with the letters in my pocket. I wish you a very good-night."

She made a low curtsey as ceremoniously as if she had been at Ranelagh, and tripped lightly off towards Clare Market; leaving Sarah and the maid to go on to Holborn together.

After this midnight interview, came a period of keenest anxiety, nay, almost of mental torture for Sarah Pawlett. Three weeks had yet to pass before she would be my Lady Bellenden. How she regretted her own persistency in having postponed the wedding—her obstinacy in having insisted upon acting until the eve of her marriage. She acted now in fear and trembling, expectant of some demonstration from the little woman in black. The little woman never missed a night in her accustomed seat in the second row of the pit. She had acquired a prescriptive right to that seat by her constant attendance, and by being always one of the first to enter the theatre. Regular pit-goers knew her by sight, and gave way to her—a dramatic enthusiast, doubtless, a little, distraught, but harmless.

Sarah's first look when she came on the stage was to that seat in the pit.

She acted the potion scene in Juliet with her eyes fixed on the little woman in black, fixed as if she had been face to face with Nemesis. It was a wonderful expression: people remembered it, and quoted it a quarter of a century afterwards as a marvel of finished art and high-wrought feeling.

Driving with Lord Bellenden in the park, or attending a fashionable auction with him, or at an afternoon water-party, Sarah was tortured by the expectation of the same haunting presence. The little woman seemed ubiquitous. Small, active, insignificant, neatly dressed, and with lady-like manners, she was able to push herself in anywhere. She tripped about auction-rooms and looked at china monsters. She had her seat in the park, as she had in the pit. She might even be seen on the river, alone with her waterman, shooting about among the crowded wherries and gaily-clad people—a creature of no more significance than a blot of ink on a gaudy flowered wall.

Sarah was always dreading an explosion; and her future husband was so devoted to her, so chivalrous, so true. His love lifted her to a calm heaven of proud contentment. To be beloved by him was to enter into a state of tranquil blessedness; just as she had pictured to herself the condition of the elect in the world to come.

Sometimes she had a mind to fall at his feet and confess everything: her romantic passion for Ned Langley, and the way she had been fooled by him—even their secret meetings in the deserted house—yes, she would have confessed all that, she would have endured that shame of it; but the idea that those letters of hers, written in all the intoxication of a first love, should be read in cold blood, read by a man of cultivated mind—those foolish, rambling sentences and reiterations, the poor little stock of words so repeated and misused, and, worst of all, the bad spelling. Yes; Sarah had been educated herself severely since her engagement to Lord Bellenden, and in the course of her studies had discovered how sorely she had erred in that matter of orthography. To think that throughout those fatal letters she had spelt affection with one f, and rapture with sh, instead of t. Orthography is such an arbitrary thing; has neither rhyme nor reason in it, Sarah thought, submitting her old lax notions to the rigid schooling of the dictionary.

And now came the wedding-day. She was to be married at St. Martin's-in-the-Fields, his lordship's house being in that parish. The wedding was to be a very quiet ceremonial. His lordship's mother, a dowager of seventy years of age, and of great dignity, of whom Sarah lived in awe, was to be the only relative present on the bridegroom's side. His best man was an old friend. On Sarah's side there were to be the four sisters, and an oafish brother. The Major was to give his daughter away, and was to have a new coat for the occasion. The eldest of her sisters was to be the bridesmaid.

After the wedding, bride and bridegroom were to step into a travelling carriage, and drive off as fast as six fine horses could take them to Tunbridge Wells, where they were to spend the honeymoon at the dowager's secluded villa near Leeds Castle. It was said to be one of the

prettiest seats in Kent on a small scale—gardens, fountains, shrubber-
ies all perfection. It had been the lady's delight in her thirty years of
widowhood to create and beautify the grounds and gardens.

"We shall be vastly quiet there, Sally," said his lordship, when he
was describing the beauties of the place. "I hope you will not get tired
of me."

"Tired of you!" She looked up at him with worshipping eyes—how
strangely different from that despairing look with which she had once
entreated him to delay their marriage!

He felt ineffably proud of his conquest. He had told himself that
he could win her, and sworn to himself to make her his in heart and
soul before the law bound her to him.

"When we are very sick of each other we can go to the Rooms or
the Pantiles to see the modish people," he said smiling at her.

"I would rather stay at home and hear you read to me," she answered
gravely. "Think how much I have to learn before I shall be worthy to
be your wife!"

"I think you have learnt the only lesson I shall ever care about
teaching you," he said.

"How do you mean?"

"I think you have learnt to love me, Sarah. That's the only wisdom
I ask of you."

"Yes, I have learnt that with all my heart. Yet when you first came
to this house I almost hated you."

"That was because you loved another. Nay"—as Sarah tried to speak—
"neither deny it nor confess it, my dear. I want to learn nothing about
the past. I am happy in the present, and confident about the future."

Sarah changed from red to pale and was silent.

How could she speak of those accursed letters after this? How could
she ever let him look into the depth of her past folly?

She was as white as sculptured marble next morning—as white as her ostrich feathers, but a bride had a privileged pallor. Nobody wondered at Sarah's colourless cheeks.

"You look frightened, my dear," said the out-spoken dowager as she kissed her in the church. "I hope you don't repent what you are doing."

"No, madam. I love your son with all my heart, and am proud with all my heart of his love."

Then the organ played a psalm, and the little procession went up to the altar rails, or the rails which defended that table which should have been an altar.

Very clear and firm and full were Sarah's accents as she gave the responses that made her George, Lord Bellenden's, wife.

"There is some advantage in having been taught to speak," thought the dowager, as she heard those rich, round tones.

Anon came the business in the vestry. The old Major was weeping for very pride that his daughter was now one of the nobility. Sarah signed herself Sarah Pawlett for the last time in her life, kissed her husband, and went out of the church leaning on his arm, happy, since he was verily hers now, and yet painfully expectant.

So far there had been no sign of the little woman in black. Sarah had looked about the church expecting to see her in the corner of a pew, or lurking behind a pillar; but she had descried the pinched little face nowhere. "How could I suppose that she would keep her promise?" thought Sarah despairingly; "she will treasure those letters as a weapon to use against me whenever the fit takes her."

But in the church porch the little woman in black pressed forward to speak to the bride, with a small brown paper parcel, very neatly packed in her hand.

"Mr. Jones, the glover, was anxious that you should have this ere you started, my lady," she said. "He could not execute your order sooner."

"Give it to one of my servants, madam," said his lordship, but Sarah snatched the parcel.

"I thank you, madam, from the bottom of my heart," she murmured, with an earnest look, while her bridegroom was giving an order to one of the outriders who were to escort them to Tunbridge Wells.

Another minute and she was in the chariot, sitting by her husband's side, the brown paper parcel in her lap.

"Shall we open it and see what the gloves are like, which the man sends you at the eleventh hour?" asked Lord Bellenden.

"No," she said, "I know all about them; I want to talk to you."

So they talked, and the parcel was not opened, and the streets and the new bridge, and the long suburban road, which in those days so soon became rustic, fleeted by them like a dream that is dreamt, a happy vision of sunlight and glancing leaves, white houses, cottage gardens—now and then a carriage, now and then a cart—and on to the woods and pastures, orchards and hop-gardens of Kent.

Before the bride dressed for dinner she burnt every one of those foolish letters—burnt them without reading a line of any of them.

"If I were to read them I should hate myself too much for my silliness in ever having written such trash," she said to herself, as she flung them into the fire, and thrust them down among the blazing coals, and held them there with the poker till not a vestige of that romantic bosh remained.

Three days afterwards Lady Bellenden received a prim little letter with the London postmark, written in a niggling hand, and beautifully spelt:

"Honoured Madam—
    "When we were talking together that night you asked me if I had a price for your letters, and I said perhaps I had.

176

"You are now Lady Bellenden. You will be a leader of fashion before long, if you play your cards cleverly. Ask me to your parties. I have long languished for modish society. The loss of that is a great deprivation to me than any of the troubles of my married life— wretched as that is. Ask me to all your parties. I shall not disgrace you. I know how to behave in company, and I shall always come in a chair.

"God bless you. I am very glad you are happily married, and have escaped that scoundrel, my husband. Be sure you send me a card for your first rout."

Lady Bellenden readily complied with this request, and Mrs. Edward Langley, of Castle-street, Leicester-square, received a card for her ladyship's first reception, and with the card a parcel of black Genoa velvet for a gown, and Spanish lace to trim the same. The little woman looked to advantage in her velvet gown, and mingled in the throng of English and foreign nobility, men about town, wits and authors, without attracting any adverse criticism. But as the years went by the little woman in black became a familiar object in Lady Bellenden's drawing-room as the looking-glasses which her lordship had brought from Venice, or the statues which his lordship had brought from Rome. She was very harmless; she listened to the music, and looked on at the dancing, and never obtruded herself upon anybody's attention. But it was observed that Lady Bellenden was always particularly kind to her, and by-the-by, when there came a bevy of sons and daughters, the little woman in black acquired the position of maiden aunt or godmother, among these young people, and spent the greater portion of her life with the Bellendens either in town or country.

Ned Langley had vanished from the stage of the world long ere this, after having dropped into disrepute as an actor in consequence of his intemperate habits.

He died in a sponging house, very suddenly, struck down by cerebral apoplexy, after a midnight drinking bout. Most people had heard the little woman in black spoken of as Mrs. Langley; but very few people knew she was the widow of handsome Ned Langley, the famous comedian.

WHITE MAGIC

Ella D'Arcy

Constance Eleanor Mary Byrne D'Arcy (1857–1937) wrote under the name Ella D'Arcy, as well as the male pseudonym, Gilbert H. Page, but was known to her friends as Goblin Ella due to the fact that she'd often appear unannounced at their houses after long silent absences. Among other publications, D'Arcy was a frequent contributor to *The Yellow Book*, a rather racy quarterly periodical which ran from 1894–1897. *The Yellow Book* was associated with Decadence, which was, in turn, associated with the erotic, the rejection of morality and "art for art's sake". The periodical's yellow cover also firmly aligned it with saucy and illicit French novels. It is therefore perhaps no surprise that D'Arcy was an advocate of sexual freedom for women, believing that this would lead to equality between the sexes. Many of her stories feature independent women who freely express sexual desire, as well as the men who fear them.

D'Arcy was one of a group of New Women writers, who include George Egerton (1859–1945) and Sarah Grand (1854–1943)—the latter first coined the term "New Woman" in 1894. New Women yearned for sexual liberation as well as independence and rights with regard to education, politics, and economics. They also argued that marriage was outdated and degrading for women. The New Woman was, unsurprisingly, the source of much controversy and was frequently lampooned in the popular press—often depicted in bloomers on a bicycle or with a phallic cigarette in hand. The criticism they received was contradictory. As Lyn Pykett famously states, "The New Woman was, by turns, a mannish amazon and a Womanly woman; she was oversexed, undersexed, or same sex identified; she was anti-maternal or a racial supermother; she was male-identified, or man-hating and/ or man-eating, or self-appointed saviour of the benighted masculinity; she was anti-domestic, or she thought to make domestic values prevail; she was radical, socialist, or revolutionary, or she was reactionary and conservative; she was the agent of social and/or radical regeneration, or symptom and agent of its decline".* Therefore, the New Woman was a threat not only to moral codes of sexual behaviour and marriage, but also to the nation more widely. New Women authors used fiction as a vehicle to advance their cause, as well as to discuss marital and sexual relationships with a frankness that had not been seen before. In keeping with her New Woman agenda of challenging the marital status quo, D'Arcy satirizes ideals of romantic love in "White Magic" in order to expose and mock gendered stereotypes.

* Pykett, Lyn, "Foreword", in Richardson, Angélique and Willis, Chris, eds., *The New Woman in Fiction and in Fact: Fin-de-siècle Feminisms* (London: Palgrave Macmillan, 2001), p. xii.

I spent one evening last summer with my friend Mauger, *pharmacien* in the little town of Jacques-le-Port. He pronounces his name Major, by-the-bye, it being a quaint custom of the Islands to write proper names one way and speak them another, thus serving to bolster up that old, old story of the German savant's account of the difficulties of the English language—"where you spell a man's name Verulam," says he reproachfully, "and pronounce it Bacon."

Mauger and I sat in the pleasant wood-panelled parlour behind the shop, from whence all sorts of aromatic odours found their way in through the closed door to mingle with the fragrance of figs, Ceylon tea, and hot *gôches-à-beurre*, constituting the excellent meal spread before us. The large old-fashioned windows were wide open, and I looked straight out upon the harbour, filled with holiday yachts, and the wonderful azure sea.

Over against the other islands, opposite, a gleam of white streaked the water, white clouds hung motionless in the blue sky, and a tiny boat with white sails passed out round Falla Point. A white butterfly entered the room to flicker in gay uncertain curves above the cloth, and a warm reflected light played over the slender rat-tailed forks and spoons, and raised by a tone or two the colour of Mauger's tanned face and yellow beard. For, in spite of a sedentary profession, his references lie with an out-of-door life, and he takes an afternoon off whenever practicable, as he had done that day, to follow his favourite pursuit over the golf-links at Les Landes.

While he had been deep in the mysteries of teeing and putting, with no subtler problem to be solved than the judicious selection of mashie and cleek, I had explored some of the curious cromlechs or *pouquelayes* scattered over this part of the island, and my thoughts and speech harked back irresistibly to the strange old religions and usages of the past.

"Science is all very well in its way," said I; "and of course it's an inestimable advantage to inhabit this so-called nineteenth century; but the mediæval want of science was far more picturesque. The once universal belief in charms and portents, in wandering saints, and fighting fairies, must have lent an interest to life which these prosaic days sadly lack. Madelon then would steal from her bed on moonlight nights in May, and slip across the dewy grass with naked feet, to seek the reflection of her future husband's face in the first running stream she passed; now, Miss Mary Jones puts on her bonnet and steps round the corner, on no more romantic errand than the investment of her month's wages in the savings bank at two and a half per cent."

Mauger laughed. "I wish she did anything half so prudent! That has not been my experience of the Mary Joneses."

"Well, anyhow," I insisted, "the Board school has rationalized them. It has pulled up the innate poetry of their nature to replace it by decimal fractions."

To which Mauger answered "Rot!" and offered me his cigarette-case. After the first few silent whiffs, he went on as follows: "The innate poetry of Woman! Confess now, there is no more unpoetic creature under the sun. Offer her the sublimest poetry ever written and the *Daily Telegraph*'s latest article on fashions, or a good sound murder or reliable divorce, and there's no betting on her choice, for it's a dead certainty. Many men have a love of poetry, but I'm inclined to think that a hundred women out of ninety-nine positively dislike it."

Which struck me as true. "We'll drop the poetry, then," I answered; "but my point remains, that if the girl of today has no superstitions, the girl of tomorrow will have no beliefs. Teach her to sit down thirteen to table, to spill the salt, and walk under a ladder with equanimity, and you open the door for Spencer and Huxley and—and all the rest of it," said I, coming to an impotent conclusion.

"Oh, if superstition were the salvation of woman—but you are thinking of young ladies in London, I suppose? Here, in the Islands, I can show you as much superstition as you please. I'm not sure that the country-people in their heart of hearts don't still worship the old gods of the *pouquelayes*. You would not, of course, find anyone to own up to it, or to betray the least glimmer of an idea as to your meaning, were you to question him, for ours is a shrewd folk, wearing their orthodoxy bravely; but possibly the old beliefs are cherished with the more ardour for not being openly avowed. Now you like bits of actuality. I'll give you one, and a proof, too, that the modern maiden is still separated by many a fathom of salt sea-water from these fortunate isles.

"Some time ago, on a market morning, a girl came into the shop, and asked for some blood from a dragon. 'Some what?' said I, not catching her words. 'Well, just a little blood from a dragon,' she answered very tremulously, and blushing. She meant of course, 'dragon's blood,' a resinous powder, formerly much used in medicine, though out of fashion now.

"She was a pretty young creature, with pink cheeks and dark eyes, and a forlorn expression of countenance which didn't seem at all to fit in with her blooming health. Not from the town, or I should have known her face; evidently come from one of the country parishes to sell her butter and eggs. I was interested to discover what she wanted the 'dragon's blood' for, and after a certain amount of hesitation she told me. 'They do say it's good, sir, if anything should have happened betwixt you and your young man.' 'Then you have a young man?' said I. 'Yes, sir.' 'And you've fallen out with him?' 'Yes, sir.' And tears rose to her eyes at the admission, while her mouth rounded with awe at my amazing perspicacity. 'And you mean to send him some dragon's blood as a love potion?' 'No, sir; you've got to mix it with water you've fetched from the Three Sisters' Well, and drink it yourself in nine sips on nine nights running, and get into bed without once looking in the glass, and then if you've done everything properly, and haven't made any mistake, he'll come back to you, an' love you twice as much as before.' 'And la Mère Todevinn (Tostevin) gave you that precious recipe, and made you cross her hand with silver into the bargain,' said I severely; on which the tears began to flow outright.

"You know the old lady," said Mauger, breaking off his narration, "who lives in the curious stone house at the corner of the market-place? A reputed witch who learned both black and white magic from her mother, who was a daughter of Hélier Mouton, the famous sorcerer of Cakeuro. I could tell you some funny stories relating to la Mère Todevinn, who numbers more clients among the officers and fine ladies here than in any other class; and very curious, too, is the history of that stone house, with the Brancourt arms still sculptured on the side. You can see them, if you turn down by the Water-gate. This old sinister-looking building, or rather portion of a building, for more modern houses have been built over the greater portion of the site, and now press upon it from either hand, once belonged to one of the finest mansions in the islands, but through a curse and a crime has been brought down to its present condition; while the Brancourt family have long since been utterly extinct. But all this isn't the story of Elsie Mahy, which turned out to be the name of my little customer.

"The Mahys are of the Vauvert parish, and Pierre Jean, the father of this girl, began life as a day-labourer, took to tomato-growing on borrowed capital, and now owns a dozen glass-houses of his own. Mrs. Mahy does some dairy-farming on a minute scale, the profits of which she and Miss Elsie share as pin-money. The young man who is courting Elsie is a son of Toumes the builder. He probably had something to do with the putting up of Mahy's greenhouses, but anyhow, he has been constantly over at Vauvert during the last six months, superintending the alterations at de Câterelle's place.

"Toumes, it would seem, is a devoted but imperious lover, and the Persian and Median laws are as butter compared with the inflexibility of his decisions. The little rift within the lute, which has lately turned all the music to discord, occurred last Monday week—bank-holiday, as you may remember. The Sunday school to which Elsie belongs and it's a strange anomaly, isn't it, that a girl going to Sunday school should still have a rooted belief in white magic?—the school was to go for an outing to Prawn Bay, and Toumes had arranged to join his sweetheart at the starting-point. But he had made her promise that if by any chance he should be delayed, she would not go with the others, but would wait until he came to fetch her.

"Of course, it so happened that he was detained, and, equally of course, Elsie, like a true woman, went off without him. She did all she knew to make me believe she went quite against her own wishes, that her companions forced her to go. The beautifully yielding nature of a woman never comes out so conspicuously as when she is being coerced into following her own secret desires. Anyhow, Toumes, arriving some time later, found her gone. He followed on, and under ordinary circumstances, I suppose, a sharp reprimand would have been considered sufficient. Unfortunately, the young man arrived on the scene to find his truant love deep in the frolics of kiss-in-the-ring. After tea in the Câterelle Arms, the whole party had adjourned to a neighbouring meadow, and were thus whiling away the time to the exhilarating strains of a French horn and a concertina. Elsie was led into the centre of the ring by various country bumpkins, and kissed beneath the eyes of heaven, of her neighbours, and of her embittered swain.

"You may have been amongst us long enough to know that the Toumes family are of a higher social grade than the Mahys, and I suppose the Misses Toumes never in their lives stooped to anything so ungenteel as public kiss-in-the-ring. It was not surprising, therefore, to hear that after this incident 'me an' my young man had words,' as Elsie put it.

"Note," said Mauger, "the descriptive truth of this expression 'having words.' Among the unlettered, lovers only do have words when vexed. At other times they will sit holding hands throughout a long summer's afternoon, and not exchange two remarks an hour. Love seals their tongue; anger alone unlooses it, and, naturally, when unloosened, it runs on, from sheer want of practice, a great deal faster and farther than they desire.

"So, life being thorny and youth being vain, they parted late that same evening, with the understanding that they would meet no more; and to be wroth with one we love worked its usual harrowing effects. Toumes took to billiards and brandy, Elsie to tears and invocations of Beelzebub; then came Mère Todevinn's recipe, my own more powerful potion, and now once more all is silence and balmy peace."

"Do you mean to tell me you sold the child a charm, and didn't enlighten her as to its futility?"

"I sold her some bicarbonate of soda worth a couple of *doubles*, and charged her five shillings for it into the bargain," said Mauger unblushingly. "A wrinkle I learned from once overhearing an old lady I had treated for nothing expatiating to a crony, 'Eh, but, my good, my good! dat Mr. Major, I don't t'ink much of him. He give away his add-vice an' his meddecines for nuddin. Dey not wort nuddin' neider, for sure.'

So I made Elsie hand me over five British shillings, and gave her the powder, and told her to drink it with her meals. But I threw in another prescription, which, if less important, must nevertheless be punctiliously carried out, if the charm was to have any effect. 'The very next time,' I told her, 'that you meet your young man in the street, walk straight up to him without looking to the right or to the left, and hold out your hand, saying these words: "Please, I so want to be friends again!" Then if you've been a good girl, have taken the powder regularly, and not forgotten one of my directions, you'll find that all will come right.'

"Now, little as you may credit it," said Mauger, smiling, "the charm worked, for all that we live in the so-called nineteenth century. Elsie came into the shop only yesterday to tell me the results, and to thank me very prettily. 'I shall always come to you now, sir,' she was good enough to say, 'I mean, if anything was to go wrong again. You know a great deal more than Mère Todevinn, I'm sure.' 'Yes, I'm a famous sorcerer,' said I, 'but you had better not speak about the powder. You are wise enough to see that it was just your own conduct in meeting your young man rather more than halfway, that did the trick—eh?' She looked at me with eyes brimming over with wisdom. 'You needn't be afraid, sir, I'll not speak of it. Mère Todevinn always made me promise to keep silence too. But of course I know it was the powder that worked the charm.'

"And to that belief the dear creature will stick to the last day of her life. Women are wonderful enigmas. Explain to them that tight-lacing displaces all the internal organs, and show them diagrams to illustrate your point, they smile sweetly, say, 'Oh, how funny!' and go out to buy their new stays half an inch smaller than their old ones. But tell them they must never pass a pin in the street for luck's sake, if it lies with its point towards them, and they will sedulously look for and pick up every such confounded pin they see. Talk to a woman of the marvels of science, and she turns a deaf ear, or refuses point-blank to believe you; yet she is absolutely all ear for any old wife's tale, drinks it greedily in, and never loses hold of it for the rest of her days."

"But does she?" said I; "that's the point in dispute, and though your story shows there's still a commendable amount of superstition in the Islands, I'm afraid if you were to come to London, you would not find sufficient to cover a threepenny-piece."

"Woman is woman all the world over," said Mauger sententiously, "no matter what mental garb happens to be in fashion at the time. *Grattez la femme et vous trouvez la folle.* For see here: if I had said to Mademoiselle Elsie, 'Well, you were in the wrong; it's your place to take the first step towards reconciliation,' she would have laughed in my face, or flung out of the shop in a rage. But because I sold her a little humbugging powder under the guise of a charm, she submitted herself with the docility of a pet lambkin. No; one need never hope to prevail through wisdom with a woman, and if I could have realized that ten years ago, it would have been better for me."

He fell silent, thinking of his past, which to me, who knew it, seemed almost an excuse for his cynicism. I sought a change of idea. The splendour of the pageant outside supplied me with one.

The sun had set; and all the eastern world of sky and water, stretching before us, was steeped in the glories of the after-glow. The ripples seemed painted in dabs of metallic gold upon a surface of polished blue-grey steel. Over the islands opposite hung a far-reaching golden cloud, with faint-drawn, up-curled edges, as though thinned out upon the sky by some monster brush; and while I watched it, this cloud changed from gold to rose-colour, and instantly the steel mirror of the sea glowed rosy too, and was streaked and shaded with a wonderful rosy-brown. As the colour grew momentarily more intense in the sky above, so did the sea appear to pulse to a more vivid copperish-rose, until at last it was like nothing so much as a sea of flowing fire. And the cloud flamed fiery too, yet all the while its up-curled edges rested in exquisite contrast upon a background of most cool cerulean blue.

The little sailing-boat, which I had noticed an hour previously, reappeared from behind the Point. The sail was lowered as it entered the harbour, and the boatman took to his oars. I watched it creep over the glittering water until it vanished beneath the window-sill. I got up and went over to the window to hold it still in sight. It was sculled by a young man in rosy shirt-sleeves, and opposite to him, in the stern, sat a girl in a rosy gown.

So long as I had observed them, not one word had either spoken. In silence they had crossed the harbour, in silence the sculler had brought his craft alongside the landing-stage, and secured her to a ring in the stones. Still silent, he helped his companion to step out upon the quay.

"Here," said I, to Mauger, "is a couple confirming your 'silent' theory with a vengeance. We must suppose that much love has rendered them absolutely dumb."

He came, and leaned from the window too.

"It's not *a* couple, but *the* couple," said he; "and after all, in spite of cheap jesting, there are some things more eloquent than speech." For at this instant, finding themselves alone upon the jetty, the young man had taken the girl into his arms, and she had lifted a frank responsive mouth to return his kiss.

Five minutes later the sea had faded into dull greys and sober browns, starved white clouds moved dispiritedly over a vacant sky, and by cricking the back of my neck I was able to follow Toumes' black coat and the white frock of Miss Elsie until they reached Poidevin's wine-vaults, and, turning up the Water-gate, were lost to view.

THE TIGER-CHARM

Alice Perrin

Alice Perrin (1867–1934) primarily wrote about the British in colonial India. She was born in Mussoorie in India in 1867 and was sent to school in England. On her return, she married Charles Perrin, an engineer in the irrigation department of the Indian Public Works, in May 1886. The couple stayed in India for sixteen years. She began writing after the birth of her only child, in part to relieve the boredom of colonial life. She wrote seventeen novels, but her most famous work is probably the short story collection, *East of Suez* (1901), in which "The Tiger-Charm" first appeared. This anthology was hugely successful in its day as the public lapped up its tales of illicit love and supernatural forces, and her writing was favourably compared with that of Rudyard Kipling. The conflict and tensions between the British and Indians played out in many of her stories' domestic settings. Perrin's attitudes toward Anglo-Indians shifted over the course of her career, moving from perceiving India to be a harmful environment filled with great horrors to a more positive view of the Anglo-Indian experience. She also spoke out against the possibility of Indian independence as she perceived Anglo-Indians to be "superior" which, in her view, justified the continuation of the British Raj regime. This makes "The Tiger-Charm" especially interesting given that it uses supernatural elements to exact a particular kind of both colonial and marital revenge.

The sun, the sky, the burning, dusty atmosphere, and the waving sea of tall yellow grass seemed molten into one blinding blaze of pitiless heat to the aching vision of little Mrs. Wingate. In spite of blue goggles, pith sun-hat and enormous umbrella, she felt as though she were being slowly roasted alive, for the month was May, and she and her husband were perched on the back of an elephant, traversing a large tract of jungle at the foot of the Himalayas.

Colonel Wingate was one of the keenest sportsmen in India, and every day for the past week had he and his wife, and their friend, Captain Bastable, sallied forth from the camp with a line of elephants to beat through the forest of grass that reached to the animals' ears; to squelch over swamps, disturbing herds of antelope and wild pig; to pierce thick tangles of jungle, from which rose peafowl, black partridge, and birds of gorgeous plumage; to cross stony beds of dry rivers—ever on the watch for the tigers that had hitherto baffled all their efforts.

As each "likely" spot was drawn a blank, Netta Wingate heaved a sigh of relief, for she hated sport, was afraid of the elephants, and lived in hourly terror of seeing a tiger. She longed for the fortnight in camp to be over, and secretly hoped that the latter week of it might prove as unsuccessful as the first. Her skin was burnt to the hue of a berry, her head ached perpetually from the heat and glare, the motion of the elephant made her feel sick, and if she ventured to speak, her husband only impatiently bade her be quiet.

This afternoon, as they ploughed and rocked over the hard, uneven ground, she could scarcely keep awake, dazzled as she was by the vista of scorched yellow country and the gleam of her husband's rifle barrels in the melting sunshine. She swayed drowsily from side to side in the howdah, her head, her eyelids closed...

She was roused by a torrent of angry exclamations. Her umbrella had hitched itself obstinately into the collar of Colonel Wingate's coat, and he was making infuriated efforts to free himself. Jim Bastable, approaching on his elephant, caught a mixed vision of the refractory umbrella and two agitated sun-hats, the red face and fierce blue eyes of the Colonel, and the anxious, apologetic, sleepy countenance of Mrs. Wingate, as she hurriedly strove to release her irate lord and master. The whole party came to an involuntary halt, the natives listening with interest as the sahib stormed at the mem-sahib and the umbrella in the same breath.

"That howdah is not big enough for two people," shouted Captain Bastable, coming to the rescue. "Let Mrs. Wingate change to mine. It's bigger, and my elephant has easier paces."

Hot, irritated, angry, Colonel Wingate commanded his wife to betake herself to Bastable's elephant, and to keep her infernal umbrella closed for the rest of the day, adding that women had no business out tiger-shooting; and why the devil had she come at all?—oblivious of the fact that Mrs. Wingate had begged to be allowed to stay in the station, and that he himself had insisted on her coming.

She well knew that argument or contradiction would only make matters worse, for he had swallowed three stiff whiskies and sodas at luncheon in the broiling sun, and since the severe sunstroke that had so nearly killed him two years ago, the smallest quantity of spirits was enough to change him from an exceedingly bad-tempered man into something little short of a maniac. She had heedlessly married him when she was barely nineteen, turning a deaf ear to warnings of his violence, and now, at twenty-three, her existence was one long fear. He never allowed her out of his sight, he never believed a word she said; he watched her, suspected her, bullied her unmercifully, and was insanely jealous. Unfortunately, she was one of those nervous, timid women, who often rather provoke ill-treatment than otherwise.

This afternoon she marvelled at being permitted to change to Captain Bastable's howdah, and with a feeling of relief scrambled off the elephant, though trembling, as she always did, lest the great beast should seize her with his trunk or lash her with his tail, that was like a jointed iron rod. Then, once safely perched up behind Captain Bastable, she settled herself with a delightful sense of security. He understood her nervousness, he did not laugh or grumble at her little involuntary cries of fear; he was not impatient when she was convinced the elephant was running away or sinking in a quicksand, or that the howdah was slipping off. He also understood the Colonel, and had several times helped her through in a trying situation; and now the sympathy in his kind eyes made her tender heart throb with gratitude.

"All right?" he asked.

She nodded, smiling, and they started again ploughing and lurching through the coarse grass, great wisps of which the elephant uprooted with his trunk, and beat against his chest to get rid of the soil before putting them in his mouth. Half an hour later, as they drew near the edge of the forest, one of the elephants suddenly stopped short, with a jerky, backward movement, and trumpeted shrilly. There was an expectant halt all along the line, and a cry from a native of "Tiger! Tiger!" Then an enormous striped beast bounded out of the grass and stood for a moment in a small, open space, lashing its tail and snarling defiance. Colonel Wingate fired. The tiger, badly wounded, charged, and sprang at the head of Captain Bastable's elephant. There was a confusion of noise; savage roars from the tiger; shrieks from the excited elephants; shouts from the natives; banging of rifles. Mrs. Wingate covered her face with her hands. She heard a thud, as of a heavy body falling to the ground, and then she found herself being flung from side to side of the howdah, as the elephant bolted madly towards the forest, one huge ear torn to ribbons by the tiger's claws.

She heard Captain Bastable telling her to hold on tight, and shouting desperate warnings to the mahout to keep the elephant as clear of the forest as possible. Like many nervous people in the face of real danger, she suddenly became absolutely calm, and uttered no sound as the pace increased and they tore along the forest edge, escaping overhanging boughs by a miracle. To her it seemed that the ponderous flight lasted for hours. She was bruised, shaken, giddy, and the crash that came at last was a relief rather than otherwise. A huge branch combed the howdah off the elephant's back, sweeping the mahout with it, while the still terrified animal sped on trumpeting and crashing through the forest.

Mrs. Wingate was thrown clear of the howdah. Captain Bastable had saved himself by jumping, and only the old mahout lay doubled up and unconscious amongst the debris of shattered wood, torn leather and broken ropes. Netta could hardly believe she was not hurt, and she and Captain Bastable stared at one another with dazed faces for some moments before they could collect their senses. Far away in the distance they could hear the elephant still running. Between them they extricated the mahout, and, seating herself on the ground, Netta took the old man's unconscious head on to her lap, while Captain Bastable anxiously examined the wizened, shrunken body.

"Is he dead?" she asked.

"I can't be sure. I'm afraid he is. I wonder if I could find some water. I haven't an idea where we are, for I lost all count of time and distance.

I hope Wingate is following us. Should you be afraid to stay here while I have a look round and see if we are anywhere near a village?"

"Oh no, I shan't be frightened," she said steadily. Her delicate, clear-cut face looked up at him fearlessly from the tangled background of mighty trees and dense creepers; and her companion could scarcely believe she was the same trembling, nervous little coward of an hour ago.

He left her, and the stillness of the jungle was very oppressive when the sound of his footsteps died away. She was alone with a dead, or dying man, on the threshold of the vast, mysterious forest, with its possible horrors of wild elephants, tigers, leopards, snakes! She tried to turn her thoughts from such things, but the scream of a peacock made her start as it rent the silence, and then the undergrowth began to rustle ominously. It was only a porcupine that came out, rattling his quills, and, on seeing her, ran into further shelter out of sight. It seemed to be growing darker, and she fancied the evening must be drawing in. She wondered if her husband would overtake them. If not, how were she and Jim Bastable to get back to the camp? Then she heard voices and footsteps, and presently a little party of natives came in sight, led by Jim and bearing a string bedstead.

"I found a village not far off," he explained, "and thought we'd better take the poor old chap there. Then, if the Colonel doesn't turn up by the time we've seen him comfortably settled, we must find our way back to the camp as best we can."

The natives chattered and exclaimed as they lifted the unconscious body on to the bedstead, and then the little procession started. Netta was so bruised and stiff she could hardly walk; but, with the help of Bastable's arm, she hobbled along till the village was gained. The headman conducted them to his house, which consisted of a mud hovel shared by himself and his family with several relations, besides a cow and a goat with two kids. He gave Netta a wicker stool to sit on and some smoky buffalo's milk to drink, while the village physician was summoned, who at last succeeded in restoring the mahout to consciousness and pouring a potion down his throat.

"I die," whispered the patient, feebly.

Netta went to his side, and he recognized her.

"A—ree! mem-sahib!" he quavered. "So Allah has guarded thee. But the anger of the Colonel sahib will be great against me for permitting the elephant to run away, and it is better that I die. Where is that daughter of a pig? She was a rascal from her youth up; but today was the first time she ever really disobeyed my voice."

He tried to raise himself, but fell back groaning, for his injuries were internal and past hope.

"It is growing dark." He put forth his trembling hand blindly. "Where is the little white lady who so feared the sahib, and the elephants, and the jungle? Do not be afraid, mem-sahib. Those who fear should never go into the jungle. So if thou seest a tiger, be bold, be bold; call him 'uncle' and show him the tiger-charm. When he will turn away and harm thee not—" He wandered on incoherently, his fingers fumbling with something at his throat, and presently he drew out a small silver amulet attached to a piece of cord. As he held it towards Netta, it flashed in the light of the miserable native oil lamp that someone had just brought in and placed on the floor.

"Take it, mem-sahib, and feel no fear while thou hast it, for no tiger would touch thee. It was my father's, and his father's before him, and there is that written on it which has ever protected us from the tiger's tooth. I myself shall need it no longer, for I am going, whereat my nephew will rejoice; for he has long coveted my seat. Thou shalt have the charm, mem-sahib, for thou hast stayed by an old man, and not left him to die alone in a Hindu village and a strange place. Some day, in the hour of danger, thy little fingers may touch the charm, and then thou wilt recall old Mahomed Bux, mahout, with gratitude."

He groped for Netta's hand, and pushed the amulet into her palm. She took it, and laid her cool fingers on the old man's burning forehead.

"Salaam, Mahomed Bux," she said softly. "Bahut, bahut, salaam." Which is the nearest Hindustani equivalent for "Thank you."

But he did not hear her. He was wandering again, and for half an hour he babbled of elephants, of tigers, of camps and jungles, until his voice became faint and died away in hoarse gasps.

Then he sighed heavily and lay still, and Jim Bastable took Mrs. Wingate out into the air, and told her that the old mahout was dead. She gave way and sobbed, for she was aching all over and tired to death, and she dreaded the return to the camp.

"Oh! my dear girl, please don't cry!" said Jim, distressfully. "Though really I can't wonder at it, after all you've gone through today; and you've been so awfully plucky, too."

Netta gulped down her tears. It was delicious to be praised for courage, when she was only accustomed to abuse for cowardice.

"How are we to get back to the camp?" she asked dolefully. "It's so late."

And, indeed, darkness had come swiftly on, and the light of the village fires was all that enabled them to see each other.

"The moon will be up presently; we must wait for that. They say the village near our camp lies about six miles off, and that there is a cart-track of sorts towards it. I told them they must let us have a bullock-cart, and we shall have to make the best of that."

They sat down side by side on a couple of large stones, and listened in silence to the lowing of the tethered cattle, the ceaseless, irritating cry of the brain fever bird, and the subdued conversation of a group of children and village idlers, who had assembled at a respectful distance to watch them with inquisitive interest. Once a shrill trumpeting in the distance told of a herd of wild elephants out for a night's raid on the crops, and at intervals packs of jackals swept howling across the fields, while the moon rose gradually over the collection of squalid huts and flooded the vast country with a light that made the forest black and fearful.

Then a clumsy little cart, drawn by two small, frightened white bullocks, rattled into view. Jim and Netta climbed into the vehicle, and were politely escorted off the premises by the headman and the concourse of interested villagers and excited women and children.

They bumped and shook over the rough, uneven track. The bullocks raced or crawled alternately, while the driver twisted their tails and abused them hoarsely. The moonlight grew brighter and more glorious. The air, now soft and cool, was filled with strong scents and the hum of insects released from the heat of the day.

At last they caught the gleam of white tents against the dark background of a mango-grove.

"The camp," said Captain Bastable, shortly.

Netta made a nervous exclamation.

"Do you think there will be a row?" he asked with some hesitation. They had never discussed Mrs. Wingate's domestic troubles together.

"Perhaps he is still looking out for us," she said evasively.

"If he had followed us at all, he must have found us. I believe he went on shooting, or back to the camp." There was an angry impatience in his voice. "Don't be nervous," he added hastily. "Try not to mind anything he may say. Don't listen. He can't always help it, you know. I wish you could persuade him to retire; the sun out here makes him half off his head."

"I wish I could," she sighed. "But he will never do anything I ask him, and the big game shooting keeps him in India."

Jim nodded, and there was a comprehending silence between them till they reached the edge of the camp, got out of the cart, and made their way to the principal tent. There they discovered Colonel Wingate, still in his shooting clothes, sitting by the table, on which stood an almost empty bottle of whisky. He rose as they entered, and delivered himself of a torrent of bad language. He accused the pair of going off together on purpose, declaring he would divorce his wife and kill Bastable. He stormed, raved and threatened, giving them no opportunity of speaking, until at last Jim broke in and insisted on being heard.

"For Heaven's sake, be quiet," he said firmly, "or you'll have a fit. You saw the elephant run away, and apparently you made no effort to follow us and come to our help. We were swept off by a tree, and the mahout was mortally hurt. It was a perfect miracle that neither your wife nor I was killed. The mahout died in a village, and we had to get here in a bullock-cart." Then, seeing Wingate preparing for another onslaught, Bastable took him by the shoulders. "My dear chap, you're not yourself. Go to bed, and we'll talk it over tomorrow if you still wish to."

Colonel Wingate laughed harshly. His mood had changed suddenly.

"Go to bed?" he shouted boisterously. "Why, I was going out when you arrived. There was a kill last night, only a mile off, and I'm going to get the tiger." He stared wildly at Jim, who saw that he was not responsible for his words and actions. The brain, already touched by sunstroke, had given way at last under the power of whisky. Jim's first impulse was to prevent his carrying out his intention of going after the tiger. Then he reflected that it was not safe for Netta to be alone with the man, and that, if Wingate were allowed his own way, it would at least take him out of the camp.

"Very well," said Jim quietly, "and I will come with you."

"Do," answered the Colonel pleasantly, and then, as Bastable turned for a moment, Mrs. Wingate saw her husband make a diabolical grimace at the other's unconscious back. Her heart beat rapidly with fear. Did he mean to murder Jim? She felt convinced he contemplated mischief, but the question was how to warn Captain Bastable without her husband's knowledge. The opportunity came more easily than she had expected, for presently the Colonel went outside to call for his rifle and give some orders. She flew to Bastable's side.

"Be careful," she panted; "he wants to kill you, I know he does. He's mad! Oh, don't go with him—don't go—"

"It will be all right," he said reassuringly. "I'll look out for myself, but I can't let him go alone in this state. We shall only sit up in a tree an hour or two, for the tiger must have come and gone long ago. Don't be frightened. Go to bed and rest."

She drew from her pocket the little polished amulet the mahout had given her.

"At any rate take this," she said hysterically. "It may save you from a tiger, if it doesn't from my husband. I know I am silly, but do take it. There may be luck in it, you can never tell; and old Mahomed Bux said it had saved him and his father and his grandfather—and that you ought to call a tiger 'uncle'—" she broke off, half laughing, half crying, utterly unstrung.

To please her he put the little charm into his pocket, and after a hasty drink went out and joined Wingate, who insisted that they should proceed on foot and by themselves. Bastable knew it would be useless to make any opposition, and they started, their rifles in their hands; but, when they had gone some distance and the tainted air told them they were nearing their destination, Jim discovered he had no cartridges.

"Never mind," whispered the Colonel. "I have plenty, and our rifles have the same bore. We can't go back now; we've no time to lose."

Jim submitted, and he and Wingate tip-toed to the foot of a tree, the low branches and thick leaves of which afforded an excellent hiding place, down-wind from the half-eaten carcass of the cow. They climbed carefully up, making scarcely any noise, and then Jim held out his hand to the other for some cartridges. The Colonel nodded.

"Presently," he whispered, and Jim waited, thinking it extremely unlikely that cartridges would be wanted at all.

The moonlight came feebly through the foliage of the surrounding trees on to the little glade before them, in which lay the remains of the carcass pulled under a bush to shield it from the carrion birds. A deer pattered by towards the river, casting startled glances on every side; insects beat against the faces of the two men; and a jackal ran out with his brush hanging down, looked round, and retired again, with a melancholy howl. Then there arose a commotion in the branches of the neighbouring trees, and a troop of monkeys fought and crashed and chattered, as they leapt from bough to bough. Jim knew that this often portended the approach of a tiger, and the moment afterwards a long, hoarse call from the river told him that the warning was correct. He made a silent sign for the cartridges; but Wingate took no notice: his face was hard and set, and the white of his eyes gleamed.

A few seconds later a large tiger crept slowly out of the grass, his stomach on the ground, his huge head held low. Jim remembered the native superstition that the head of a man-eating tiger is weighed down by the souls of its victims. With a run and a spring the creature attacked its meal, and began growling and munching contentedly, purring like a cat, and stopping every now and then to tear up the earth with its claws.

A report rang out. Wingate had fired at and hit the tiger. The great beast gave a terrific roar and sprang at the tree. Jim lifted his rifle, only to remember it was unloaded.

"Shoot again!" he cried excitedly, as the tiger fell back and prepared for another spring. To his horror, Wingate deliberately fired the second barrel into the air, and, throwing away the rifle, grasped him by the arms. The man's teeth were bared, his face distorted and hideous, his purpose unmistakeable—he was trying to throw Bastable to the tiger. Wingate was strong with the diabolical strength of madness, and they swayed till the branches of the tree cracked ominously. Again the tiger roared and sprang, and again fell back, only to gather itself together for another effort. The two men rocked and panted, the branches cracked louder with a dry, splitting sound, then broke off altogether, and, locked in each other's arms, they fell heavily to the ground.

Jim Bastable went undermost, and was half stunned by the shock. He heard a snarl in his ear, followed by a dreadful cry. He felt the weight of Wingate's body lifted from him with a jerk, and he scrambled blindly to his feet. As in a nightmare, he saw the tiger bounding away, carrying something that hung limply from the great jaws, just as a cat carries a dead mouse.

He seized the Colonel's rifle that lay near him; but he knew it was empty, and that the cartridges were in the Colonel's pocket. He ran after the tiger, shouting, yelling, brandishing the rifle, in hopes of frightening the brute into dropping its prey; but, after one swift glance back, it bounded into the thick jungle with the speed of a deer, and Bastable was left standing alone.

Faint and sick, he began running madly towards the camp for help, though he knew well that nothing in this world could ever help Wingate again. His forehead was bleeding profusely, either hurt in the fall or touched by the tiger's claw, and the blood trickling into his eyes nearly blinded him. He pulled his handkerchief from his pocket as he ran, and something came with it that glittered in the moonlight and fell to the ground with a metallic ring.

It was the little silver amulet. The tiger-charm.

ONE REMAINED BEHIND

A ROMANCE À LA MODE GOTHIQUE

Marjorie Bowen

Gabrielle Margaret Vere Long (1885–1952; née Campbell) was a prolific writer of historical romances, supernatural stories, popular history, and biography. She wrote under many pseudonyms, including Joseph Shearing, George R. Preedy, John Winch, Robert Payne, and Margaret Campbell. However, the bulk of her work was published under the pen name of Marjorie Bowen. Bowen was born on Hayling Island in Hampshire, England in 1885 to an unaffectionate mother and an alcoholic father who deserted his impoverished and bohemian family. Nevertheless, she was able to study at the Slade School of Fine Art in London, as well as in Paris. Her first book, *The Viper of Milan* (1906), a historical novel written as Marjorie Bowen, was published to great success when she was sixteen. Her writing enabled her to support her family. She continued to write at a great pace and produced over 150 books, mostly under the Bowen name. "One Remained Behind" was first published in *Help Yourself!* annual in 1936. It features an ancient grimoire filled with black magic. Grimoires have been with us since writing began and are books that contain magic spells, instructions for making amulets and talismans, ancient wisdom, elaborate rituals, and magical symbols; often, the grimoire itself is said to be invested with supernatural abilities and magical powers. In Bowen's ghastly tale of would-be revenge, the "infernal rites" contained within the grimoire, along with a cursed ring, lead to dire consequences for Rudolph and a "detestable" young bride, as the devil and his dark arts cannot be outwitted.

Rudolph quarrelled fiercely with M. Dufours, the antique dealer, but in low tones so as not to be overheard in the street. "If you do not sell it to me—and cheaply—I shall report you to the police," he whispered, firmly clasping the large book bound in wood and brass that he had found on a top shelf in the little room at the back of the shop.

"I do not think, M. Rudolph, that you would care to go to the police," retorted the old man, sucking in his toothless mouth with fury. "I would not part with the *grimoire*, no, not for fifty thousand francs."

"You will, however," sneered Rudolph, "sell it to me for fifty francs. I have no objection to informing the police that you are a receiver of stolen goods, a moneylender at an exorbitant rate of interest, a dealer in dangerous drugs, charms and black magic—"

"Ah, indeed," replied the shopkeeper, trying to be sarcastic but really rather uneasy. "And pray what are *you*, M. Rudolph? Unless I am very much mistaken *your* reputation is none too pure."

"Bah! What does it matter about my reputation? The police have nothing against me. I am a poor student, a poet, a philosopher, and I intend to have this treasure that I have discovered on your shelf."

"You admit that it is a treasure!" raged the old man. "And yet you offer me a miserable fifty francs for it!"

"It is no treasure for you," replied Rudolph scornfully. "You are a pitiful dabbler in the black arts. You would never have the courage to proceed far along this dangerous, fascinating road! You do not even understand the secrets concealed here!" He tapped with elegant soiled white fingers the cover of the disputed book. "I doubt if you can even read the title."

Overcome by curiosity, the old man asked:

"What is this volume that you think so highly of, M. Rudolph?"

"Ha! ha! And just now you said you wanted fifty thousand francs for it!"

"Well, I know that it is an ancient *grimoire*, and therefore valuable."

"It is," sneered the student. "The *Grimoriam Veram*, written by Alibeck the Egyptian and printed at Memphis in 1517—together with this are bound several other treatises exceedingly rare."

"What do you want with these things?" demanded the antique dealer suspiciously. "You have no skill to interpret those signs and wonders—"

"Nor have you, or you would not be living here in this shabby shop, existing by petty crimes!"

"I might say the same of you, M. Rudolph! It is obvious that the study of black magic has not done you much good—your shirt is darned, your coat shiny at the elbows, your trousers are ragged round the hems, and one of your shoes is split!"

The student's eyes gleamed with malice.

"Nevertheless, perhaps I might surprise you, sordid old miser that you are! Please have the goodness to look into this!"

Still retaining the *grimoire* under his arm, the young man whipped out a small mirror that seemed to be of polished metal from his breast and flashed it in front of the reluctant gaze of M. Dufours.

He found, however, that it was impossible to avoid the metallic disc; his bleary eyes, worn by age and counting over the contents of his money-bags, stared, without his volition, into the magic mirror.

On the surface of this appeared a little cloudy figure, curled up like a bird in the nest, that gazed back at the old man with small black eyes that glittered vindictively.

"There is nothing in my shop," muttered the curio dealer drowsily, "like that—what can it be a reflection of?"

The student laughed and the little figure flew out of the mirror and hung between it and the frightened face of M. Dufours; then, with a buzz like that of an angry insect, it rushed at the curio dealer's nose and pinched it violently until the old man howled with fear and pain. Rudolph laughed and returned the metal disc to his pocket, upon which the spirit vanished.

"It was some wasp or bee flew in," muttered M. Dufours, rubbing his red, smarting nose.

"Was it?" sneered the student. "Kindly look round your filthy shop."

The old man obeyed, fascinated by the brilliant black eyes, pallid face and mocking lips of M. Rudolph.

His jaw dropped and a trembling ran through all his shrunken limbs at what he saw—every object in his shop was transformed into something devilish. The old coats on their pegs waved their sleeves at him, the pawned trousers kicked as if prancing in a polka, grimacing faces peered from the blotched, cracked mirrors, the cupidons on the tarnished candelabra that hung from the cob-webbed rafters began to fly about like pigeons, and a lady in a very bad portrait by Legros, the art student, winked rudely at M. Dufours and shook at him her bouquet of miserably drawn roses which really resembled pickled onions.

M. Dufours rubbed his eyes and when he looked round again everything was normal.

"You see," remarked Rudolph, "that I know a few tricks. I shall keep the *grimoire* and owe you the fifty francs."

With an air of disdain he picked up his dusty, frayed beaver hat, that he thrust on the side of his head jauntily above his long jet-black locks, and strode into the street; M. Dufours shook a lean fist after him, but dare not raise a hue and cry. There was really something Satanic about M. Rudolph—that nip on the nose, now, surely he had not imagined that!

The student went gloomily along the street, the *grimoire* clasped tightly under his arm; the sky was a pale violet colour above the roofs that were shining wet from a shower of rain, and a delicate breeze from the hills beyond the town stirred the rubbish in the gutter.

Outside the wineshop several students were sitting over their pints of claret, discussing their work and love affairs, joyously speculating as to their chances of prizes, of kisses, of distinction, and of monies that might be sent from their relatives.

As Rudolph strode past without taking any notice of them, they fell into a silence and stared after him. How poor and proud he was! No one knew much about him and everyone was slightly afraid of him; he was morose, haughty and had no friends—how was it that he could afford to pay for the courses at the University?

He was brilliant at his work, but was not likely, the professors said, to be successful, for he attended so few of the lectures.

How did he spend his time?

The students often asked one another this question and were afraid to answer it; the rumour was that Rudolph wasted his days and imperilled his soul by studying the forbidden arts.

They craned their necks after him in awe and admiration; he was so handsome with his high brow, black hair and cavernous eyes; every Fifi and Mimi in the town was in love with him and he never as much as glanced at any of them.

The other students admired his courage, too; he never concerned himself with any kind of civility and they were envious of his top hat—that *chapeau en haute forme* that he wore instead of the usual college cap.

True, this fashionable headgear was old and had probably been bought secondhand *chez Dufours*, but it had the address of a maker in the *rue St. Honoré* inside the brim and was undoubtedly elegant.

Sourly gratified by these admiring glances that he affected not to notice, Rudolph proceeded to his poor lodgings, which were in an inconvenient part of the town, a long way from the University.

Not only poverty, however, persuaded Rudolph to live in this remote quarter; he liked the solitude of the deserted street where the tumble-down houses huddled beneath the broken walls of the town, where at night it was silent save for the hoot of an owl or so that strayed in from the woods and brooded on the roof-tops, and dark save for the yellow spurts of light from the few dirty street lamps.

Holding the *grimoire* tightly, he mounted the twisting staircase to his attic; he was the sole lodger in the ancient house. An old woman and her grandchild owned the crazy building and dwelt on the ground floor.

Rudolph locked his door (he had fashioned the lock himself and carefully fixed it in place of the rude latch), and seating himself by the window in the lean-to roof, began to read his book eagerly.

There were many curious objects in the attic, stacked away in dark corners and under the dusty chairs and truckle-bed; on a bare table stood a lamp, a desk, on a shelf was a row of books; there were hanging cupboards, pegs for clothes and a number of boxes.

Rudolph read long in the *grimoire*, until the sun declined behind the roofs of the town, dusk filled his garret, and Jeanette, the landlady's grandchild, knocked at the door, crying out, in her thin, piping voice, that she had brought up the supper.

Rudolph, startled from his self-absorption, whispered a malediction, tossed the tangled hair from his eyes, rose and unlocked the door.

The little tin lamp on the stairs had been lit; this feeble light showed the broken banister rails, rotting floor boards and dust everywhere.

Jeanette, who looked like a white rat, hurried timidly into the room and placed Rudolph's supper on the table—a pint of wine, two slices of black bread, a dish of salted ham and pickled onions, and a withering apple; she then lit his lamp.

"Ha, little misery!" exclaimed the student wildly. "How is it that thou canst continue this wretched existence, unworthy of a human being who owns a mortal soul?"

"Indeed, Monsieur, I don't know," stammered the girl, trying to drop a curtsey; her skirts were so scanty that she could not achieve much elegance, and when she bent her knee it stuck through a hole in her rags. "Grandmother says that if you could pay the rent—"

"Begone," scowled Rudolph, waving his elegant hand. "I have my studies awaiting me."

Jeanette hurried away, glad to escape, and Rudolph pondered deeply on what he had read in the *grimoire*.

It certainly was a treasure, that book! It contained secrets that he had long been seeking to discover and directions for conjurations and divinations that he longed to try immediately. Unfortunately all these required expensive materials, new-born infants, kids, black or white cocks, costly drugs, shew stones, tables of sweet-wood and squares of undyed wool taken from a spotless lamb and woven by a maiden.

Rudolph knew a great deal about black magic, but he had never made any money from either that or the poetry which stood in dusty stacks against the walls; indeed, most of his meagre substance had gone in buying ingredients or articles for his forbidden studies.

He frowned gloomily, staring with disgust at the coarse food on the table. How he longed for luxury, a splendid castle, troops of liveried servants, a carriage with six white horses, a superb mistress clad in Venetian velvet!

Again he opened the *grimoire* and carefully re-read something that had greatly taken his fancy; as he perused the badly printed page his pallid face gradually assumed a diabolical expression, for Rudolph wished evil to all mankind, and all his experiments—mostly taken from the *Clavicle of King Ptolomeus*—had been of the following kinds: "Of hatred and destruction"—"Of mocks and gainful seeking"—"Of experiments extraordinary that be forbidden of good men."

What fascinated him now was the description of certain rites whereby four strangers could be brought to the celebrant's room and one of them forced to do his will—even to the revealing of hidden treasure, the gift of luck at cards and success in a chosen career.

Rudolph nibbled an onion and brooded over this prospect; he decided at once on three of the people whom he would summon in this manner, so humiliating to them and so gratifying to himself.

First he would force Saint Luc, the arrogant young aristocrat who had so often sneered at him and whom he so greatly detested, to appear in his wretched garret; second he would bring the vicious old professor, Maître Lachaud, who had so often told him, Rudolph, that he was idle, stubborn and a disgrace to the University; and third he would drag along by his magic spells M. Lecoine, the fat banker who had laughed in his, Rudolph's face, when he had asked for a loan.

But here again expensive materials were required, and the experiment might fail and all the money and effort be wasted.

Rudolph ate his bread and ham, then went to the window and glared out at the sky from which all daylight had now receded. A full moon was appearing above the house-tops and a few dark clouds that might have been witches impatiently flying off for nocturnal delights showed beneath it. As Rudolph gazed a great longing took possession of him to make the experiment of which he had read in the *grimoire*; not only did he earnestly desire to vex and terrify three people whom he detested, he was dazzled by the hope of luck in cards, in his career, and the finding of a hidden treasure.

"I shall be the greatest poet in the world and I shall have more money than any man ever had before."

Such a prospect was worth a large sacrifice.

Rudolph turned back into the room and dragged an ancient carpet-bag from under his bed; he opened it, unfastening the cumbrous lock, while he sighed deeply and from swathes of old silk rags he took out a large golden ring set with a pale stone that gave out more light than the dirty lamp fed by cheap oil.

This jewel had been given to Rudolph by his great-grandfather with strict charges never to part with it—"except from the purest motives" the old man had said. He had been a famous roué in his time and had squandered all the family fortune on English jockeys, boxers and Italian dancers.

Rudolph disliked the thought of parting with the ring because the possession of such a gem increased his self-esteem and also because he was afraid of his great-grandfather's curse; he decided, however, to do so, and thrusting the ring in his bosom left the attic and turned to the fashionable part of the town beyond the University buildings that, rising directly in front of the moon, looked as if they were cut out of black paper.

The shutters were just being put up in front of the shop of M. Colcombet, the jeweller, but Rudolph dashed through the door and laid his ring on the counter, on the length of black velvet that covered the glass that contained flashing parures in heart-shaped boxes lined with satin.

"This is a family piece," said the student haughtily. "It is worth a good sum."

M. Colcombet was doubtful, however, both of the ring and the customer; he peered suspiciously, first at the sardonic young man, then at the white jewel which was brighter than any diamond in the shop.

"It is a beryl," he remarked.

"Not an ordinary beryl," replied Rudolph, contemptuously flashing the ring about in his hand so that in the light of the well-trimmed silver lamp the stone cast out flames of blue, green and crimson.

"Well," admitted M. Colcombet, who seemed fascinated by the stone, "I daresay the Comtesse Louise would like it for her wedding *toilette*."

"Ha, is the Comtesse Louise to be married?" asked Rudolph, who remembered with anger this haughty beauty who had stared through him when her carriage has passed him in the street, covering him with mud.

"Yes, to the Prince de C——; it is to be a splendid affair," gossiped the jeweller. "At her father's château, you know—the chapel is hung with cloth of gold and there is to be a festival for all the neighbour-hood. Many of the students have had cards of invitation, and some of them have been in here to buy their presents—M. le Marquis de Saint Luc, for instance. Perhaps you yourself, Monsieur?" he added with an inquisitive glance at Rudolph's shabby clothes.

"What do you offer for the ring?" demanded the student fiercely.

"It is white," said the jeweller, "but not, I am sure, a diamond—reset it would look very handsome, perhaps in the centre of a tiara or on a corsage ornament—"

"How much? I am in a hurry."

M. Colcombet, who felt rather embarrassed and confused, stammered:

"Two thousand francs, Monsieur."

"It is worth far more, but I was not born to bargain—give me the money."

As Rudolph flung down the ring he disarranged the black cloth over the show case and revealed a set of pearl and diamond ornaments in cases of pale blue satin.

"It is the wedding parure of the Comtesse Louise," said M. Colcombet as he counted out the notes from his pocket-book; Rudolph took up the money and passed out into the street that, when the shutters were all up in front of the shops, was lit only by the light of the rising moon; the small dark clouds had now disappeared and the sky was pale and pure.

The student returned in a melancholy, bitter mood to his lodgings; although he had two thousand francs in his pocket he felt poorer than when he had been in possession of the beryl ring.

The mention of the Comtesse Louise had considerably vexed him; how he detested that proud girl with her little sneering mouth and large, slightly prominent blue eyes! He had several times seen her driving in the town, and once he had come face to face with her in a bookshop where she was buying foolish novels and he was trying to sell some Aldine volumes with superb sepia-coloured initials; on that occasion he had held open the door for her, and she had passed him with the most icy of unspoken rebukes in her lofty carriage and set sweetness of glance.

He had, however, seen her leaning on the arm of Saint Luc, that ostentatious dandy who spent more in a year on his trousers and *gilets* than the whole of Rudolph's annual income.

Hatred and another dark emotion that was almost despair inspired the student with a diabolic plan; absenting himself from all classes and lectures he devoted all his time to carrying out precisely the instructions in the *grimoire* published at Memphis in 1517.

He made his plans carefully and arranged for his great experiment to take place on the evening of the wedding day of the Comtesse Louise and Prince de C——.

First he provided himself with a magic wand by going into the woods and cutting two twigs, one of hazel and one of elder from trees that had never borne fruit; at the end of these he placed steel caps magnetized with a lodestone; then he took from the carpet-bag some ink made from sprigs of fern gathered on St. John's Eve and vine twigs cut in the March full moon which had been ground to powder and mingled with river water in a fair glazed earthen pot; this mixture had been boiled up over a fire of virgin paper.

Rudolph also possessed a phial of pigeon's blood and a male goose quill and a bloodstone which possessed the virtue of protecting the wearer from evil spirits; he had always found this a very necessary precaution.

On the third day of the new moon Rudolph purchased a black cock and a white cock from the market place and kept them in his garret until nightfall; he then put the birds in a wicker cage, his paraphernalia in the carpet-bag, and set out beyond the town, beyond the woods until he came to an open space that surrounded the ruins of an Abbey reputed to be haunted by the spirits of monks who had been unfaithful to their vows.

Here the grass was short and scarred by stones and rocks; an ancient thorn tree, sacred to heathen deities, stood bleak and twisted by a small pool. The Gothic windows of the Abbey showed a black framework against the luminous sky; the bats flew in and out of the crisp, dark ivy; several noxious fungi grew round the pool, which was covered by a dull red floating weed so that it did not reflect any light.

Rudolph had often visited this place before; it was exactly what the *grimoires* said was required for infernal rites—"a desolate spot free from interruptions."

With mutterings to himself, while the sweat gathered on his high, pallid brow, the student made the grand Kabbalistic circle. From his carpet-bag he took out his rods, a goatskin, two garlands of Vervain, two candles of virgin wax made by a virgin—Jeanette whose meagre charms guaranteed her chastity—a sword of blue steel, two candlesticks of massive silver, two flints, tinder, a flask of *eau-de-vie*, some camphor, incense, and four nails from the coffin of a child—which last item Rudolph had paid Pierre, the coffin-maker, very highly for, for it had been necessary to go to the burial vaults of Saint Jean to obtain them.

With this material Rudolph made his grand circle of goatskin, sprinkling the incense and camphor in a wheel shape and kindling his fire of wood (that he fed with the cognac) in the centre, then, with his right arm bared to the shoulder, he sacrificed the two cocks, burning them on the fire while he muttered his evocations.

The bats and owls fled from the ruins, the moon veiled in the sky, the earth shook, the red scum of weeds on the lake became agitated; Rudolph pressed the bloodstone to his cheek and muttered an even more powerful spell.

The water was troubled furiously and a lovely boy rose to the surface of the lake and in a pleasant voice demanded of the student what he wished.

Rudolph was not deceived by this civility; he knew that the apparition was Lucifer himself, the most violent of the evil spirits who would tear the celebrant to pieces if he were to step out of the circle or to drop his bloodstone. Astaroth came, Rudolph was well aware, in the shape of a black and white ass, Beelzebub in hideous disguises, Belial seated in a flaming chariot, and Beleth on a white horse preceded by a company of musicians.

"What is your will?" asked Lucifer gently, but puffing out his red cheeks with rage.

"Monsieur," said the student respectfully, "I am about—at the end of the month, to be exact—to make a great experiment, that described on page twenty-three of the *Grimoire* of Alibeck the magician, published at Memphis in 1517."

"A rare edition," remarked Lucifer. "You were fortunate to find it."

While he spoke he was carefully watching to see if the student made the least mistake, so that he might seize him and pull him to shreds, but Rudolph was prudent and kept well within the centre of the magic circle with the bloodstone pressed to his cheek.

"I want to know, Monsieur, if you will assure me that the experiment will be successful?"

"You seem to know a few tricks," smiled the fiend. "No doubt, if you will fulfil all the requirements given in the *grimoire*, the experiment will be successful. You will take the consequences, of course."

"If I can have four strangers in my room to do my bidding, discover a hidden treasure, become a famous poet and lucky at cards, I shall require nothing more," sneered Rudolph, who even when talking to a devil could not for long maintain a submissive tone.

"All that you shall have," promised the lovely child in a sweet voice, but his pretty little eyes were sparkling with fury at this insolence.

"I ask no more!" cried Rudolph, shaking his magic hazel wand at the lake. "Foul fiend begone!"

With a dreadful hiss the boy sank into the lake, the red weed closed over the place where he had been, the moon came to a standstill in the sky, the bats and owls flew back to the ruins, and the student stepped out of the magic circle and began to pack away his materials into the carpet-bag.

When he returned through the town he heard the violinists above the music shop of M. Kuhn practising for the wedding festivities of the Comtesse Louise.

As the time drew near for the great experiment Rudolph made his final preparations; these had cost him nearly all the money he had received for the beryl ring and the suspicious looks of his fellow students.

He had paid his rent and given Jeanette a present to bribe her to sweep and clean out his chamber so that no dirt remained anywhere; he had then perfumed it with mastic and aloes and hung clean white curtains at the window, furnished the bed with fair linen, woollen coverlets and a mattress of goose down.

He bought also a table and four chairs of plain white wood, four platters of white damask. To rid himself of the curiosity of Jeanette he declared that these preparations were for a visit from his mother and two sisters that he was expecting.

For three days before the date fixed for the wedding of the Comtesse Louise, Rudolph fasted and looked to his room, making sure that there were no hangings, nor indeed any objects, set crosswise, that no clothes were on pegs, that there was not a birdcage in any corner of the room, and that everything was scrupulously clean.

On the evening of the great day itself the student set his four chairs round his table, placed out on the fair damask cloth the four platters with a wheaten loaf on each, and the four glass beakers full of clear water. Beside his bed he set his old armchair, and the windows he opened wide onto the moonlit night.

In the centre of the table he placed a shaker of goatskin, three black and one white bean, then, everything being in readiness, he cast himself on his knees and uttered the powerful conjuration given in page twenty-three of the *grimoire* of Alibeck. Then he lay down on his bed, wearing a handsome chamber-robe that he had bought for the occasion.

He heard the church clock strike midnight, and then the moonlight in the attic began to quiver a little and Professor Lachaud floated in through the open window, not moving his feet nor looking to right nor left, but stiffly passing along; taking no heed of Rudolph, the dry little *savant* seated himself at the table and gazed in front of him through his silver-rimmed spectacles.

The next arrival was the banker, M. Lecoine; with an expression of surprise on his chubby face he floated in from the outer moonlight, a table napkin tucked under his chin and a pen in his hand; without speaking he seated himself opposite Lachaud. Almost at once the window was darkened again as M. Saint Luc appeared wearing a fashionable evening costume with a superb *gilet* of sky-blue *moiré anglaise*, in silence he occupied the third place at the table.

Rudolph felt ill with excitement; the white curtains blew out in the moonlight and a lady all in white entered—the Comtesse Louise, or rather the Princesse de C——, in her bridal gown of silver and satin with her wreath of myrtle and her parure of diamonds and pearls; on the thumb of her right hand was the beryl ring.

She took the fourth place at the table and the four strangers began to eat and drink; their movements were stiff and jerky like those of automata, and they were silent, without seeming to notice anything.

"One remains behind," whispered Rudolph from the bed. "One remains behind."

The four strangers ate the wheaten loaves to the last crumb and drank the crystal water to the last drop; then the professor took up the goatskin shaker and put inside it the three black and one white bean, so that they might draw lots as to who should stay behind.

It was the lady who took out the white bean; the three men then rose and, still in silence, floated out of the window one after the other, the professor's robe, the youth's frac coat and the banker's napkin fluttering for a second in the night breeze as they disappeared into the moonlight.

The Comtesse Louise then rose, and crossing the room without moving her feet, seated herself in the armchair beside Rudolph's bed. There were many things that the student would have liked to have asked the bride, but he remembered the danger of deviating from the formula of Alibeck, so he said:

"Confer on me luck at cards."

She slipped the beryl ring off her thumb, handed it to him and replied:

"As long as you wear this you shall have luck at cards."

"Confer on me the gift of fame."

"You shall be the most famous poet alive."

The lady answered clearly and promptly, but she ignored Rudolph as utterly as she had ignored him when she had met him in the bookshop or the street; this angered him and he made his third demand very haughtily:

"Reveal to me some hidden treasure."

She rose.

"Come with me."

The student left his bed and followed her out of the window, walking on the air as if it had been curdling foam with firm sand beneath it. They passed over the house-tops, Rudolph in his bedgown that floated out behind him and his pearl-grey trousers, the lady in her bridal dress and the long veil that billowed into the moonlight until it seemed part of the silver vapour of night.

When they reached the market square the lady descended like a ray of light and paused before the great iron-studded door of the Church; when she saw that Rudolph was behind her, she passed through the door, and the student found no difficulty in doing the same.

The Church was cold and dim; as these two entered all the lamps before the shrines burnt very low, but the spell held.

The Comtesse Louise paused on a gravestone in the chancel; it sunk beneath her, and Rudolph, who was close behind, descended with her to the vaults.

Here the only light was that which emanated from the brilliant figure of the bride, who hovered over the rows of coffins like a will-o'-the-wisp.

Over one of these that was covered with a rotting pall cloth she hung motionless, and her voice, hollow as an echo in a shell, broke the silence of the vault.

"Here is your treasure."

Rudolph wrenched at the wooden coffin lid, then at the leaden shell beneath, and found that both came away like paper in his hands; the supernatural light cast by the Comtesse Louise enabled him to see a skeleton, livid with the hues of decay, lying in a tattered shroud; under the skull was a cluster of diamonds and sapphires arranged like a pillow; these had been enclosed in a silken case which had frayed to a few faded threads.

The student despoiled the coffin, filling the pockets of his *robe de chambre*, of his waistcoat and trousers with the gems. When he had grubbed up the last of the jewels he harshly told the lady to lead him back to his garret.

She instantly rose through the stone floor of the Church and passed down the aisle, through the wooden door and into the public square; without moving her feet, without speaking, without glancing to right or left, she led him over the roofs to his garret.

Rudolph did not think of her at all until he had packed all the jewels into his carpet-bag and hair-cord trunk; then he looked at her standing immobile in her wedding splendour, gazing in front of her with her blue, slightly prominent eyes, and he felt a twinge of compassion for her.

"You may return to your bridegroom," he said disdainfully.

She did not, however, move, and Rudolph could not recall what the formula of dismissal was in this conjuration.

He searched in the *grimoire* and could find nothing on this point: "One remains behind" was all that was written in the instructions.

The student did not greatly concern himself about this, however;

225

he felt very drowsy and cast himself on his bed. "No doubt she will be gone in the morning."

When Rudolph awoke the sun was bright in his room and Jeanette was at his bedside with coffee and rolls; on the tray was a letter with the Parisian postmark.

The student tore the envelope open and found inside an enthusiastic letter from a publisher to whom he had submitted his poems a year ago. This gentleman had, it seemed, printed the poems without telling the author, and the thin volume had been a *succès fou*. "You are acclaimed as the greatest poet of the century, far beyond Lamartine or Byron."

Rudolph sprang out of bed in an excess of joy, which was checked however when he saw the bride still standing where he had left her last night, erect by the table staring in front of her with her blue, slightly prominent eyes.

He now perceived that she was as transparent as the lace that she wore and that she looked as if sketched with white chalk on the dark background of the room; he saw also that she was perceptible to himself only, since Jeanette had not only taken no notice of her, but, in leaving the room, had walked right through her. Rudolph then realized that the four strangers had been spectres or phantoms, not, as he had thought, the human beings themselves.

He felt that he had humiliated the lady sufficiently—besides, he was becoming bored with her company; so he again commanded her to depart, and, when she took no heed of him, he once more consulted the *grimoire*. This authoritative work, however, had one serious defect—it offered no advice on how to be rid of spirits, ghosts, wraiths or supernatural appearances that had outstayed their welcome.

Rudolph was, however, too excited and too anxious to put his good fortune to the test to concern himself very much about the phantasm that had already done him such good service.

"Pray please yourself, Madame la Princesse," he said with a sarcastic bow, and hastened into the street, the lady floating behind him with feet that were motionless and with a fixed gaze.

As he passed the University the student saw a knot of his fellows gathered round the steps. One of them hailed him:

"Rudolph, have you heard the news?"

"About the success of my poems?" asked the student haughtily.

"Your poems? No, indeed—poor Professor Lachaud died suddenly last night. He was shut up in his library to study as usual, and this morning he was found stiff in his chair!"

Rudolph passed on in silence; he felt rather disturbed.

M. Colcombet and some friends were gossiping outside his shop.

"Oh, M. Rudolph, have you heard, what a dreadful tragedy? Last night, just as the bride—the Comtesse Louise—was being conducted to the bridal chamber, she fell down dead! Yes, dead as a stone! And what do you think, at the same moment one of the guests, M. Saint Luc, had a stroke of apoplexy, and he too fell dead, with a glass of champagne in his hand!"

Rudolph looked over his shoulder at the phantom, that gazed ahead serenely; he thought—"the *grimoire* did not state that the spell would cause the death of the four strangers. But perhaps if it had I should not have hesitated."

As he passed the Bank he saw the black shutters being put up; in the doorway were clerks fastening black bands to their arms. "Someone dead?" asked Rudolph drily.

"M. Lecoine himself! He retired to his counting-house, as he always does on Friday evenings, at ten minutes to twelve—old Auguste took him in his cup of soup, and he was alive then—this morning he was dead in his chair, with his napkin under his chin and his empty cup on his desk!"

"What a number of deaths in this town!" remarked Rudolph sarcastically. "I hope that it isn't the plague!"

Although at first he had been shocked to learn of the dreadful results of his spell, he soon consoled himself; the four dead people were all detestable—perhaps one might be a little sorry for the bride, until one remembered how cold and haughty she had been, how insulting with her icy looks.

No, everything was as it should be; the only difficulty was how to be rid of this phantom that followed him so closely—"One remains behind."

"Eh, well," thought Rudolph, "no one can see her but myself, and no doubt she will soon tire of following me about or I shall be able to find a spell to dismiss her."

So, being strong-minded as well as hard-hearted, he contrived to forget the filmy-white shape that was the dead bride, and that never left him, day or night. Everywhere that he went she accompanied him, and when he returned home in the evenings she seated herself by his bed in the worn armchair.

The phantom was the last thing he saw at night, the first thing he saw in the morning, and though he searched his whole library through he could not discover any spell to be rid of her; he was also debarred from any magical ceremonies, divinations or conjurations, for it is well-known that the company of a ghost is fatal on these occasions.

His good fortune, however, prevented him from troubling much about this inconvenience; not only had he the treasure taken from the vaults of Saint Jean, but his fame as a poet spread over the entire country, and he found that whenever he played at cards, when wearing the beryl ring he was lucky, so that his winnings at play afforded him a considerable income.

He soon moved to Paris, where he became the centre of a crowd of admirers; all the ladies were singing his verses to harps or guitars, all the gentlemen copied his waistcoats and the manner in which he tossed his long black hair off his pallid brow.

The student now enjoyed almost everything that he had ever wished for; he had a handsome apartment, liveried servants, a smart *phaeton*—but he had no mistress.

All the women adored him, but if he tried to make love to any one of them, she seemed repelled, frightened, and always ended by running away.

Rudolph cursed and wished that he had asked for luck in love instead of luck in cards, for the sale of the treasure trove would supply him with all the money he needed. He knew why the women avoided even the slightest intimacy with him—they could not perceive the ghost of the bride, but they felt it, a miasma of death that killed their rising passion, a bitter chill that cooled their warm hearts and withered the kisses on their lips.

The student used all the arts at his command in the hope of destroying the phantom, but nothing was of any avail; sometimes she was so pale as to be scarcely visible, sometimes she was as solid as a living woman; but she was always there and Rudolph's nerves began to quiver every time he looked over his shoulder—"One remains behind" he would mutter, gazing up into her glassy eyes. He tried to argue out the matter with her, to appeal to her compassion, even to make love to her, but she never took any more notice of him than she had taken when she had passed him in the bookshop or in the streets of the University town.

There were other flaws in the student's good fortune; his publisher continually implored him to write some more poems.

"You know there are only ten poems in that little volume, and everyone in France knows them by heart! Soon people will begin to say that you are incapable of writing anything else!"

This was precisely what had happened; whenever Rudolph sat down to write, the spectre of the bride glided round to the other side of the table, and seated there, stared at him with her blue, slightly prominent eyes, and while she gazed at him he found it impossible to compose a single line.

With relief he remembered the sheaves of paper, all covered by verses, that he had, in his excitement, left behind in his garret, so he wrote to Jeanette telling her to send them at once. The girl had, however, used the papers to light the kitchen fire, and the student uttered a bitter malediction when he received the ill-spelt letter in which she gave him this news.

Gradually his popularity waned; the Parisians became tired of his ten poems, of his gloomy, preoccupied airs, and began to laugh at his failures in love. He was too successful at cards, and so found himself avoided, not only at the gambling parties in private houses, but even at the halls in the *Palais Royal*.

One morning he was seated over his coffee pondering how he should be rid of the phantom when his eye caught a line in the *Gazette* that his English valet had left on the table beside his service of coffee, rolls and fruit.

In the University town of S—— a horrible outrage had been discovered; a sacrilegious robbery had been committed in the Church of Saint Jean—a tomb had been broken open and a vast treasure was stolen.

The student read this account with a good deal of interest.

"I never heard any of this," he commented bitterly, "when I was in that detestable town."

The ancient Church, it seemed, possessed a vast treasure, largely consisting of offerings at the miraculous shrine of Ste. Pelagie, which had been hidden in the coffin of that saint during the dangers of the late revolutions; all record of this had been lost, and for a generation people had searched in vain for the hidden treasure; then a paper found in the sacristy had given them the clue and the coffin with the gems had been discovered.

They had been left there while the Bishop was consulted as to the propriety of moving them; His Grace had not only given his consent to this, but had come in person to see this remarkable discovery—only to learn that the jewels had been stolen by thieves who had broken into the vault. At first the police had kept the matter hushed up in order that they might pursue their investigations more at ease, now they decided to make the matter public.

"Ah, Madame!" cried Rudolph, addressing the phantom that hovered over his breakfast table. "You have deceived me grossly!"

He morosely decided to leave Paris. The jewels might be traced and he did not dare to try to sell those that he had left; on consulting with his major-domo he found that he was short of money—he had been living most extravagantly, spending thousands of francs on horses, dogs, furniture, pictures and other things that he did not care for in the least.

So in order to raise the money for his travelling expenses, he put on the beryl ring and went to one of the worst gambling dives in Paris where accomplished gamblers nightly stripped newcomers to the capital.

Rudolph entered this den of vice. As he threw off his long black cloak there was a murmur of admiration for his superb blue *gilet* in *moiré anglaise*.

He was not, however, very welcome even in that dreadful place, for even these hardened gamblers, coarsened by debauchery, felt uneasy in his presence; the phantom spread a chill about her that surrounded Rudolph like a cold sea mist and caused those who came near him to shiver. These scoundrels, however, could not for long resist the lure of the piles of gold that the student flung down on the long green baize table—these represented the last remnants of his ready money, the rest of his fortune was contained in the stolen treasure that he dare not dispose of in France.

When he had been playing and winning for an hour, a huge pile of gold pieces was massed in front of him, and hellish looks of black hatred were cast on him by the *habitués* of the gambling dive.

Rudolph felt depressed and took little pleasure in his fortune, that was more than sufficient to take him to Vienna or Rome or some other city where he could sell the stolen gems; his head ached and the flames of the ring of candles above the table seemed to penetrate his brain like hot nails, all the vicious, greedy faces sneering about him seemed to float detached from their bodies in the thick, foul air.

The phantom of the bride had become quite solid; it seemed impossible to Rudolph that she was invisible to the company as she hovered over the piles of dirty cards, her wedding splendour floating about her like a cloud of moonshine.

"Madame," he said between his teeth, "have the goodness to leave me—this is not a fit place for a gentlewoman. But, if you do not cease plaguing me, I shall take you to worse—"

"What are you muttering?" asked his companion, a stout man whose face was covered by carbuncles and whose breath was hot as flame.

"Oh, nothing, I was merely counting my winnings," sneered Rudolph with his hands over the pile of gold.

"Pray," said he of the carbuncles, "have another cast of the dice with this young gentleman," and he nudged the student in the ribs to let him know that here was another pigeon to be plucked.

Rudolph saw a spruce youth with a baby face bowing before him, and he thought: "This is a fool fresh from college, he reminds me of Saint Luc. I may as well have his money."

So he agreed to play with the young stranger, who had a pleasant lisping voice, a cheek as smooth as a girl's and slightly reddened eyes.

"Surely," thought the student, "I have seen him before." He was tormented by this likeness to someone whom he had once known and so did not observe that the bride had made a movement for the first time since she had followed him; always she had moved through the air in one piece, like a floating statue, now she leaned forward and drew from his finger the beryl ring.

The student played carelessly, certain of his luck, and lost all his winnings to the youth with the baby face.

"Ah!" he shrieked, "I have been deceived!"

He stared closer at the young man who was gathering up the gold; now he recognized him—it was Lucifer who had appeared to him on the weed-covered pond outside the ruined abbey.

With a yell echoed in the mocking laughter of the gamblers, Rudolph rushed into the street, the bride floating after him, the great beryl glittering on her pale finger.

When the student reached his luxurious apartment he found that the police were in possession; the stolen jewels had been traced to him. His publisher was also waiting for him in the antechamber.

"You are a cheat as well as thief, M. Rudolph," he declared severely. "I do not believe that you wrote those poems, or you would be able to write others. Ah, he could rob a church, the dead, is capable of anything! Tomorrow I shall publish a statement in the *Gazette* to the effect that you are not the author of the poems, and you will be the laughing stock of Paris!"

Rudolph did not stay to hear these indignant words; he fled out into the night with the *agents de police* lumbering after him, and reeling along under the moon that shone above the house-tops, reached the river that dark as ink flowed between houses white as paper.

The phantom pressed close to the student, like a cold fog in his lungs. For the first time she spoke:

"You cannot complain. All the promises in the *grimoire* have been fulfilled."

"Do not let us, Madame, waste words," replied Rudolph. "Will you return me my beryl ring?"

"Never!"

"Will you leave me?"

"Never! One remains behind!"

The student then perceived that he had come to the end of his story; he jumped into the river. As he sank he raised his top hat and said politely:

"Goodbye, Madame la Princesse de C——."

The phantom remained hovering over the spot where he had disappeared, then slowly dissolved into air, her pearls and diamonds turning into drops of rain, her veils and laces into wisps of vapour, the beryl ring being caught up into a shaft of moonshine.

This romantic suicide made Rudolph very popular again in Paris; it was believed that he had written the poems after all, and the fashionable colour for that season became a faded green named *vert Rudolph*. The police became disliked for their hasty action in raiding the apartments of the sensitive poet, for it was discovered that the so-called gems in his possession were mere paste and had nothing to do with the treasure trove in the vaults of Saint Jean.

M. Dufours travelled to Paris and bought back the *grimoire* from the sale of Rudolph's effects and returned it to the shelf at the back of his shop where it soon became again covered with dust.

THE LADY OF THE
HOUSE OF LOVE

Angela Carter

Angela Carter (1940–1992) is famous for her reimaginings, as well as gathering, of fairy tales. Carter smashed the dominance of Victorian didactic retellings to pieces by uncovering "bloody" and "bawdy" tales from all over the world in her *Book of Fairy Tales* (1990), as well as returning them to their original dark, chaotic, and troubling roots in her short story collection, *The Bloody Chamber* (1979). "The Lady of the House of Love" was first published in the Summer/Autumn issue of the *Iowa Review* in 1975 having emerged out of Carter's script for the radio play, *Vampirella* (broadcast on BBC Radio 3 in 1976). Both versions are based on Sleeping Beauty, transforming it from a rather creepy "romance" to a work of explicit horror. "The Lady of the House of Love" reverses the roles played out in the well-known fairy tale as the female character becomes a blood-sucking Countess who, in a mockery of a virgin bride, wears "an antique bridal gown" while she waits for her Prince, now in the guise of a soldier, to sleepwalk into disaster. However, this predatory "queen of the vampires" cuts a tragic figure as she is also "a girl who is both death and the maiden". The image of Death and the Maiden was a common motif in Renaissance art, which usually depicted a beautiful young woman being seized by the personification of death, often in the shape of a skeleton. These frequently eroticized images act as a sort of memento mori, a reminder that death is always with us, and death and pain in all its brutality and gore is indeed woven throughout this tragic love affair. Carter's self-acknowledged "overblown, purple, self-indulgent prose" infects this doomed romance with the grotesque, the visceral, and the monstrous. Read it, if you dare.

At last the revenants became so troublesome the peasants abandoned the village and it fell solely to the possession of subtle and vindictive inhabitants who manifest their presences by shadows that fall almost imperceptibly awry, too many shadows, even at midday, shadows that have no source in anything visible; by the sound, sometimes, of sobbing in a derelict bedroom where a cracked mirror suspended from a wall does not reflect a presence; by a sense of unease that will afflict the traveller unwise enough to pause to drink from the fountain in the square that still gushes spring water from a faucet stuck in the mouth of a stone lion. A cat prowls in a weedy garden; he grins and spits, arches his back, bounces away from an intangible on four fear-stiffened legs. Now all shun the village below the chateau in which the beautiful queen of the vampires helplessly perpetuates her ancestral crimes.

Wearing an antique bridal gown, the beautiful queen of the vampires sits all alone in her dark, high house under the eyes of the portraits of her demented and atrocious ancestors, each one of whom through her, projects a baleful, posthumous existence; she is counting out the Tarot cards, ceaselessly construing a constellation of possibilities as if the random fall of the cards on the red plush tablecloth before her could precipitate her from her chill, shuttered room into a country of perpetual summer and obliterate the perennial sadness of a girl who is both death and the maiden.

Her voice is filled with distant sonorities, like reverberations in a cave. Now you are at the place of annihilation, now you are at the

237

place of annihilation. And she is herself a cave full of echoes; she is a system of repetitions, she is a closed circuit. "Can a bird sing only the song it knows or can it learn a new song?" She draws her long, sharp fingernail across the bars of the cage in which her pet lark sings, rousing in the metal a plangent twang like that of the plucked heartstrings of a woman of metal. Her hair falls down like tears.

The castle is mostly given over to ghostly occupants but she herself has her own suite of drawing room and bedroom. Closely-barred shutters and heavy, velvet curtains keep every leak of natural light out. There is a round table on a single leg covered with a red plush cloth on which she lays out her inevitable Tarot; this room is never more than faintly illuminated by a heavily shaded lamp on the mantelpiece and the dark red figured wallpaper is obscurely, distressingly patterned by the rain that drives in through the neglected roof and leaves behind it random areas of dreadful staining, ominous marks like those left on the sheets of beds of anthropophagous lovers. Depredations of rot and fungus everywhere. The unlit chandelier is so heavy with dust the individual prisms no longer show any shapes; industrious spiders have woven canopies in the corners of this ornate and rotting place, have trapped the porcelain vases on the mantelpiece in soft, grey nets. But the mistress of all this disintegration notices nothing. She sits in a chair covered in moth-ravaged burgundy velvet at a low, round table and distributes the cards; sometimes the lark sings, but more often remains a sullen mound of drab feathers. Sometimes the Countess will wake it for a brief cadenza by strumming the bars of its cage; she likes to hear it announcing how it cannot escape.

The querent approaches the arcana. She wakes up when the sun sets and goes immediately to her table, where she plays her game of patience until she grows hungry, until she becomes ravenous. She is so beautiful she is unnatural; her beauty is an abnormality, a deformity, for none of her features exhibit any of those touching imperfections that reconcile us to the imperfection of the human condition. Her beauty is a symptom of her disorder, of her soullessness.

The white hands of the tenebrous belle deal the hand of destiny. Her fingernails are longer than those of the mandarins of ancient China and each is pared to a fine point. These and teeth as fine and white as spikes of spun sugar are the visible signs of the destiny she wistfully attempts to evade via the arcana; her claws and teeth have been sharpened on centuries of corpses, she is the last bud of the poison tree that sprang from the loins of Vlad the Impaler who picnicked on corpses in the forests of Transylvania.

The walls of her bedroom are hung with black satin, embroidered with tears of pearl. At the room's four corners are funerary urns and bowls which emit slumbrous, pungent fumes of incense. In the centre is an exceedingly elaborate catafalque, in ebony, surrounded by long candles in enormous silver candlesticks. In a white lace negligee stained a little with blood, the Countess climbs upon the catafalque at dawn each morning and lies down to sleep in an open coffin.

A chignonned priest of the Orthodox faith staked out her wicked father at a Carpathian crossroad before her milk teeth grew. Now she possesses all the haunted forests and mysterious habitations of his vast domain; she is the hereditary commandant of the army of shadows who camp in the village below her chateau, who penetrate the woods in the form of owls, bats and foxes, who make the milk curdle and the butter refuse to come, who ride the horses all night on a wild hunt so they are sacks of skin and bone in the morning, who milk the cows dry and, especially, torment pubescent girls with fainting fits, disorders of the blood, diseases of the imagination.

But the Countess herself is indifferent to her own weird authority. She believes that, by ignoring it, she can abnegate it. More than anything, she would like to be human; but she does not know if that is possible. The Tarot always shows the same configuration: always she turns up La Papesse, Le Mort, Le Tour Abolie, wisdom, death, dissolution.

On moonless nights, her keeper lets her out into the garden. This garden, an exceedingly sombre place, bears a strong resemblance to a burial ground and all the roses her pathetic mother planted have grown up into a huge, spiked wall that incarcerates her in the castle of her inheritance. When the back door creaks open, the Countess will sniff the air and howl. She drops, now, on all fours. Crouching, quivering, she catches the scent of her prey. Delicious crunch of the fragile bones of rabbits and small, furry things she pursues with fleet, four-footed speed; she will creep home, whimpering, with blood smeared on her cheeks. She pours water from the ewer in her bedroom into the bowl, she washes her face with the wincing, fastidious gestures of a cat.

The voracious margin of huntress' nights in the gloomy garden, crouch and pounce, surrounds her habitual tormented somnambulism, her life, or imitation of life. The eyes of this nocturnal creature enlarge and glow. All claws and teeth, she strikes, she gorges; but nothing can console her for the ghastliness of her condition, nothing. She resorts to the magic comfort of the Tarot pack and shuffles the cards, lays them out, reads them, gathers them up with a sigh, shuffles them again, constantly constructing hypotheses about a future which is irreversible.

An old mute looks after her, to make sure she never sees the sun, that all day she sleeps in her coffin, to keep mirrors and all reflective surfaces from her—in short, to perform all the functions of the servants of vampires. Everything about this beautiful and ghastly lady is as it should be, queen of night, queen of terror, except her horrible reluctance for the role.

Nevertheless, if an unwise adventurer pauses in the square of the deserted village to refresh himself at the fountain, a crone in a black dress and white apron presently emerges from a house. She will invite you with smiles and gestures; you will follow her. The Countess wants fresh meat. When she was a little girl, she was like a fox and contented herself entirely with baby rabbits that squeaked piteously as she bit into their necks with a nauseated voluptuousness, with voles and field mice that palpitated for a bare moment between her embroideress' fingers. But now she is a woman, she must have men. If you stop too long at the giggling fountain, you will be led by the hand to the Countess' larder.

All day, she sleeps in her coffin in a negligee of bloodstained lace; when the sun drops behind the mountains, she yawns and stirs and puts on the only dress she has, her mother's wedding dress, to sit and read her cards until she grows hungry. She loathes the food she eats; she would have liked to take the rabbits home with her, feed them on lettuce, pet them and make them a nest in her red-and-black lacquer chinoiserie escritoire but hunger always overcomes her. She can eat nothing else. She sinks her teeth into the neck where an artery throbs with terror; she will drop the deflated skin from which she has extracted all the nourishment with a small cry of both pain and disgust. And it is the same with the shepherd boys and gypsy lads who, foolhardy or ignorant, come to wash the dust from their feet in the water of the fountain; the Countess' governess brings them into the drawing room where the cards on the table always show the Grim Reaper. She herself will serve them coffee in tiny, cracked cups of precious porcelain and little sugar cakes. The hobbledehoys sit with a spilling cup in one hand and a biscuit in the other, gaping at the beautiful Countess in her satin finery as she pours from a silver pot and chatters distractedly to put them at their fatal ease. A certain desolate stillness of her eyes indicates she is inconsolable. She would like to caress their lean, brown cheeks and stroke their ragged hair. When she takes them by the hand and leads them to her bedroom, they can scarcely believe their luck.

Afterwards, her governess will tidy the remains into a neat pile and wrap it in its own discarded clothes. This mortal parcel she then discreetly buries in the garden. The blood on the Countess' cheeks will be mixed with tears; her keeper probes her fingernails for her with a little silver toothpick, to get rid of the fragments of skin and bone that have lodged there.

> Fee fie fo fum
> I smell the blood of an Englishman.

One hot, ripe summer in the pubescent years of the present century, a young officer in the British army, blond, blue-eyed, heavy-muscled, after a visit to friends in Vienna, decided to spend the rest of his furlough exploring the little-known uplands of Rumania. When he quixotically decided to travel the rutted cart-tracks by bicycle, he saw all the humour of it: "on two wheels in the land of the vampires." So, laughing, he sets out on his adventure.

He has the special quality of virginity, most and least ambiguous of states; ignorance, yet, at the same time, power in potentia, and, further-more, unknowingness, which is not the same as ignorance. He is more than he knows—and has about him, besides, the special glamour of that generation for whom history has already prepared a special, exemplary fate in the trenches of France; history, then, is about to collide with the timeless Gothic eternity of the vampiress, for whom all is as it always has been and will be, whose cards always fall in the same pattern.

Although so young, he is also rational. He has chosen the most rational mode of transport in the world for his trip round the Carpathians. To ride a bicycle is in itself some protection against superstitious fears, since the bicycle is the product of pure reason applied to motion. Geometry at the service of man! Give me two spheres and a straight line and I will show you how far I can take them. Voltaire himself might have invented the bicycle, since it contributes so much to man's well-being and nothing at all to his bane. Beneficial to the health, it emits no harmful fumes and permits only the most decorous speeds. A bicycle is not an implement of harm.

A single kiss woke the Sleeping Beauty in the Wood.

The waxen fingers of the Countess, fingers of a holy image, turn up the card called L'Amoureux. Never, never before... never before has the Countess cast herself a fate involving L'Amoureux. She shakes, she trembles, her great eyes close beneath her finely veined, nervously throbbing eyelids; the lovely cartomancer has, this time, the first time, dealt herself a hand of love and death.

> Be he alive or be he dead
> I'll grind his bones to make my bread.

At the mauvish beginnings of evening, the English m'sieu toils up the hill to the village he glimpsed from a great way off; he must dismount and push his bicycle before him, the path too steep to ride. He hopes to find a friendly inn to rest the night; he's hot, thirsty, weary, dusty... at first, such disappointment to discover the roofs of all the cottages caved in and tall weeds thrusting through the piles of fallen tiles, shutters banging disconsolately from their hinges; an entirely uninhabited place. And the rank vegetation whispers, one could almost imagine twisted faces appearing momentarily beneath the crumbling eaves, if one were sufficiently imaginative... but the adventure of it all, and the comfort of the poignant brightness of the hollyhocks still bravely blooming in the shaggy garden, and the beauty of the flaming sunset, all these considerations soon overcome his disappointment, assuage the faint unease he'd felt. And the fountain where the village women used to wash their clothes still gushes out bright, clear water; he gratefully washes his feet and hands, applies his mouth to the faucet, lets the icy stream run over his face.

When he raised his dripping, gratified head from the lion's mouth, he saw, silently arrived beside him in the square, an old woman who smiled eagerly, almost conciliatorily, at him. She wore a black dress and a white apron, with a housekeeper's key-ring at the waist; her grey hair was neatly coiled in a chignon beneath the white linen headdress worn by elderly women of that region. She bobbed a curtsey at the young man and beckoned him to follow her. When he hesitated, she pointed towards the great bulk of the mansion above them, whose façade loured over the village, rubbed her stomach, pointed to her mouth, rubbed her stomach again and sighed, clearly miming an invitation to supper. Then she beckoned him again, this time turning determinedly on her heel as though she would brook no opposition.

A great, intoxicated surge of the heavy scent of red roses blew into his face as soon as they left the village, inducing a sensuous vertigo; a blast of rich, faintly corrupt sweetness strong enough, almost, to fell him. Too many roses. Too many roses bloomed on the enormous thickets of roses that lined the path, roses equipped with vicious thorns, and the flowers themselves, were almost too luxuriant, their huge congregations of plush petals somehow obscene in their excess, their whorled, tightly budded cores outrageous in their implications. The façade of the mansion emerged grudgingly from this jungle.

In the subtle and haunting light of the setting sun, that golden light rich with nostalgia for the day that is just past, the sombre visage of the place, part manor house, part fortified farmhouse, immense, rambling, a dilapidated eagle's nest atop the crag down which its attendant village meandered, reminded him of childhood tales on winter evenings, when he and his brothers and sisters scared themselves half out of their wits with ghost stories set in just such places, and then had to have candles to light them up the stairs to bed, so overworked had their imaginations become. He could almost have regretted accepting the crone's unspoken invitation; but now, standing before the great door of time-eroded oak while she selected a huge, iron key from the clanking ringfull at her waist, he knew it was too late to turn back and, besides, he was not a child any more, to be scared of bricks and mortar.

The old lady unlocked the door, which swung back on melodramatically creaking hinges, and fussily took charge of his bicycle, in spite of his vigorous protests; he felt a certain sinking of the heart to see his beautiful two-wheeled symbol of rationality vanishing into the dark entrails of the mansion, to some outhouse where they would not oil it or check the tyres. But, in for a penny, in for a pound—in his youth and strength and blond beauty, in the invisible, even unacknowledged pentacle of his virginity, the young man stepped over the threshold of Nosferatu's castle and did not shiver in the blast of cold air, as from the mouth of a grave, that emanated from the lightless, cavernous interior.

The crone took him to a little chamber where there was a black oak table spread with a clean white cloth and this cloth was carefully laid with heavy silverware, a little tarnished, as if someone with foul breath had breathed on it, but laid with one place only. Curiouser and curiouser; invited to the castle for dinner, now he must dine alone. Still, he sat down as she bade him. Although it was not yet dark outside, the curtains were closely drawn and only the sparing light trickling from a single oil lamp showed him how dismal his surroundings were. The crone bustled about to get him a bottle of wine and a glass from an ancient cabinet of wormy oak; while he bemusedly drank his wine, she disappeared but soon returned bearing a steaming platter of the local spiced meat stew with dumplings, and a shank of black bread. He was hungry after his long day's ride, he ate heartily and polished his plate with the crust but this coarse food was hardly the entertainment he'd expected at such a mansion and he was puzzled by the assessing glint in the dumb woman's eyes as she watched him eating; but she darted off to get him a second helping as soon as he'd finished the first one and she seemed so friendly and helpful, besides, that he knew he could count on a bed for the night in the castle, as well as his supper, so he sharply reprimanded himself for his own sudden lack of enthusiasm for the eerie silence, the clammy chill of the place.

Then, when he'd put away the second plate, the old woman came and gestured he should leave the table and follow her once again. She made a pantomime of drinking; he deduced he was now invited to take after-dinner coffee in another room with some more elevated member of the household who had not wished to dine with him but, all the same, wanted to make his acquaintance.

He was surprised to find how ruinous the interior of the house was—cobwebs, worm-eaten beams, crumbling plaster; but the mute crone resolutely wound him on the spool of light she'd taken from the dining room down endless corridors, up winding staircases, through the galleries where the painted eyes of family portraits briefly flickered as they passed, eyes that belonged, he noticed, to faces one and all of a quite memorable beastliness. At last she paused and, behind the door where they'd halted, he heard a faint, metallic twang as of, perhaps, a chord struck on a harpsichord and then, wonderfully, the liquid cascade of the song of a lark, bringing to him, in the heart—had he but known it—of Juliet's tomb, all the freshness of morning. The crone rapped with her knuckles on the panels; the most beautiful voice he had ever heard in all his life softly called, in heavily accented French, the adopted language of the Rumanian aristocracy: "Entrez."

First of all, he saw only a moony gleam, a faint luminosity that caught and reflected from its tarnished surfaces what little light there was in the ill-lit room: of all things, a hoop-skirted dress of white satin draped here and there with lace, a dress fifty or sixty years out of fashion but once, no doubt, intended for a wedding; and its wearer a girl with the fragility of the skeleton of a moth, a being of such a famished leanness that the garment seemed to him to hang suspended, untenanted, in the dank air, a fabulous lending, a self-articulated gown. And then, as his eyes grew accustomed to the half-dark, he saw how beautiful and how very young the scarecrow inside the amazing dress was, and he thought of a child dressing up in her mother's clothes, perhaps a child putting on clothes of a dead mother in order to bring her, however briefly, to life again.

The Countess stood behind a low table, beside a pretty, silly, gilt-and-wire birdcage on a stand, in an attitude, distracted, almost of flight; she looked as startled by their entry as if she had not requested it. Only a low lamp with a greenish shade on a distant mantelpiece illuminated her so that, with her stark white face, her lovely death's head surrounded by long, dark hair that fell down as straight as if it were soaking wet, she looked like a shipwrecked bride. Her enormous, dark eyes almost broke his heart with their waif-like, lost look; yet he was disturbed, almost repelled by her extraordinarily fleshy mouth, a mouth with wide, full, prominent lips of a vibrant, purplish-crimson, a morbid mouth, even—but he put the thought away from him immediately—a whore's mouth. She shivered all the time, a starveling chill, a malarial agitation of the bones. He thought she must be only sixteen or seventeen years old, no more, with the hectic, unhealthy beauty of a consumptive. She was the chatelaine of all this decay.

The crone raised the light she held to show his hostess her guest's face and at that the Countess let out a faint, cawing cry and made a blind, appalled gesture with her hands, as if pushing him away, so that she knocked against the table and a butterfly dazzle of painted cards fell to the floor. Her mouth formed a round "o" of woe, she swayed a little and then sank into her chair, where she lay as if now scarcely capable of moving. A bewildering reception. Tsk'ing under her breath, the crone busily poked about on the table until she found an enormous pair of dark glasses such as blind beggars wear and perched them on the Countess' nose.

He went forward to pick up her cards for her from a carpet that, he saw to his surprise, was part rotted entirely away, partly encroached upon by all kinds of virulent-looking fungi. He retrieved the cards and shuffled them together; strange playthings for a young girl, grisly picture of a skeleton... he covered it with a happier one, two young, he supposed, lovers, smiling at one another, and put her toys back in a hand so slender you could almost see the frail net of bone beneath the translucent skin, hands with fingernails as long, as finely pointed as banjo picks. (She had been strumming on the birdcage again.)

At his touch, she seemed to revive a little and almost smiled, raising herself upright.

"Coffee," she said. "You must have coffee." And scooped up her cards in a pile so that the crone could set before her a silver spirit kettle, a silver coffee pot, cups, cream jug, sugar-basin, all on a silver tray, a strange touch of elegance, even if discoloured, in this devastated interior in which she ethereally shone with a blighted, submarine radiance.

The crone found him a chair and, tittering noiselessly, departed.

While the young lady attended to the coffee-making, he had time to contemplate with some distaste a further series of family portraits which decorated the stained and peeling walls of the room; these livid faces all seemed contorted with a febrile madness and the blubber lips, the huge, demented eyes they all held in common bore a disquieting resemblance to those of the hapless victim of inbreeding now patiently filtering her fragrant brew. The lark, its chorus done, had long ago fallen silent; no sound but the chink of silver on china. Soon, she held out to him a tiny cup of rose-painted china.

"Welcome," she said in her voice with the rushing sonorities of the ocean in it. "Welcome to my chateau. I rarely receive visitors and that's a misfortune, nothing animates me half as much as the presence of a stranger... This place is so lonely, now the village is deserted, and my one companion, alas, she cannot speak. Often I am so silent I think I, too, will soon forget how to talk."

She offered him a sugar biscuit from a Limoges plate; her fingernails struck carillons from the antique china. Her voice, issuing from those red lips like the obese roses in her garden, lips that do not move, her voice is curiously disembodied; she is like a doll, he thought, a ventriloquist's doll. And the idea she was an automaton, an ingenious construction of white velvet and black fur and crimson plush that could not move of its own accord never quite deserted him. The carnival air of her white dress emphasized her unreality, like a sad Columbine who lost her way in the wood a long time ago and never reached the fair.

"And the light, I must apologize for the lack of light... a hereditary affliction of the eyes..."

Her blind spectacles gave him his handsome face back to himself twice over; if he presented himself to her naked gaze, he would dazzle her like the sun she is forbidden to look at because it would shrivel her up at once, poor night bird. Night bird, butcher bird.

Vous serez ma proie.

You have such a fine throat, like a column of marble. When you came through the door retaining about you the golden light of the summer's day of which I know nothing, nothing, the card called "L'Amoureux" has just emerged from the tumbling chaos of imagery before me; it seemed to me you had stepped off the card into my darkness and, for a moment, I thought perhaps you might irradiate it.

I do not mean to hurt you. I shall wait for you in my bride's dress in the dark.

The bridegroom is come, he will go into the chamber which has been prepared for him.

I am condemned to solitude and dark; I do not mean to hurt you. I will be very gentle.

(And could love free me from the shadows? Can a bird sing only the only song it knows, could I not learn a new song?)

See, how I'm ready for you, I've always been ready for you; I've been waiting for you in my wedding dress, why have you delayed so long... it will all be over very quickly.

You will feel no pain, my darling.

She herself is a haunted house. She does not possess herself; her ancestors sometimes come and peer out of the windows of her eyes and that is very frightening. She has the mysterious solitude of ambiguous states; she hovers in a no man's land between life and death, sleeping and waking, behind the hedge of spiked flowers, Nosferatu's sanguinary rosebud. The beastly forebears on the walls condemn her to a perpetual repetition of their passions.

(One kiss, however, and only one, woke up the Sleeping Beauty in the Wood.)

Nervously, to conceal her inner voices, she keeps up a front of inconsequential chatter in French while her ancestors leer and grimace on the walls; however hard she tries to think of any other, she only knows of one kind of consummation.

He was struck, once again, by the bird-like, predatory claws which tipped her marvellous hands; the sense of strangeness that had been growing on him since he buried his head under the streaming water in the village, since he entered the dark portals of the fatal castle, now fully overcame him. Had he been a cat, he would have bounced backwards from her hands on four fear-stiffened legs; but he is not a cat, he is a hero.

A fundamental disbelief in what he sees before him sustains him, even in the boudoir of Countess Nosferatu herself; he would have said, perhaps, that there are some things which, even if they are true, we should not believe possible. He might have said, it is foolish to believe one's eyes. Not so much that he does not believe in her; he can see her, she is real. If she takes off her dark glasses, from her eyes will stream all the images that populate this vampire-haunted land, but, since he himself is immune to shadow, due to his virginity—he does not yet know what there is to be afraid of—and due to his heroism, which makes him like the sun, he sees before him, first and foremost, an inbred, highly-strung girl-child, fatherless, motherless, kept in the dark too long and as pale as a plant that never sees the light, half-blinded by some hereditary condition of the eyes. And though he feels unease, he cannot feel terror; so he is like the boy in the folk-tale, who does not know how to shudder and not spooks, beasties, the Devil himself and all his retinue could do the trick.

This lack of imagination gives his heroism to the hero.

He will learn to shudder in the trenches. But this girl cannot make him shudder.

Now it is dark. Bats swoop and squeak outside the tightly shuttered windows that have not been opened for five hundred years. The coffee is all drunk, the sugar biscuits gone. Her chatter comes trickling and diminishing to a stop; she twists her fingers together, picks at the lace of her dress, shifts nervously in her chair. Owls shriek; the impedimenta of her condition squeak and gibber all around us. Now you are at the place of annihilation, now you are at the place of annihilation. She turns her head away from the blue beams of his eyes; she knows no other consummation than the only one she can offer him. She has not eaten for three days. It is dinner-time. It is bed-time.

> *Suivez-moi.*
> *Je vous attendais.*
> *Vous serez ma proie.*

The raven caws on the accursed roof. "Dinner-time, dinner-time," clang the portraits on the walls. A ghastly hunger gnaws her entrails; she has waited for him all her life without knowing it.

The handsome bicyclist, scarcely believing his luck, will follow her into her bedroom; the candles around her sacrificial altar burn with a low, clear flame, light catches on the silver tears stitched to the wall.

> "My clothes have but to fall and you
> will see before you a succession of
> mysteries."

She has no mouth with which to kiss, no hands with which to caress, only the fangs and talons of a beast of prey. To touch the mineral sheen of the flesh revealed in the cool candle gleam is to invite her fatal embrace; in her low, sweet voice, she will croon the infernal *Liebestod* of the House of Nosferatu.

Embraces, kisses; your golden head, of a lion although I have never seen a lion, only imagined one, of the sun, even if I've only seen the picture of the sun on the Tarot card, your golden head of L'Amoureux whom I dreamed would one day free me, this head will fall back, its eyes roll upward in a spasm you will mistake for that of love and not of death. The bridegroom bleeds on my inverted marriage bed. Stark and dead, poor bicyclist; he has paid the price of a night with the Countess and some think it too high a fee while some do not.

Tomorrow, her keeper will bury his bones under the roses. The food her roses feed on gives them their rich colour, their swooning odour that breathes lasciviously of forbidden pleasures.

Suivez-moi.

The handsome bicyclist, fearful for his hostess' health, her sanity, gingerly follows her into the other room; he would like to take her into his arms and protect her from the ancestors who leer down from the walls.

What a macabre bedroom!

His colonel, an old goat with jaded appetites, had given him the visiting card of a brothel in Paris where, the satyr assured him, ten louis would buy just such a lugubrious bedroom, with a naked girl upon a coffin; offstage, the brothel pianist played the *dies irae* on a harmonium and, amidst all the perfumes of the embalming parlour, the customer took his necrophiliac pleasure of a pretended corpse. He had good-naturedly refused the old man's offer of an initiation; how can he now take criminal advantage of the disordered girl with fever-hot, bone-dry, taloned hands and eyes that denied all the erotic promises of her body with their terror, their sadness, their dreadful, baulked tenderness?

So delicate and damned, poor thing. Quite damned.

Yet I do believe she scarcely knows what she is doing.

She is shaking as if her limbs were not efficiently joined together. She raises her hands to unfasten the neck of her dress and her eyes fill with tears, they trickle down beneath the rim of her dark glasses. She can't take off her dress without taking off her glasses; when she takes off the dark glasses, they slip from her fingers and smash to pieces on the tiled floor. This unexpected, mundane noise breaks the wicked spell in the room, it disrupts the fatal ritual of seduction; she gapes blindly down at the splinters and ineffectively smears the tears across her face with her fist. When she kneels to try to gather the fragments of glass together, a shard pierces deeply into the pad of her thumb; she cries out. She kneels among the broken glass and watches the bright bead of blood form a drop. She has never seen her own blood before, not her own blood.

Into this macabre and lascivious room, the handsome bicyclist brings the innocent remedies of the nursery; in himself, by his presence, he is an exorcism. He gently takes her hand away from her and dabs away the blood with his own handkerchief, but still it spurts out; and so he puts his mouth to the wound, he will kiss it better for her.

All the silver tears fall from the wall with a flimsy tinkle. Her painted ancestors turn away their eyes and grind their fangs.

How can she bear the trauma of becoming human?

The end of exile, the end of being.

He was awakened by larksong. The shutters, the curtains, even the long-closed windows of the horrid bedroom were all opened up and light and air streamed into the room; now you could see how tawdry it was, how thin and cheap the satin, the catafalque not ebony at all but black-painted paper stretched on struts of wood, as in the theatre. The wind had blown droves of petals from the roses outside into the room and this ominous crimson residue swirled about the floor. The candles had blown out and the Countess' pet lark perched on the edge of the silly coffin and sang him an ecstatic morning song. His bones were stiff and aching; he'd slept on the floor, with his bundled-up jacket for a pillow, after he'd put her to bed.

But now there was no trace of her to be seen except, lightly tossed across the crumpled black satin bedcover, a lace negligee soiled with blood, as it might be from a woman's menses, and a rose that must have come from the fierce bushes nodding through the window. The air was heavy with incense and roses, it made him cough. The Countess must have got up early to enjoy the sunshine, slipped outside to pull him a rose. He got to his feet, coaxed the lark onto his wrist and took it to the window. At first, it exhibited the reluctance for the sky of a long-caged thing but, when he tossed it up onto the currents of the air, it spread its wings and was up and away into the clear, blue bowl of the heavens; he watched its trajectory with a lift of joy in his heart.

Then he padded into the boudoir, his mind occupied with plans. We shall take her to Zurich, to a clinic; she will be treated for nervous hysteria. Then to an eye specialist for her photophobia, and to a dentist to draw her teeth. A manicurist, to deal with her claws... we shall turn her into the lovely girl she is, I shall cure her.

The heavy curtains are pulled back, to let in brilliant fusillades of early morning light; in the desolation of her boudoir, at her round table she sits, in her white wedding dress with the cards laid out before her. She has dropped off to sleep over the cards of destiny, the Lover, the Grim Reaper droop from her dreaming hand. Gently, a kiss upon her sleeping forehead...

She is not sleeping.

In death, she looked far older, less beautiful and so, for the first time, fully human.

I will vanish in the morning light, I was only an invention of the darkness.

And I give you as a souvenir the dark fanged rose I plucked from between my thighs, like a flower laid on a grave. On a grave.

My keeper will attend to everything.

Nosferatu always attends
his own obsequies.

After a search in some foul-smelling outhouses, he discovered his bicycle and, abandoning his holiday, rode directly to Bucharest where, at the post-restante, he found a telegram summoning him to rejoin his regiment at once; history asserted itself. Much later, when he changed back into uniform in his quarters, he discovered he still had the Countess' sad rose, he'd tucked it into the breast pocket of his tweed cycling jacket. Curiously enough, the flower did not seem quite dead and, on impulse, because the girl had been so lovely and her heart-attack so unexpected and pathetic, he decided to try to resurrect the rose; he filled his tooth-glass with water from the carafe on his locker and popped the rose into it, so that its shaggy head floated on the top.

When he returned from the mess that evening, the heavy fragrance of Count Nosferatu's roses drifted down the stone corridor of the barracks to greet him, and his spartan quarters brimmed lasciviously with the reeling odour of a glowing, velvet, monstrous flower whose petals had regained all their former bloom and elasticity, their corrupt and brilliant splendour.

Next day, his regiment embarked for France.

THE GLASS BOTTLE TRICK

Nalo Hopkinson

Nalo Hopkinson was born in Jamaica in 1960 but has spent most of her life in Toronto in Canada. She currently holds a professorship in Creative Writing at the University of British Columbia. Her first novel, *Brown Girl in the Ring* (1998), won the Warner Aspect First Novel Contest in 1998, and she has continued to collect writing accolades, including the Sunburst Award for Canadian Literature of the Fantastic, the World Fantasy Award, the Gaylactic Spectrum Award, the Inkpot Award, and the Octavia E. Butler Memorial Award. She has received honorary Dr. of Letters degrees from Anglia Ruskin University and the Ontario College of Art and Design University. Hopkinson's writing foregrounds non-normative voices and experiences, and embeds African, Caribbean, and Creole folklore into both the Science Fiction and Fantasy genres. "The Glass Bottle Trick" features a duppie, a restless malevolent ghost. Many of the original duppie, or duppy, Caribbean folklore stories have their roots in the slave trade. In this unsettling narrative, Hopkinson moves the Bluebeard myth into the West Caribbean landscape and blends it with a duppie to ramp up the sense of dread in this story of an unhappy marriage cursed by the husband's racist disgust towards darker skin tones.

T he air was full of storms, but they refused to break. In the wicker rocking chair on the front veranda, Beatrice flexed her bare feet against the wooden slat floor, rocking slowly back and forth. Another sweltering rainy season afternoon. The arid heat felt as though all the oxygen had boiled out of the parched air to hang as looming rainclouds, waiting.

Oh, but she loved it like this. The hotter the day, the slower she would move, basking. She stretched her arms and legs out to better feel the luxuriant warmth, then guiltily sat up straight again. Samuel would scold if he ever saw her slouching like that. Stuffy Sammy. She smiled fondly, admiring the lacy patterns the sunlight threw on the floor as it filtered through the white gingerbread fretwork that trimmed the roof of their house.

"Anything more today, Mistress Powell? I finish doing the dishes." Gloria had come out of the house and was standing in front of her, wiping her chapped hands on her apron.

Beatrice felt the shyness come over her as it always did when she thought of giving the older woman orders. Gloria was older than Beatrice's mother. "Ah... no, I think that's everything, Gloria..."

Gloria quirked an eyebrow, crinkling her face like running a fork through molasses. "Then I go take the rest of the afternoon off. You and Mister Samuel should be alone tonight. Is time you tell him."

Beatrice gave an abortive, shamefaced "huh" of a laugh. Gloria had known from the start, she'd had so many babies of her own. She'd been mad to run to Samuel with the news from since. But Beatrice had already decided to tell Samuel. Well, almost decided. She felt irritated, like a child whose tricks have been found out. She swallowed the feeling. "I think you right, Gloria," she said, fighting for some dignity before the older woman. "Maybe... maybe I cook him a special meal, feed him up nice, then tell him."

"Well, I say is time and past time you make him know. A picknie is a blessing to a family."

"For true," Beatrice agreed, making her voice sound as certain as she could.

"Later then, Mistress Powell." Giving herself the afternoon off, not even a by-your-leave. Gloria headed off to the maid's room at the back of the house to change into her street clothes. A few minutes later, she let herself out the garden gate.

"That seems like a tough book for a young lady of such tender years."

"Excuse me?" Beatrice threw a defensive cutting glare at the older man. He'd caught her off guard, though she'd seen his eyes following her ever since she entered the bookstore. "You have something to say to me?" She curled the Gray's Anatomy *possessively into the crook of her arm, price sticker hidden against her body. Two more months of saving before she could afford it.*

He looked shyly at her. "Sorry if I offended, Miss," he said. "My name is Samuel."

Would be handsome, if he'd chill out a bit. Beatrice's wariness thawed a little. Middle of the sun-hot day, and he wearing black wool jacket and pants. His crisp white cotton shirt was buttoned right up, held in place by a tasteful, unimaginative tie. So proper, Jesus. He wasn't that much older than she.

"Is just... you're so pretty, and it's the only thing I could think of to say to get you to speak to me."

Beatrice softened more at that, smiled for him, and played with the collar of her blouse. He didn't seem too bad, if you could look beyond the stocious behaviour.

Beatrice doubtfully patted the slight swelling of her belly. Four months. She was shy to give Samuel her news, but she was starting to show. Silly to put it off, yes? Today she was going to make her husband very happy, break that thin shell of mourning that still insulated him from her. He never said so, but Beatrice knew that he still thought of the wife he'd lost, and tragically, the one before that. She wished she could make him warm up to life again.

Sunlight was flickering through the leaves of the guava tree in the front yard. Beatrice inhaled the sweet smell of the sun-warmed fruit. The tree's branches hung heavy with the pale yellow globes, smooth and round as eggs. The sun reflected off the two blue bottles suspended in the tree, sending cobalt light dancing through the leaves.

When Beatrice first came to Sammy's house, she'd been puzzled by the two bottles that were jammed onto branches of the guava tree.

"Is just my superstitiousness, darling," he'd told her. "You never heard the old people say that if someone dies, you must put a bottle in a tree to hold their spirit, otherwise it will come back as a duppie and haunt you? A blue bottle. To keep the duppie cool, so it won't come at you in hot anger for being dead."

Beatrice had heard something of the sort, but it was strange to think of her Sammy as a superstitious man. He was too controlled and logical for that. *Well, grief make somebody act in strange ways.* Maybe the bottles gave him some comfort, made him feel that he'd kept some essence of his poor wives near him.

"That Samuel is nice. Respectable, hard-working. Not like all them other ragamuffins you always going out with." Mummy picked up the butcher knife and began expertly slicing the goat meat into cubes for the curry.

Beatrice watched the red lumps of flesh part under the knife. Crimson liquid leaked onto the cutting board. She sighed, "But, Mummy, Samuel so boring! Michael and Clifton know how to have fun. All Samuel want to do is go for country drives. Always taking me away from other people."

"You should be studying your books, not having fun," her mother replied crossly.

Beatrice pleaded, "You well know I could do both, Mummy." Her mother just grunted.

Is only truth Beatrice was talking. Plenty men were always courting her, they flocked to her like birds, eager to take her dancing or out for a drink. But somehow she kept her marks up, even though it often meant studying right through the night, her head pounding and belly queasy from hangover while some man snored in the bed beside her. Mummy would kill her if she didn't get straight As for medical school. "You going have to look after yourself, Beatrice. Man not going do it for you. Them get their little piece of sweetness and then them bruk away."

"Two patty and a King Cola, please." The guy who'd given the order had a broad chest that tapered to a slim waist. Good face to look at, too. Beatrice smiled sweetly at him, made shift to gently brush his palm with her fingertips as she handed him the change.

A bird screeched from the guava tree; a tiny kiskedee, crying angrily, "Dit, dit, qu'est-ce qu'il dit!" A small snake was coiled around one of the upper branches, just withdrawing its head from the bird's nest. Its jaws were distended with the egg it had stolen. It swallowed the egg whole, throat bulging hugely with its meal. The bird hovered around the snake's head, giving its pitiful wail of, "Say, say, what's he saying!"

"Get away!" Beatrice shouted at the snake. It looked in the direction of the sound, but didn't back off. The gulping motion of its body as it forced the egg further down its own throat made Beatrice shudder. Then, oblivious to the fluttering of the parent bird, it arched its head over the nest again. Beatrice pushed herself to her feet and ran into the yard. "Hsst! Shoo! Come away from there!" But the snake took a second egg.

Sammy kept a long pole with a hook at one end leaned against the guava tree for pulling down the fruit. Beatrice grabbed up the pole, started jooking it at the branches as close to the bird and nest as she dared. "Leave them, you brute! Leave!" The pole connected with some of the boughs. The two bottles in the tree fell to the ground and shattered with a crash. A hot breeze sprang up. The snake slithered away quickly, two eggs bulging in its throat. The bird flew off, sobbing to itself.

Nothing she could do now. When Samuel came home, he would hunt the nasty snake down for her and kill it. She leaned the pole back against the tree.

The light breeze should have brought some coolness, but really it only made the day warmer. Two little dust devils danced briefly around Beatrice. They swirled across the yard, swung up into the air, and dashed themselves to powder against the shuttered window of the third bedroom.

Beatrice got her sandals from the veranda. Sammy wouldn't like it if she stepped on broken glass. She picked up the broom that was leaned against the house and began to sweep up the shards of bottle. She hoped Samuel wouldn't be too angry with her. He wasn't a man to cross, could be as stern as a father if he had a mind to.

That was mostly what she remembered about Daddy, his temper—quick to show and just as quick to go. So was he; had left his family before Beatrice turned five. The one cherished memory she had of him was of being swung back and forth through the air, her two small hands clasped in one big hand of his, her feet held tight in another. Safe. And as he swung her through the air, her Daddy had been chanting words from an old-time story:

> Yung-Kyung-Pyung, what a pretty basket!
> Margaret Powell Alone, what a pretty basket!
> Eggie-law, what a pretty basket!

Then he had held her tight to his chest, forcing the air from her lungs in a breathless giggle. The dressing-down Mummy had given him for that game! "You want to drop the child and crack her head open on the hard ground? Ee? Why you can't be more responsible?"

"Responsible?" he'd snapped. "Is who working like dog sunup to sundown to put food in oonuh belly?" He'd set Beatrice down, her feet hitting the ground with a jar. She'd started to cry, but he'd just pushed her toward her mother and stormed out of the room. One more volley in the constant battle between them. After he'd left them Mummy had opened the little food shop in town to make ends meet. In the evenings, Beatrice would rub lotion into her mother's chapped, work-wrinkled hands. "See how that man make us come down in the world?" Mummy would grumble. "Look at what I come to."

Privately, Beatrice thought that maybe all Daddy had needed was a little patience. Mummy was too harsh, much as she loved her. To please her, she had studied hard all through high school: physics, chemistry, biology, describing the results of her lab experiments in her copy book in her cramped, resigned handwriting. Her mother greeted every "A" with a non-committal grunt and anything less with a lecture. Beatrice would smile airily, seal the hurt away, pretend the approval meant nothing to her. She still worked hard, but she kept some time for play of her own. Rounders, netball, and later, boys. All those boys, wanting a chance for a little sweetness with a light-skin browning like her. Beatrice had discovered her appeal quickly.

"Leggo beast..." Loose woman. The hissed words came from a knot of girls that slouched past Beatrice as she sat on the library steps, waiting for Clifton to come and pick her up. She willed her ears shut, smothered the sting of the words. But she knew some of them. Marguerita, Deborah. They used to be friends of hers. Though she sat up proudly, she found her fingers tugging self-consciously at the hem of her short white skirt. She put the big physics textbook in her lap, where it gave her thighs a little more coverage.

The farting vroom of Clifton's motorcycle interrupted her thoughts. Grinning, he slewed the bike to a dramatic halt in front of her. "Study time done now, darling. Time to play."

He looked good this evening, as he always did. Tight white shirt, jeans that showed off the bulges of his thighs. The crinkle of the thin gold chain at his neck set off his dark brown skin. Beatrice stood; tucked the physics text under her arm; smoothed the skirt over her hips. Clifton's eyes followed the movement of her hands. See, it didn't take much to make people treat you nice. She smiled at him.

Samuel would still show up hopefully every so often to ask her to accompany him on a drive through the country. He was so much older than all her other suitors. And dry? Country drives; Lord! She went out with him a few times; he was so persistent and she couldn't figure out how to tell him no. He didn't seem to get her hints that really she should be studying. Truth to tell though, she started to find his quiet, undemanding presence soothing. His eggshell-white BMW took the gravelled country roads so quietly that she could hear the kiskedee birds in the mango trees, chanting their query: "Dit, dit, qu'est-ce qu'il dit?"

One day, Samuel brought her a gift.

"These are for you and your family," he said shyly, handing her a wrinkled paper bag. "I know your mother likes them." Inside were three plump eggplants from his kitchen garden, raised by his own hands. Beatrice took the humble gift out of the bag. The skins of the eggplants had a taut, blue sheen to them. Later she would realize that that was when she'd begun to love Samuel. He was stable, solid, responsible. He would make Mummy and her happy.

Beatrice gave in more to Samuel's diffident wooing. He was cultured and well-spoken. He had been abroad, talked of exotic sports: ice hockey; downhill skiing. He took her to fancy restaurants she'd only heard of, that her other young, unestablished boyfriends would never have been able to afford, and would probably only have embarrassed her if they had taken her. Samuel had polish. But he was humble too, like the way he grew his own vegetables, or the self-deprecating tone in which he spoke of himself. He was always punctual, always courteous to her and her mother. Beatrice could count on him for little things, like picking her up after class, or driving her mother to the hairdresser's. With the other men, she always had to be on guard: pouting until they took her somewhere else for dinner, not another free meal in her mother's restaurant; wheedling them into using the condoms. She always had to hold something of herself shut away. With Samuel, Beatrice relaxed into trust.

"Beatrice, come! Come quick, nuh!"

Beatrice ran in from the backyard at the sound of her mother's voice.

Had something happened to Mummy?

> Her mother was sitting at the kitchen table, knife still poised to crack
> an egg into the bowl for the pound cake she was making to take to the
> shop. She was staring in openmouthed delight at Samuel, who was fretfully
> twisting the long stems on a bouquet of blood-red roses. "Lord, Beatrice;
> Samuel say he want to marry you!"
>
> Beatrice looked to Sammy for verification. "Samuel," she asked
> unbelievingly, "what you saying? Is true?"
>
> He nodded yes. "True, Beatrice."
>
> Something gave way in Beatrice's chest, gently as a long-held breath.
> Her heart had been trapped in glass, and he'd freed it.

They'd been married two months later. Mummy was retired now;
Samuel had bought her a little house in the suburbs, and he paid for
the maid to come in three times a week. In the excitement of planning
for the wedding, Beatrice had let her studying slip. To her dismay she
finished her final year of university with barely a "C" average.

"Never mind, sweetness," Samuel told her. "I didn't like the idea
of you studying, anyway. Is for children. You're a big woman now."
Mummy had agreed with him too, said she didn't need all that now.
She tried to argue with them, but Samuel was very clear about his
wishes, and she'd stopped, not wanting anything to cause friction
between them just yet. Despite his genteel manner, Samuel had just
a bit of a temper. No point in crossing him, it took so little to make
him happy, and he was her love, the one man she'd found in whom
she could have faith.

Too besides, she was learning how to be the lady of the house, trying
to use the right mix of authority and jocularity with Gloria the maid
and Cleitis, the yardboy who came twice a month to do the mowing
and the weeding. Odd to be giving orders to people when she was
used to being the one taking orders, in Mummy's shop. It made her

feel uncomfortable to tell people to do her work for her. Mummy said she should get used to it, it was her right now.

The sky rumbled with thunder. Still no rain. The warmth of the day was nice, but you could have too much of a good thing. Beatrice opened her mouth, gasping a little, trying to pull more air into her lungs. She was a little short of breath nowadays as the baby pressed on her diaphragm. She knew she could go inside for relief from the heat, but Samuel kept the air-conditioning on high, so cold that they could keep the butter in its dish on the kitchen counter. It never went rancid. Even insects refused to come inside. Sometimes Beatrice felt as though the house was really somewhere else, not the tropics. She had been used to waging constant war against ants and cockroaches, but not in Samuel's house. The cold in it made Beatrice shiver, dried her eyes out until they felt like boiled eggs sitting in their sockets. She went outside as often as possible, even though Samuel didn't like her to spend too much time in the sun. He said he feared that cancer would mar her soft skin, that he didn't want to lose another wife. But Beatrice knew he just didn't want her to get too brown. When the sun touched her, it brought out the sepia and cinnamon in her blood, overpowered the milk and honey, and he could no longer pretend she was white. He loved her skin pale. "Look how you gleam in the moonlight," he'd say to her when he made gentle, almost supplicating love to her at night in the four-poster bed. His hand would slide over her flesh, cup her breasts with an air of reverence. The look in his eyes was so close to worship that it sometimes frightened her. To be loved so much! He would whisper to her, "Beauty. Pale Beauty, to my Beast," then blow a cool breath over the delicate membranes of her ear, making her shiver in delight. For her part, she loved to look at him, his molasses-dark skin, his broad chest, the way the planes of flat muscle slid across it. She imagined tectonic plates shifting in the earth. She loved the bluish-black cast the moonlight lent him. Once, gazing up at him as he loomed above her, body working against and in hers, she had seen the moonlight playing glints of deepest blue in his trim beard.

"Black Beauty," she had joked softly, reaching to pull his face closer for a kiss. At the words, he had lurched up off her to sit on the edge of the bed, pulling a sheet over him to hide his nakedness. Beatrice watched him, confused, feeling their blended sweat cooling along her body.

"Never call me that, please, Beatrice," he said softly. "You don't have to draw attention to my colour. I'm not a handsome man, and I know it. Black and ugly as my mother made me."

"But Samuel…!"

"No."

Shadows lay between them on the bed. He wouldn't touch her again that night.

Beatrice sometimes wondered why Samuel hadn't married a white woman. He could have met someone while he was studying abroad. She thought she knew the reason, though. She had seen the way that Samuel behaved around white people. He smiled too broadly, he simpered, he made silly jokes. It pained her to see it, and she could tell from the desperate look in his eyes that it hurt him too. For all his love of creamy white skin, Samuel probably couldn't bring himself to approach a white woman the way he'd courted her.

The broken glass was in a neat pile under the guava tree. Time to make Samuel's dinner now. She went up the veranda stairs to the front door, stopping to wipe her sandals on the coir mat just outside the door. Samuel hated dust. As she opened the door, she felt another gust of warm wind at her back, blowing past her into the cool house. Quickly, she stepped inside and closed the door, so that the interior would stay as cool as Sammy liked it. The insulated door shut behind her with a hollow sound. It was airtight. None of the windows in the house could be opened. She had asked Samuel, "Why you want to live in a box like this, sweetheart? The fresh air good for you."

"I don't like the heat, Beatrice. I don't like baking like meat in the sun. The sealed windows keep the conditioned air in." She hadn't argued.

She walked through the elegant, formal living room to the kitchen. She found the heavy imported furnishings cold and stuffy, but Samuel liked them.

In the kitchen she set water to boil and hunted a bit—where did Gloria keep it?—until she found the Dutch pot. She put it on the burner to toast the fragrant coriander seeds that would flavour the curry. She put on water to boil, stood staring at the steam rising from the pots. Dinner was going to be special tonight. Curried eggs, Samuel's favourite. The eggs in their cardboard case made Beatrice remember a trick she'd learned in physics class for getting an egg unbroken into a narrow-mouthed bottle. You had to boil the egg hard and peel it, then stand a lit candle in the bottle. If you put the narrow end of the egg into the mouth of the bottle, it made a seal, and when the candle had burnt up all the air in the bottle, the vacuum it created would suck the egg in, whole. Beatrice had been the only one in her class patient enough to make the trick work. Patience was all her husband needed. Poor, mysterious Samuel had lost two wives in this isolated country home. He'd been rattling about in the airless house like the egg in the bottle. He kept to himself. The closest neighbours were miles away, and he didn't even know their names.

She was going to change all that, though. Invite her mother to stay for a while, maybe have a dinner party for the distant neighbours. Before her pregnancy made her too lethargic to do much.

A baby would complete their family. Samuel would be pleased, wouldn't he? She remembered him joking that no woman should have to give birth to his ugly black babies, but she would show him how beautiful their children would be, little brown bodies new as the earth after the rain. She would show him how to love himself in them.

It was hot in the kitchen. Perhaps the heat from the stove? Beatrice went out into the living room, wandered through the guest bedroom, the master bedroom, both bathrooms. The whole house was warmer than she'd ever felt it. Then she realized she could hear sounds coming from the outside, the cicadas singing loudly for rain. There was no whisper of cool air through the vents in the house. The air conditioner wasn't running.

Beatrice began to feel worried. Samuel liked it cold. She had planned tonight to be a special night for the two of them, but he wouldn't react well if everything wasn't to his liking. He'd raised his voice at her a few times. Once or twice he had stopped in the middle of an argument, one hand pulled back as if to strike, to take deep breaths, battling for self-control. His dark face would flush almost blue-black as he fought his rage down. Those times she'd stayed out of his way until he was calm again.

What could be wrong with the air conditioner? Maybe it had just come unplugged? Beatrice wasn't even sure where the controls were. Gloria and Samuel took care of everything around the house. She made another circuit through her home, looking for the main controls. Nothing. Puzzled, she went back into the living room. It was becoming thick and close as a womb inside their closed-up home.

There was only one room left to search. The locked third bedroom. Samuel had told her that both his wives had died in there, first one, then the other. He had given her the keys to every room in the house, but requested that she never open that particular door.

"I feel like it's bad luck, love. I know I'm just being superstitious, but I hope I can trust you to honour my wishes in this." She had, not wanting to cause him any anguish. But where else could the control panel be? It was getting so hot!

As she reached into her pocket for the keys she always carried with her, she realized she was still holding a raw egg in her hand. She'd forgotten to put it into the pot when the heat in the house had made her curious. She managed a little smile. The hormones flushing her body were making her so absentminded! Samuel would tease her, until she told him why. Everything would be all right.

Beatrice put the egg into her other hand, got the keys out of her pocket, opened the door.

A wall of icy, dead air hit her body. It was freezing cold in the room. Her exhaled breath floated away from her in a long, misty curl. Frowning, she took a step inside and her eyes saw before her brain could understand, and when it did, the egg fell from her hands to smash open on the floor at her feet. Two women's bodies lay side by side on the double bed. Frozen mouths gaped open; frozen, gutted bellies too. A fine sheen of ice crystals glazed their skin, which like hers was barely brown, but laved in gelid, rime-covered blood that had solidified ruby red. Beatrice whimpered.

> "But Miss," Beatrice asked her teacher, "how the egg going to come back out the bottle again?"
>
> "How do you think, Beatrice? There's only one way; you have to break the bottle."

This was how Samuel punished the ones who had tried to bring his babies into the world, his beautiful black babies. For each woman had had the muscled sac of her womb removed and placed on her belly, hacked open to reveal the purplish mass of her placenta. Beatrice knew that if she were to dissect the thawing tissue, she'd find a tiny foetus in each one. The dead women had been pregnant too.

A movement at her feet caught her eyes. She tore her gaze away from the bodies long enough to glance down. Writhing in the fast congealing yolk was a pin-feathered embryo. A rooster must have been at Mister Herbert's hens. She put her hands on her belly to still the sympathetic twitching of her womb. Her eyes were drawn back to the horror on the beds. Another whimper escaped her lips.

A sound like a sigh whispered in through the door she'd left open. A current of hot air seared past her cheek, making a plume of fog as it entered the room. The fog split into two, settled over the heads of each woman, began to take on definition. Each misty column had a face, contorted in rage. The faces were those of the bodies on the bed. One of the duppie women leaned over her own corpse. She lapped like a cat at the blood thawing on its breast. She became a little more solid for having drunk of her own life blood. The other duppie stooped to do the same. The two duppie women each had a belly slightly swollen with the pregnancies for which Samuel had killed them. Beatrice had broken the bottles that had confined the duppie wives, their bodies held in stasis because their spirits were trapped. She'd freed them. She'd let them into the house. Now there was nothing to cool their fury. The heat of it was warming the room up quickly.

The duppie wives held their bellies and glared at her, anger flaring hot behind their eyes. Beatrice backed away from the beds. "I didn't know," she said to the wives. "Don't vex with me. I didn't know what it is Samuel do to you."

Was that understanding on their faces, or were they beyond compassion?

"I making baby for him too. Have mercy on the baby, at least?"

Beatrice heard the *snik* of the front door opening. Samuel was home. He would have seen the broken bottles, would feel the warmth of the house. Beatrice felt that initial calm of the prey that realizes it has no choice but to turn and face the beast that is pursuing it. She wondered if Samuel would be able to read the truth hidden in her body, like the egg in the bottle.

"Is not me you should be vex with," she pleaded with the duppie wives. She took a deep breath and spoke the words that broke her heart. "Is... is Samuel who do this."

She could hear Samuel moving around in the house, the angry rumbling of his voice like the thunder before the storm. The words were muffled, but she could hear the anger in his tone. She called out, "What you saying, Samuel?"

She stepped out of the meat locker and quietly pulled the door in, but left it open slightly so the duppie wives could come out when they were ready.

Then with a welcoming smile, she went to greet her husband. She would stall him as long as she could from entering the third bedroom. Most of the blood in the wives' bodies would be clotted, but maybe it was only important that it be *warm*. She hoped that enough of it would thaw soon for the duppies to drink until they were fully real. When they had fed, would they come and save her, or would they take revenge on her, their usurper, as well as on Samuel?

Eggie-law, what a pretty basket!

COULD YOU WEAR MY EYES?

Kalamu ya Salaam

Kalamu ya Salaam was born in New Orleans on 24th March 1947. Originally known as Val Ferdinand III, he later changed his name to Kalamu ya Salaam, meaning "pen of peace" in Kiswahili. He has had a prolific and wide-ranging career as poet, educator, editor, playwright, essayist, and activist, who has spoken out on many racial and human rights issues. He left school in 1964 and joined the United States army where he served in Korea. On leaving, he returned to New Orleans to gain his associate degree. In 1968, along with writer Tom Dent, he established BLKARTSOUTH, a community writing and acting workshop, which provides a place for Black poets and playwrights to both show and produce their work. Salaam was a member of the Free Southern Theatre, a community group which was part of the newly emerging Black Theatre Movement. Salaam also participated in the Black Arts Movement (BAM) which resulted in new and radical art, poetry, music, and plays during the 1960s and 1970s, much of which focused on addressing issues surrounding Black identity and Black liberation. This movement extended out from the artistic achievements of the Harlem Renaissance in the 1920s and 1930s. Salaam was heavily influenced by Langston Hughes (1901–1967), leader of the Harlem Renaissance and poet; writer, James Baldwin (1924–1987); and poet and founder of BAM, Amiri Baraka (1934–2014). He was also inspired by the civil rights movement, which sought to end racial segregation

COULD YOU WEAR MY EYES?

and discrimination during the mid-twentieth century. "Could You Wear My Eyes?" was first published in 2000 as 'Can You Wear My Eyes' in the anthology *Dark Matter: A Century of Speculative Fiction from the African Diaspora*, and was later retitled for its appearance on the author's blog Neo-Griot in 2014. It is a masterpiece in bodily horror, which offers a warning to impetuous lovers who fail to think through the consequences of their romantic gestures.

A t first Reggie wearing my eyes after I expired was beautiful; a sensitive romantic gesture and an exhilarating experience. For him there was the awe of seeing the familiar world turned new when viewed through my gaze, and through observing him I vicariously experienced the rich sweetness of visualizing and savouring the significance of the recent past.

I'm a newcomer to the spirit world, so occasionally I miss the experience of earth feelings, the sensations that came through my body when I had a body. I can't describe the all-encompassing intricate interweave of spirit reality—"reality" is such a funny word to use in talking about what many people believe is so unreal. I can't really convey to you the richness of the spirit world nor what missing human feelings is like. I'm told eventually we permanently forget earth ways, sort of like when we were born and forgot all those pre-birth months we spent gestating in our mother's womb, in fact, most of us even forget what it feels like to be a baby. Well the spirit world is something like always being a baby, constant wonder and exploration.

Reggie must have had an inkling of the immensity of the fourth dimension—which is as good a name as any for the spirit world—or maybe Reggie guessed that there was a meta-reality, or intuited that there was more to eyes than simply seeing in the physical sense. But then again, he probably didn't intuit that this realm exists because, like most men, centring on his intuition was difficult for Reggie, as difficult as lighting a match in a storm or imagining being a woman.

277

In fact, his inability to adapt to and cope with woman-sight is why he's blind now.

I was in his head and I don't mean his memories. I mean literally checking his thoughts, each one existing with the briefness of a mayfly as Reg weighed the rationality of switching eyes. This was immediately following those four and a half anaesthetized days I hung-on while in the hospital after getting blindsided by a drunk driver a few blocks beyond Chinese Kitchen where I had stopped to get some of their sweet and sour shrimp for our dinner. Through the whole ordeal Reggie never wavered. Two days after my death and one day before the operation, Reginald woke up that Monday morning confident as a tree planted by the water. Reggie felt that if he took on my eyes then he would be able to have at least a part of me back in his life.

He assumed that with my eyes he maybe could stop seeing me when he brushed, combed and plaited Aiesha's thick hair or sat for over an hour daydreaming at her bedside while she slept, looking at our daughter but thinking of me; or maybe once my chestnut-coloured pupils were in his head then my demise wouldn't upset him so much he'd have to bow his head like he was reverently praying when a woman jumps up in church to testify—like sister Carol had done the day before—and has on a dress the same colour as the one I often wore.

Reginald was so eager to make good as a husband and father, to redeem whatever he thought was lost because of the way he came up. I am convinced he didn't really know me. He had this image, this ideal and he wanted that in the worse way. Wanted a family, a home. And I was the first woman he ever loved and who ever loved him. All the rest had been girls still discovering themselves. We married. I had his child. And for him everything was just the way it was supposed to be. For me, well, let us just say, some of us want more out of life without ever really identifying what that more is and certainly without ever attaining that more. So, in a sense, I settled—that's the woman Reginald married. And in another sense, there was a part of me that remained restless. I hid that part from Reginald. But I always knew. I always, always knew me and yes, that was what really disoriented Reginald. He loved me and I could live with his love, but until he wore my eyes he never got a glimpse of the other me.

I used to think there was something wrong with me. I should have been totally happy. Of course, I loved our daughter. I loved my husband. I could live with the life we had, but… But this is not about me. This is about the man whom I married. I married Reginald more because he loved me so much than because I loved him back like that—I mean I loved him and all but I would never have put his eyes into my head if he had been killed and I had been the one still alive.

After we went through all the organ donation legal rigmarole, we actually celebrated with a late night seafood dinner; that was about eight and a half months before Aiesha was born. Just like getting married, the celebration was his idea, an idea I went along with because I had no good reason not to even though I had a vague distaste, a sort of uneasiness about the seriousness that Reginald invested into his blind allegiance to me. You know the discomfort you experience when you have two or three forkfuls left on your plate and you don't feel like eating any more, but you have always been taught not to waste food so you eat that little bit more. Eating a few more morsels is no big thing but nonetheless forcing yourself leaves you feeling uneasy the rest of the evening. I can see how I was, how I hid some major parts of myself from Reginald and how difficult I must have been to live with precisely because he didn't really know the whole person he was living with, and he would be so sincerely worshipping the part of me that he envisioned as his wife, while inside I cringed and he never knew that despite my smiles how sad I sometimes felt because I knew he didn't know and

I knew I was concealing myself from him. Besides, what right did I have not to eat two little pieces of chicken or not to go celebrate my husband's decision to dedicate his life to me?

In hindsight I came to realize I shouldn't have let him give me things I didn't want. Reginald would have died if he had known that having or not having a baby didn't really make that much difference to me. He wanted... You know, this is really not about me. When we went to celebrate our signing of the donation papers, I didn't know then that I was pregnant but even if I had, we wouldn't have done anything differently; stubborn Reginald had his mind made up and, at the time, I allowed myself to be mesmerized by the sincerity and dedication of Reg's declaration—my husband's pledge to wear my eyes was unmatched by anything I had previously imagined or heard of. When somebody loves you like that you're supposed to be happy and if you aren't well then you just smile and, well, I think when he saw the world through my eyes he saw both me and the world in ways he never imagined.

The doctors told Reginald there usually weren't any negative side effects, although in a rare case or two there were some unexplained hallucinations but, even for those patients, counselling smoothed out the transition. The first week after the operation went ok and then the intermittent double visions started. For Reggie it was like he had second sight. He saw what was there but then he also saw something else.

Sometimes he would go places he never knew I went and get a disorienting image flash from a source about which he previously would never have given a second thought, like the svelte look of a waiter at a cafe, a guy whose sleek build I really admired. Reginald never envisioned me desiring some other man. I don't know why, but he just never thought of me fantasizing sex with someone else and now suddenly Reginald looks up from a menu and finds himself staring at a man's behind. Needless to say, such sightings were disconcerting. Or like how the night I got drunk on Tequila would flash back every time I saw limes. Reginald is in a supermarket buying apples and imagines himself retching, well, he thinks he's imagining dry heaves but he's really seeing the association of being drunk with those tart green, lemon-shaped fruit. And on and on, till Reggie's afraid to go anywhere new, afraid he'll run into another man I had made love to that he never knew about, like this person he saw in a bookstore one day, a bookstore Reginald never went in but which I used to frequent. That's how I had met Rahsaan. Reggie just happened to be passing the place, looked inside the big picture window and immediately peeped Rahsaan. When he looked into the handsome obsidian of Rahsaan's face with its angular lines that resembled an elegant African mask, Reginald got the shock of his naive life. He didn't sleep for two whole days after that one.

And when he closes our eyes to sleep, it's worse. A man should never know a woman's secret life; men cannot stand so much reality. Their fragile egos can't cope. It's like they say in Zimbabwe: men are children and women are mothers. Being a child is about innocence, about not knowing the realities that adults deal with every day. Men just don't know the world of women. So after Reginald adopted my eyes, you can just imagine how often he found himself laying awake at night, staring into the dark trying to make sense out of the complex of images he was occasionally seeing: awakened by the terror of a particularly vivid dream in which he saw how he had treated me, sometimes abusing me when he actually thought he was loving me—like when we would make mad love and he wanted me to suck him, he would never say anything, just shove my head down to his genitals. Sex didn't feel so exquisitely good to him to see his dick up close, the curl of his pubic hair.

Although the major episodes kept him awake and eventually drove him down to the riverside, it was the unrelenting grind of daily life's thousands of tiny tortures that propelled poor Reg over the edge.

Looked like every time he turned around in public he felt unsafe, felt vulnerable to assault from men he previously would never have bothered to notice. Seemed like my eyeball radar spotted potential invaders everywhere Reg looked: how to dodge that one, don't get on an elevator with this one, make sure there's always another person nearby when you're in a room with so-and-so. And even though as a man Reg was immune to much of the usual harassment, it became a real drag having to expend a ton of precautionary emotional energy in the course of taking a casual stroll down the block to buy some potato chips. The strain of always being on guard was too much for Reg; he became outraged: nobody should have to live like this is the conclusion he came to.

He never knew when the second sight would kick in and the visioning never lasted too long but the incidents were always so viscerally jolting that they emotionally disoriented him. In less than two weeks it had reached the point that just looking at makeup made Reg sick. He unconsciously reacted to seeing some shades of lipstick by wetting his lips with his tongue, like there was something inappropriate about him having unpainted lips—a vague but powerful feeling that he was wrong for being like he was started to consume him. And he couldn't bear to watch cable any more.

The morning Reginald blinded himself, he stood on the levee staring into the sun without squinting. Silent tears poured profusely down his cheeks. He kept saying he had always thought our life together was beautiful, and he never knew I had suffered so. And then he threw a twelve-ounce glass, three-quarters full of battery acid onto his face, directly into our unblinking eyes. A jogger that morning found Reginald on his knees, shrieking. The runner ran to a house and begged the people who lived there to call an ambulance for a Black guy folded over on the levee screaming about he didn't want to see any more, couldn't stand to see anything else.

I'LL BE YOUR MIRROR

Tracy Fahey

Tracy Fahey is one of Ireland's most striking and original horror writers. Her collections *I Spit Myself Out* (2021) and *The Unheimlich Manoeuvre* (2020) were both shortlisted for Best Collection at the British Fantasy Awards. Her latest book, *They Shut Me Up*, is a feminist folklore novella which was published in 2023. "I'll Be Your Mirror" is taken from *I Spit Myself Out*, where the female narrators unpeel horrors to reveal the visceral truths that reside under the surface of the skin in a terrifying striptease. Fahey's collection is influenced by French theorist, Julia Kristeva's essay "The Powers of Horror", specifically "the way [Kristeva] explores the notion of the *abject*; that which is of us, but which the body casts off."* "I'll Be Your Mirror" slowly dissects the brutality of a doomed love affair through the organs and membranes of the female body in the form of an Anatomical Venus. Life-sized wax cadavers, the Anatomical Venuses, were produced in the eighteenth-century by Clemente Susini and Felice Fontana in Florence as a means to study human anatomy. Reclining in erotic poses, the Anatomical Venus can be dismembered and all parts of the body—heart, lungs, kidney, intestines, pancreas—removed one-by-one until a tiny foetus is revealed sleeping

---

* Fahey, Tracy, "Guest Article: Tracy Fahey Discusses Contemporary Body Horror in Literature and her Collection, *I Spit Myself Out*.", hookofabook. wordpress.com.

in her womb. Uncomfortably straddling the scientific and the voyeur-istic, these imitation cadavers reduce a woman to her composite parts. Also known as "Slashed Beauties" or "Dissected Graces", the models are both hauntingly sensuous and macabre.

I. OVERLAY

From the moment I saw her I was in love. The Anatomical Venus. Her smooth face locked in a dream, the contours of her shining body interrupted by the line of her breastplate. Beneath the glass coffin, she sleeps, a waxen Snow White; crowned with human hair, a lustrous string of pearls twined around her delicate throat.

"The *pièce de résistance* has arrived." Derek smiles proudly. "Now if you could move it a little over to the right here," he says to the art handlers, who obey. One unloads the special plaque and places it carefully to one side. "Clemente Susini. 1870. La Specola." I dream of it sometimes, late at night, that Wunderkammer of a wax workshop in the Florentine Museum of Zoology and Natural History. She was born there, together with her sisters, the Slashed Beauty and the Dissected Graces.

"It'll really draw the crowds in, won't it?" His face is happy and anxious. I know the cost of the loan, the endless calculations behind this request.

I take off my glasses and wipe them. *All the better to see you with*, I think, touching the plaque with one careful finger.

"Yes," I say.

The Anatomical Venus. More beautiful and disturbing than I ever imagined.

It's a Friday and a few minutes to closing. Derek is kneeling on the floor beside the case, one eye on the old grandfather clock as it ticks away the seconds to 6pm. He has a date tonight; I know because he's changed into the freshly ironed shirt he brought in on a hanger, and his shoes are bright and hopeful with polish.

"You're on tomorrow morning, right? We're not quite done here, so can you look after her?" He gestures at the Anatomical Venus. "Do a once-over? Check everything is intact?" This wouldn't have been a question a few months ago, but an assumption.

He gets up and brushes the dust off his knees with short, sharp smacks. It smoke-puffs in the air. His gaze is meaningful; heavy. In the last few weeks I've been different. I've overslept. I've deleted emails by mistake. I've made him coffee with trembling hands; forgetting the sugar, adding too much milk.

I don't want to get this wrong. It's important. I need to look as responsible as I can. "Yes." I say, sliding my glasses down from the top of my head. I blink at him through thick lenses. "Yes, of course."

As long as I can remember I've always been obsessed with anatomy. During the summer hush of holidays; long days spent indoors in the book-must of old books, I find the entry for H for Human Body in the *World Book Encyclopaedia*. Slowly, reverently, I turn the plastic overlays. The notation at the bottom boasts "Especially in Trans Vision!" Transparent pages separate the skeleton from the organs from the skin. Turning the page of the skin reveals a panoply of wonders. Long, pink muscles and ligaments cling to the bones. I turn another slick plastic page. Mysterious organs surface, hidden deep inside.

It was my first anatomical peep-show and I loved it.

The door shuts with a neat *click*. I lift the glass coffin and touch her face. Biology class at school, *Gray's Anatomy*, dissection class at university; I've loved many anatomical specimens in my time.

But she—I reach out and stroke a pale, immobile arm—*she* is special. A thousand circuses hum to life under her waxen skin.

2. THE BODY

As I touch her pallid cheek, the museum recedes.

I'm ten. A day out at the fairground; music and sunlight and shouts from the rides. The sweet fluff of candyfloss sticks to my teeth. Tents spring from the flattened grass.

"Come inside!" A man stands outside a tent. I wiggle inside. It's dark except for a bright light at the front. The crowd smells hot; a mingled scent of sweat and crushed grass.

"See me saw the lady in half!" The white-gloved magician wears a red spangled waistcoat. His moustache is glossy and curled. The glossy assistant, all teased blonde hair and bright red dress, climbs inside the wooden box. Her legs protrude from the end; red shoes with scuffed heels. She lies prone in the too-small coffin. He brandishes a saw above her head. Her head slowly rotates; blue eyes lock with mine.

"See me saw the lady in half!" I move to the front of the dark crowd.

Close up, his face is carved with wrinkles. There are sequins missing from his waistcoat. His white gloves are smudged with dirt. My mother's hand closes over mine in the darkness, tight and warm. "It's not suitable for you." Her voice is tight and hard.

As we leave I look back. He saws at the wood; a harsh, grating sound. Her face is still tilted to one side; eyes blue, expressionless.

Upstairs I can hear the sounds of the university shut down, doors close, the heavy footsteps of medical students echo down the tiled stairs. Slowly the noises recede, swallowed by silence. It's just me and her now. I touch her hair, that startlingly real, human hair that flows in two fat brown plaits over her shoulders.

She lies still, uncaring. Her pearl necklace is softly iridescent in the gloom of the museum. Pearls for wisdom, for purity, for the moon. I think of their genesis; grit in the shell.

She was born in the warmth of La Specola. I picture the careful hands of the apprentices, modelling the pale body in a delicate soap of heated wax. Her face carries the residual warmth of the day held within it, like sand underfoot at the seaside. My fingers lie where those of thousands of medical students and tourists have rested; on the surface of her mysterious skin, closed tight around the seeds of her organs.

She is the goal of the Grand Tourist, the ancestor of the medical cadaver, the legacy of the Murder Act; she is the buried treasure dug by grave robbers under the cold eye of the moon. I watch her open-eyed sleep as she dreams her waxen dreams.

And then I do what I've wanted to do all afternoon. I slide my fingernails under the breastplate and lift it. *See me saw the lady in half!*

The last rays of the sunlight pool on her body, gilding the nestled organs within. I touch the keys in my pocket. "We've got all night," I say softly. Her eyes stare at me; glassy, unblinking.

2.1 STOMACH

I close my eyes as my fingers slide down inside her. *Come inside.* It's Halloween, and we're playing that game, you know the one, Withered Corpse, where we sit in the dark and pass body parts to each other. I remember the slick shudder of touching the peeled grapes for eyes, the warm slipperiness of spaghetti for guts. My fingertips remember the ridged contours of cauliflower brains, the soft curled ears of dried apricot.

But this is different. The waxen parts slide under my hands. I plunge deep into the abdominal cavity and my fingers close around my goal. The stomach.

I weigh it in my palm. I know already from anatomy class that it's a surprisingly solid object. Looking at it, I imagine my own. I see my last meal, a gluey mess of macaroni cheese, slide inexorably down my oesophagus, the digestive juices rising to meet it. A wave of bile washes upwards, quick and sour.

No. I promised myself I wouldn't do it again.

Come inside.

I'm an anxious thirteen when they bring me to the doctor. His cold hands palpate my skin; brush the downy hair on my arms.

"She's very under-nourished." My mother. The skin of her face is stretched on the tight bone beneath. "She won't listen to us." I stand there, ashamed. He ignores me and talks to her instead. They speak of food, of nutrients, of reason. I see the bodies of the girls I want to be, skinny and sun-warmed in bikinis. Food is the enemy. It lines up before me; tempting and colourful. I remember the guilty, sweet slickness of chocolate and the joy of expulsion.

No.

I replace the stomach with a shiver.

2.2 BLOOD

I run a finger down the tracery of veins and arteries. In the stillness of the dust and silence of the museum I can hear the soft pounding of my blood as it travels around my own subterranean highways.

I stopped being bulimic but continued to eat.

And my body ripened and bulged. Great seams of stomach poked through the intersection between my jeans and t-shirt. My skin stretched in red, angry marks that whitened to a delicate silver. I was lost inside my body, insulated by flesh, buried and deadened.

I became fascinated by my own blood. Late at night I would listen to it; that soft drumbeat in my ears. Fingers pressed to the side of my neck, I would feel my artery pulse blood around my body. I stuck pins in it, measuring myself in pain. I cut into the yielding envelope of my flesh, the pale softness of my thighs, the marshmallow insides of my upper arms. Red blood welled up, dark and beautiful; the ritual of punishment calming me.

I look at the Anatomical Venus as I stroke her tangle of veins. Her sleepy, orgasmic face betrays no emotion. I envy her that sense of repose, the still calm of a beach after a storm.

I put my hands inside her and close my eyes. The Withered Corpse game, played in wax. My fingers touch the smooth surface of an organ. I lift it out.

The pancreas.

2.3 PANCREAS

I eat and eat until my body rebels. But instead of getting bigger, I start to fade. My thick limbs deflate, my stomach sinks inward. I'm so thirsty now, all the time. At first I think it's the hot summer. All I want to do is drink; my insides like concrete cracked in the heat. And then all night I want to urinate. As I sit on the cold porcelain my vision blurs and fades. A sick eddy of stars when I stand up.

I have to crawl back to my bed. My mother finds me in the corridor, slumped against the wall.

We're back at the doctor. A different one. She has warm cocoa skin and her eyes are soft and brown. She talks directly to me, ignoring the staccato bursts of my mother. I understand I have battled my own pancreas; killed off cells that produce insulin.

The war is over. I start to heal my injured body. With the help of the kind doctor, we measure the sugar in my blood, we inject insulin. Now the only blood that wells up is from the punctures on my fingertips.

Physician, heal thyself. "I want to be a doctor," I tell my parents. Their faces are wary, uncertain. But I know it's right for me.

I look at the wax pancreas in my hand, and picture my own, floating now like a dead fish in the warm sea of my body.

I replace it. Lucky dip time. And I feel them then, like secret wings under the flesh, the lungs of the Venus.

2.4 LUNGS

Medical school is difficult, more difficult than I anticipate. I thought my own experience, my apprenticeship with my body, would transmute itself into my brain, my fingertips. But instead there are long nights of tense study, the memorization of Latin terms. I feel panic rise in my body, hard and bright and horrible. Sometimes, late at night, I can't breathe. The air is soup, my throat closes. In my head I hear the dark drumbeat of my heart.

But then, things start to flower. First, there's the job in the museum of pathology. I treasure my time there; those quiet days spent relabelling specimens under Derek's watchful eye. We have a marvellous collection of faux anatomical specimens; yellowed jars of malformed limbs, diseased organs, even the twisted bodies of strange, never-born children. These linen and wax simulacra around me were created by clever artists, studying cadavers side by side with medical students.

"We still do it, you know. Bring in artists." Derek is proud of the tradition. "Maybe you'd like to cover their session on Saturdays?" He's seen my scribbled sketches, even admired them on occasion.

"Sure." He's making it sound like he's doing me a favour, but I know he wants to get the time off for whatever mysterious Derek-life he leads. And that leads me to the second thing. The important thing.

You. I'm there when you come in, talking away to a girl with blonde hair. I couldn't breathe. Your wavy brown hair, your dark, direct gaze, the stubble erupting coarse and dark from tanned skin. Those details crush out the air from my body. I can only stand and stare. My lungs hurt.

"Hey," you say.

I can't answer.

You. My throat closes at the memory; dusty air is thick in my mouth. I slide the lungs back into their cavity, cover them up. I rock back on my heels. Her glass eyes stare under heavy lids; Brown eyelashes almost touch her candle-smooth cheeks.

2.5 EYES

"You are beautiful," you say, your artist's eye moving over me in a practised manner, dissecting me. You ignore the flaws, the white marks, the stretch of damaged skin over my insides. I am transformed; tiny echoes of a pretty self sparkle in the twin, black fastness of your retinas.

Your pencil makes me beautiful. The *slish-slash* of graphite on rough paper. You remake me, stroke by stroke. A mess of lines straightens out to reveal the long curves of my body.

We spend time together. Not just the Saturdays when you sit sketching, your bold eyes meeting mine. You cook for me; long nights spent pouring red wine as you fuss over the perfect sauce. Curled up on the sofa we play Operation; I laugh at your rage when your tweezers touch the edges of the Charley Horse slot. I sit in your studio and watch you draw, the surety of your line bringing me a sense of peace.

And for a while it is perfect.

I swallow and look away. Only for a while. I touch my sternum and then the chest of the Venus.

I lift out her heart.

2.6 HEART

Such a small organ, so powerful. It sits in my hand like an apple.

You are insistent you want it. You tell me you love me, that your heart is mine. *Come inside.* I am wary of your warmth. Beneath the veneer of my skin, I am an ugly puzzle, a game of Withered Corpse gone wrong.

Come on. The impatience is scribbled stark on your face.

And under the weight of it all—those subtitled movie marathons, holding hands in a gallery, the picnics on the beach—under it all I feel my dark self unravel and soften like spaghetti in water. I give in. You stand in my kitchen and eat leftovers from my fridge. Your hair is a black tangle in my drain. I find flecks of paint on my sofa.

Yet your flesh is still alien to me. I stroke it in the moonlit nights when I can't sleep, when panic clusters round my mouth and nose. Your shoulders are smooth, your chest furred with dense hair. I listen to your soft, purring snores and marvel at the otherness and togetherness of being us.

After six months I give you my heart. You hold it in hands smudged with charcoal, the nails never completely clean.

I think I have your heart in return. But just when I want it most, you take it away.

"I'm sorry," you tell me. "It's over. There's someone else." In your eyes I see it. The unmistakeable glitter of the magician's gaze. *See me saw the lady in half!*

There are tears on my face now. The sun is gone, and the room is filled with velvet greyness. Colour leaches from the Anatomical Venus. I place her heart back inside. It touches her ribs and I imagine the whole of her body lighting up with an electric buzz.

But I haven't finished yet. Underneath everything, there is the grit in the pearl. That seed at the centre. I open up the case of the womb and touch the tiny, curled foetus inside.

2.7 WOMB

You didn't just take my heart. You took this too. You wanted me to love you, to dream of the future. You held my hand and talked to me about our children.

"They'll have your eyes." You stare into mine. "Green like glass."

"No, yours. They're so dark and beautiful." I am in love. I am recklessly free, unbounded by hesitancy, buttressed by your affection.

But no more. Now there's someone else. That someone else has a name. It's Amanda, the blonde girl from your class. Her hair is long and straight, her body firm as those of the bikini girls I tried to purge myself to be. I see you together on Saturdays. It's a special kind of torture; your brown hands on her pale shoulders.

And then, one day, I see it. A clear and unmistakable bump, poking out the top of her baggy combats. Like everything else about her, it is small and pert. I stare at the murky jars of twisted embryos. I hex the bump. I long for it to hide a hideous secret. A chimera. But I know it ripens within; succulent and perfect as the golden skin that envelops it.

I'm always lonely now. I stop eating. I survive on black coffee. My blood glucose dips; I roller-coaster it with lumps of sugar. My bed fills with anatomy textbooks, their covers chill to the touch.

"How could you?" I can't hold back the words when I see you on your own one Saturday morning. You frown.

"How could you?" I repeat. You act like you can't hear me, like you don't understand. You always hated being wrong.

"Don't be hysterical." Your voice is cold and clear. I feel the madness spread inside me, leaking poison from my unwanted womb, curdling the blood in my veins.

She comes in and sets out her brushes. Her eyes meet mine; warm and triumphant. They rake my imperfections. I am withered, an inferior husk; dry and desiccated as the imitation diseased limbs around us.

I return her gaze with the blank, empty eyes of the magician's assistant.

I'm always lonely now. Till she comes. My wonderful Anatomical Venus. I'm in love. I can't stop touching her. Her tranquil face. Under my fingertips, her hair is warm to the touch. I trace a gentle finger from her womb to her brain.

3. THE REVEAL

I take off my clothes in the gloom of the museum. The darkness hides my imperfections; the stretch marks, the punctures on my fingers, the scars on my arms and legs, all the evidence of my own flawed life. I drag my clothes onto her waxen, unyielding body until she is covered, finally. Her long striptease has ended.

I move her to one side and lie down on the empty plinth. My flesh is chill and marble to the touch. I am laid bare. No wooden case, no glass box. I close my eyes.

It's quiet here. There's no sound but the ticking of the old grandfather clock. My eyelids waver and stutter. The long nights of sleeplessness catch up with me; pull me under into the darkness. My organs grow cold, harden into wax. My skin grows over them, pure and perfect and smooth to the touch. I feel their eyes on me, those centuries of men, their warm hands on my cold body. Now I am the *World Book Encyclopaedia*, dissected in those slick plastic sheets, filed under H for Human. Colours swirl and ebb. Now I am the woman in the dark tent, eyes slack with ennui, limbs curled up in the fake box. More swirls. Now I am the Operation Game. I see hands above me, holding the tweezers. My nose buzzes a bright and cheery red.

And then, all too soon, I'm surfacing to the sound of footsteps. Behind my eyelids it's pink; sunlight spilling into the museum. Saturday morning.

I try to move, but I can't. My limbs are cold and heavy as lead.

Come inside I hear his voice. The magician stands over me. *See me saw the lady in half!* My skin envelope peels back to reveal the intimate clockwork of my body. I am a wax doll, a magician's assistant, a withered corpse.

There's the sound of voices. I hear the fluorescent bulb overhead hum and stutter into being.

Come inside.

The show has begun...

2022

DANCEHALL DEVIL

V. Castro

V. Castro is one of the most exciting voices in horror. She was born in Texas to Mexican American parents but is now based in the U.K. She has been twice nominated for the Bram Stoker award for *The Queen of the Cicadas* (2022) and *The Goddess of Filth* (2021). "Dancehall Devil" is taken from her short story collection *Mestiza Blood*, published by Flame Tree Press in 2022. Her most recent release is *The Haunting of Alejandra* (2023), a sinister story of grief and revenge, and a woman who is haunted by the Mexican folk demon, La Llorona. She has also written a Science Fiction novel for the *Alien* film franchise, entitled *Alien: Vasquez*, which was published in 2022. Her Latinx narratives are influenced by Mexican folklore and the urban legends of Texas. Her writing pulsates with violent and erotic expressions of female rage and power, and their blood-drenched plot lines reveal intergenerational and colonial traumas. "Dancehall Devil" is one such weird and gory tale of sexual vengeance.

They say she is a beauty, with hair that will tangle you in tendrils of brown as you spin her around. Before you know it, you are as helpless as a spider's next meal. Her lips are so wet and inviting you might mistake them for forbidden fruit you can't help but want to taste. That shine is poison. Eyes are obsidian. Black as a sky without a moon or stars. You will be forever lost and forget you ever wanted anything else but her if you stare too long. But it is her feet that are the tell-tale sign you are dancing with the devil. She will bury your bones beneath hooves of a goat stained with blood that looks like nail polish. This is just what they say. I tend the bar at the dancehall where she was last seen, and let me tell you, she is very real.

This is what happened when that devil of a woman walked in with her friends.

It was Friday night, payday. It was crowded with men and women wanting to unwind from a hard week or hoping to find an easy fuck. Both are good enough reasons to come out. The band plays merengue and salsa every Friday. It's a crowd of Wrangler jeans, hats, tight dresses and boots. The music is loud and hot, something they would play in hell because the bodies are packed so tight there is no room between them. Grinding bodies, slithering bodies, bodies that should be in a motel room because their mouths are kissing so passionately you wonder why they aren't already naked. As the night wears on, the more drinks stream down gullets, the more freedom everyone feels.

Every bar has its regulars. Most of them are nice, respectful, leave a little tip for the lady working weekends so she can save for college for her teenage son. Then there was that one. That one who felt entitled to every woman who passed by. The one who always wanted to pick a fight if a dude looked at him wrong. He was a bully of the worst kind. No matter how many times I complained to management about the comments he made to me or other patrons, I was told as long as he was a paying customer, the money was good enough here. None of the bar staff, male or female, wanted to serve him. It goes without saying, he always came in alone.

A group of five women stood at the bar. Each wore a dress in a different colour with a matching faux flower in their hair half pinned up. Their makeup and hairstyle were both old-school, like they'd walked out of the 1940s; classic pachucas, so beautiful and timeless. They toasted with shots of Mezcal while dancing in place and chatting with each other.

Paulo walked past me. "I'm going on break. You know who just walked in. I want to keep my job, so you deal with him. Last time I almost jumped over the bar and punched him in the face."

I rolled my eyes. Paulo was good people. He didn't need trouble so I wouldn't hold this sudden abandonment against him. This job was paying for his wife's notary classes.

The troublesome customer decided to shoulder his way to the bar next to the group of five women. He looked them up and down, not even trying to disguise his lust.

"Oye, baby. Let me buy you a drink." He chose to bother the woman in red. Her dress was off the shoulders with a ruffle over the bust, fitted to the waist then fell loose just above the knee.

She stared at him hard so he would get the message. "No thank you, vato. I'm here with friends."

I could feel something about to happen. It was nearly midnight and he was already decently drunk.

He slipped his hand to the side of her hip.

She turned her head to the side again, eyes narrowing. They looked completely black to me, but I thought it was a trick of the light. Her friends stopped their conversation and drinking. "I said no, cabron. I'm here with my friends and I want to have a good time."

He positioned his body so that he was standing directly behind her, too close for a total stranger. "Baby, I'll show you a good time. Once I'm inside of you. I got my truck outside with an extended cab. Just a dance first. I know you chicks like foreplay."

I expected her to walk away or call security. How could any woman allow a man to talk to her like that? But was I any better for not speaking up? What could I do? All my complaints went ignored.

She looked at her silent friends, who watched expressionless, their eyes dead as the beer sign behind me reflected in the sheen of the blackness of their eyes. In unison they nodded to their friend in red.

"Okay, hombre, you think you know what I want? Come dance with me. Then maybe I will let you inside as you so romantically put it."

The man made my stomach turn. His cologne smelled worse than his machismo. I wanted to stab him with a corkscrew or string him up with his bolo tie. A smug smile stretched across his face. You could tell he thought he had won.

He wrenched the woman's arm to the dance floor and forcefully pulled her hips to his own. Their bodies twisted and turned as he grinded against her, trying to show off, but it was when he tried to squeeze her ass that things got interesting.

As he fingers worked to pull up her dress, she grabbed his hands with such force the bones in his fingers crumbled. It looked like she held a rubber glove. She began to lead the dance over his screams while the band played a merengue song. They spun faster and faster, so fast they looked like an out-of-control top made of hair and red fabric. People cleared the way so as not to get knocked over. She just laughed over his cries for help. The band quit their playing as they watched.

Then a scream.

Her dress floated like a bright hibiscus flower in full bloom, showing her thong and thighs, but that wasn't what made the band stop playing or caused the people to scream. The bottom half of her legs were those of a goat. Her feet were cloven hooves with a spiked horn jutting from the back of each. When she noticed the band had stopped, she and her four friends looked their way.

The singer panicked and shouted into the microphone, "¡Uno, dos, tres!"

A horn started a new song. The four women joined her on the dance floor. Their legs and feet were those of a goat, too. They danced round the man, laughing, shouting gritos, with their thongs, thighs and fishnet stockings held up by garters in full view, not caring who saw because they were having the time of their lives.

How I wanted to join them. To spin in merengue oblivion. It must be just as satisfying to dance around your tormentor in pain as it is to dance on their grave.

As he begged for them to stop, his dance partner unfurled a forked tongue as long as a whip. His eyes widened upon seeing it float in front of his face. He didn't know what it would do next. With the quickness of a scorpion's pinch, it plucked out his eyes. Blood oozed from empty sockets as he screamed for help, but there was no one to come to his aid. The other women had tongues just as long and teased the man by whipping his body or lapping up his blood. When he could no longer stand, they stopped their dance. The band threw down their instruments and ran out the door.

The five women stood in a circle, looking down on the crushed man. The woman in red put one cloven hoof on his belly. "I won't kill you but now you may never have the pleasure or privilege of looking at or touching another woman again."

There were sounds of sirens approaching. I waved my hands in the air to get the goat women's attention. They turned their heads towards me then galloped on their hooves to the back of the bar.

"This way. Come quick!" Before leaving, the woman in red pulled out a one-hundred-dollar bill from beneath the bust of her dress. "Until next time." She gave me a wink that almost made me fall in love with her.

Now, Friday night is Ladies' Night and men are always on their best behaviour.

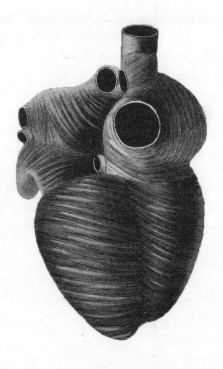

For more Tales of the Weird titles
visit the British Library Shop (shop.bl.uk)

We welcome any suggestions, corrections or feedback you may have, and will
aim to respond to all items addressed to the following:

The Editor (Tales of the Weird), British Library Publishing,
The British Library, 96 Euston Road, London NW1 2DB

We also welcome enquiries through our Twitter account, @BL_Publishing.